PART ONE

MARY

HERD OF THE HILLS

I

JOHNNIE GILLIES was away!
He strode down the white ribbon of the glen-road, a little stocky figure of a man in an old grey suit, a stick in his right hand, a waterproof slung over his shoulder and under the opposite arm, tied up with string. His cap was tilted on the side of his head, jauntily at an angle, a song and a jest in a piece of cloth. Two collie dogs trotted at his heels: an old black smooth-coated bitch, slender and close-set to the ground; a dog, black and larger, her son.

Johnnie Gillies turned his head, raised the cap from his raven curls, waved it in the air with a flourish. His deep-set brown eyes were sorrowful, his twisted mouth, made for glad laughter, was sad. He waved a last time, swung round, settled to the long hill-stride which would take him down the winding road, out of the narrow glen to the wide valley beyond.

Behind him was the red sun setting in the November evening, a thread of smoke rising from a whitewashed cottage, and Mary Maclean staring with wet eyes at the lad who was leaving her. She stood there in blue print blouse and short grey skirt, her sleeves rolled up to show the strong red arms—in her black woollen stockings and her worn black shoes. Her fair skin was browned by the summer

9

that was gone, there were large freckles at the side of her upturned nose. The wide mouth was kindly, the blue eyes steady and grave under the broad brow, the skin of the neck smooth and soft where the collar had shielded her. She had a woman's work to do, and it had stamped her face with a woman's cares. But the fair hair, which caught the sun's low rays, was waved and shingled. Mary Maclean was eighteen years old, and she would go to the town once a month to have her hair done, no matter what her father might say.

She turned slowly in the unhurried country way. She walked up the beaten earth path to the green door of the cottage, to go in to the stone-flagged kitchen and to the work she had left undone. All about her were the lonely hills, raising their vast bulk to a blood-red sky; silence, and the deep hush of a windless evening. Far away down the glen a tiny figure was moving, two dots following at his heels—Johnnie Gillies leaving the glen. A hoodie-crow, black, menacing, flapped with infinite leisure across the flaming background of sunset.

Mary crossed the kitchen to the little window which would not open, to take one last look of the valley. Then she lit the paraffin lamp, the flame running across the trimmed wick with a splutter and smoke, burning flickeringly, then settling to quietness under the glass chimney. She placed the lamp on the sill by the little window, to shine out through the gathering darkness. It was a signal and direction to her father, who was out on the hill. She went to the range, stirred the fire to a red glow, put on the kettle. Moving quietly, as she always did, she arranged the cups

and saucers on the bare deal table, then the bread, the butter, the oatcakes and the scones, getting tea ready against her father's return. But she had no heart in her work that night, because little Johnnie Gillies had gone away.

II

Big Hugh Maclean was high out on the hill. His blue eyes were tired, his brown beard wet with dew, his footsteps lagging from fatigue. He raised the fifth fingers of his big red hands to his mouth, forced the corners outwards to a line, blew through his strong white teeth a command to stop.

The shrill, far-carrying whistle echoed over the heather to the hill-tops, up round the shoulder of the Craig to the Corriemore. The sheep turned their black faces and hazel eyes towards the man below. Far away, where the clear springs rise at the burn's beginning, a stag raised his antlers to the sky and with soft moist muzzle tasted the wind. A dog, circling wide of the sheep, stopped in his tracks, tilted a white face down the brae, cocked two black inquiring ears—waited. A second whistle, louder, more urgent, frightened the sheep to a brisk trot. The stag galloped to the peat-hags where the hinds were resting, halting at intervals, turning back to face the danger that might come. The black-and-white dog turned to his master and for home.

Hugh Maclean had been out all afternoon looking for a tup that had strayed. It was a costly Cranok ram, a shearling, and he had put it on the East-end

the management, the buying and selling to do, for a shepherd's wage. Sixty pounds a year he had in cash, a cow and its keep, a ton of coals, oatmeal, peats, and the right to keep poultry. The house was rent-free and slated, five rooms and a pantry, with thick stone walls that could stand to the storm. But the place was needing pointing, and the two windows that could open rattled in the wind. All in one storey, four-square and squat, the house had faced the drifting snow and lashing rains of a century.

It had looked a tidy place on the May term when Hugh had brought his wife and bairn to the glen, with the swallows about the byres and the golden whins on the low hills. His wife had died two years after their coming there, when they were hoping for a boy after fourteen years, and when Mary, their girl, was near done with the school. On a warm July day, when the men were at the clipping, she had died of a haemorrhage. Hugh, coming in to his dinner, had found her lying, her fingers against the door she had been beating on for help.

He had got Mary excused the school, and she had come to keep house for him when she was thirteen. Five long years were by, and still she was with him, mending, cleaning, milking, baking—and all for her keep. He did not want to lose her now, so little Johnnie Gillies had gone.

Hugh Maclean fell asleep, his great limbs stretched, his square brown beard heaving with the movements of his chest, his grey socks steaming, his grey shirt open at the neck. His lips moved gently as he dreamt, muttering commands to his dogs.

By candle-light, Mary washed up after tea. The single tap in the sink dripped cold water, the drops falling rhythmically on the piled plates. The boiling water from the kettle sent up a cloud of steam. Mary wondered who would come in Johnnie's place. She had never dared ask her father.

That night, when Mary was in bed, she stared through the small window to the strip of sky she could see. A full moon was up, resting its yellow edge on the crest of a hill. The wind was rising in the west, the window rattled when the gusts came. White clouds were drifting like driven sheep across the clear sky, rushing to meet the moon.

Round the house the hill burns were whispering down, a quiet and restful rippling. The branches of the rowans on the stream's edge sighed in the light winds. The moonlight crept in a broad beam across the worn rug to the bed, now clear, now falling into shadow. Delicate feathers of ice grew and multiplied on the window-panes. Over the mountains great stillness lay.

Mary turned over to sleep on the hard pillow. She was glad that somewhere the same moon was shining on a dark head.

III

Seven o'clock of a cold morning, quietness, and a grey flicker of dawn. Hugh Maclean rose to light the kitchen fire and to give a call to Mary, who still slept. He padded softly across to the range, groped on the mantelshelf for the matches, running his hand over its surface until he touched the box. Two sharp scrapes on its side, a point of yellow flame

shyness of the hills she would fain have flown, and have left the intruder to the empty echoing house. But that she dared not do, she who was her father's housekeeper and not just Mary Maclean.

Jack Knight had left the grey halls and green playing fields of his public school with a fixed determination. He would never, given the continued indulgence of his mother, be caged in a room again. His resolution had led him to farming, to Glendarroch, and the heaped mountains of the West. Mr Knight he was called by the servants, but he was only a boy newly from school, in his brown tweed jacket, breeches and leggings, with his short brown hair and clear skin, and his grey eyes seeking adventure. He raised his deer-stalker's cap when Mary met him at the door, smiling his question with gentility's charm :

'Are you Miss Maclean ? '

'Aye ; you'll be Mr Knight, sir ? '

The boy suffered a flat feeling of disappointment. He had painted mental pictures of the shepherd's daughter at Glendarroch. He had imagined her a sturdy, sunburnt milkmaid, but with the grace and beauty of an actress in revue. He found her short and shabby, with freckled face and upturned nose, crumpled stockings and badly shingled hair. He could not see the warmth and blueness of her eyes, for they were lowered, in her shyness, to the ground.

'If you will come in, sir,' said Mary, 'I will show you to your room. My father is out.'

Jack Knight went through the lobby to the best parlour on its right, and thence to the little back room where Johnnie Gillies had slept. He felt the damp depression of the unused sitting-room, and

sensed the absurdity of its useless adornments. It was crowded with straight-backed red-plush chairs, small tables, bureaus buried in photographs, and a shabby stuffed fox with yellow glass eyes. But the bedroom was in keeping with the house, the bare boards scrubbed, the iron bedstead spread with warm white blankets, and the single window, propped open by a wooden block, looking out to the birches and rowans beside a tumbling burn.

The chauffeur put the cases down with a bump on the plank floor and went out. Mary was alone with Jack Knight for the first time. She felt oppressed by the nearness of him, by his tall handsomeness and searching eyes. She imagined that if she turned suddenly he might hold her, smiling down at her with easy condescension. She wished, for a moment, that her father had been home.

Jack broke the spell of strained uneasy silence.

' I like this room very much,' he said.

Mary turned with thankfulness because he had spoken first, and in doing so showed him the soft blueness of her eyes. ' Excuse me,' she said, brushing past him to the door.

Safe in the kitchen, she listened to him unpacking his things, while she prepared the dinner. She hoped that he would stay in the bedroom until her father came home. Jack lingered over the arranging of shirts and ties with the same thought in his heart.

Hugh Maclean was all smiles and joviality when he stepped in. The shepherd Mackenzie had met him on the high watershed with the glad news of the Cranok tup's safety in Strathord. Mackenzie would have some better lambs in the spring than he deserved, but the fine beast itself was unharmed.

IV

Next day, in the early morning, a small gust of wind struck the cottage, making all the windows rattle together. An outhouse door slammed to; a wisp of straw blew across the frozen cobbles of the yard; the hens turned uneasily on their perches. Far up in the corries the red deer huddled together in the comfort of the herd, turned dark inquiring noses to the north, tasted the quality of the wind. Breaking into trot, a grizzled stag in the van, they turned downwards, making for the low hills.

Earlier than by custom the sheep rose one by one from the high places where they sleep, shaking damp fleeces in the cold air. Each one, moving away, left a dark patch of flattened grass, staring like a scar in the dead, white face of the frost. By twos and threes, following the winding sheep-tracks down the slopes, they sought shelter from the ice wind rising in their rear. Grouse—packs, couples, or single birds—sailed with stilled wings over the crest of the hills, broke into powerful agitated flight, drifted down to the safety of the valley. Small trees by the watercourses bent and sighed before the wind as though in supplication.

Hugh Maclean, turning in his sleep, dimly sensed the new motion that stirred outside, breaking the month-long stillness of the frost. He felt the cold air that whispered through the room, stealing under the blankets to his shivering skin. Hugh Maclean knew the snow was coming.

He thought of the new-bought tups on the hill, that would not know where to shelter when the drifts were blowing, and he roused himself to

vigour. His great hands crept to the chair by his bedside to find a match, in order to see the time on the heavy watch ticking through the darkness.

It was barely five o'clock—two hours and more before dawn. Hugh lay in wakeful watchfulness, praying that daylight might precede the storm. Faint gusts had changed to buffets and the wind's low whispering to a howl, when a thinning of darkness in the east showed where the sun would rise. Hugh sprang from bed, thankful to end an anxious inactivity. His bedroom door opened directly to the lobby beyond the parlour's entrance. He paused there, because he had promised the laird that young Knight should work like any herd. He had intended to call him in the early morning. But, with a snow wind blowing, it would be enough to see to the helpless sheep without being cumbered with an equally helpless boy. Hugh hurried to light the fire, to knock on Mary's door, and to stride out to the stable for his dogs.

When Mary awoke she knew she had been cold for a long time. The wind had crept over her as she slept; her legs were heavy and aching, her feet half frozen, her body lifeless and numbed. She heard the snow wind howling like a lost dog around the house, stifling the life of the glen with a cold threat. She listened for the crackling movement of burning sticks, but there was no sound. Hugh Maclean, in his haste to be with the sheep, had performed the first task of the day with carelessness. In a rustle of charred paper the fire had died down to blackness and to dust.

Shivering in her flannel night-gown, Mary made haste to relight it. She was kneeling before the

range, coaxing a trembling spark to flame, when she heard footsteps. Instinctively she pulled the end of her gown over her bared ankles. Turning, she saw that it was Mr Knight.

'Good-morning,' he said. 'Can I help you with the fire?'

'No, thanks,' she answered; 'I can manage.'

She felt helpless and awkward, kneeling in her night-dress, with the tall figure of the boy, fully clothed, behind her.

'Where is your father?'

'He's out.'

'He said he would waken me and show me the morning's work.'

'He would be thinking it would be too coarse a day for you to be out.'

'I'm used to rough weather. I'll follow him.'

Mary jumped up. 'No, no!' she said. 'It's coming on snow. You might be losing your way on the hill and never come back.'

'You seem very anxious about me,' he laughed.

In the grey twilight of the room his shyness had gone.

'My father'd be in trouble if anything was to come over you,' she explained.

'I see. Then what can I do until he comes back?'

'You might be watching the fire until I'm dressed.'

'Right, Mary. Give me the matches.'

He helped her with the work that morning, finding fun in its novelty. He was clumsy with his untrained hands, asking how everything should be done, his fingers fumbling in their frozen stiffness.

'God! it's cold here,' he exclaimed when they

went out to the yard, and his face was stung by the whip-lash of the wind.

'It'll be milder when the snow comes,' she shouted.

Piled masses of smoke-grey clouds drifted over the sky. Doors and windows banged and rattled in the outbuildings. The square house with its smoking chimney seemed a tramp steamer sailing to battle with tempestuous seas.

The shelter of the byre was warm haven from the storm, a place of stillness where soft hay rustled and the cud was chewed. The cows rose gladly as in answer to an invitation. Over the slated slope of the roof the wind whistled as though searching for prey. Jack Knight watched Mary milk the cows, her strong hands moving rhythmically upwards and downwards, her brow resting lightly on the warm hide. The squirting streams of white milk beat a tattoo on the pail's side.

'I'd like to learn to do that,' Jack said.

'It's easy enough to learn.'

'Will you let me try it?'

'You might coup the pail.'

'But I'm here to learn things.'

'It'll be the sheep you're here to learn about, Mr Knight. The cows are my work, and milking's no' a job for a gentleman.'

'Couldn't you forget that I'm a gentleman while I'm here?'

'It's no' possible.'

Jack Knight laughed.

'Am I to take that as a compliment?' he asked.

'It's the truth,' said Mary, as she lifted the pail clear of the cow's feet.

When they came from the byre the darkness had increased. Low-flying clouds had drifted across the young face of the sun: the hills were hidden in the drifting blackness of the storm. The boy and girl staggered across the yard, the pail between them, leaning backwards to the wind, resting their weight on their heels. They fought against the kitchen door to close it in the teeth of the gale. The contrasting quietude of the house had the weird hushed deadness of the tomb. Mary was troubled and afraid.

'It's a coorse day for father to be out,' she said.

'I wish I'd gone with him.'

'That would have made things worse.'

The bleak greyness of the morning drifted slowly towards midday. An hour past the usual time Mary and Jack breakfasted together in the strained silence of waiting. A small bird dashed against the window and fell dead beside the door. Mary shivered in fear.

'I can't stand this any longer,' said Jack, 'I must go out to look for your father. I'm not a woman, to sit here beside the fire and do nothing.'

'And where would you be looking for him, not knowing the hill? You'd be lost yoursel' before you were away an hour.'

'Well, what can we do, Mary? We *must* do something.'

'I was thinking that if father's no' back within the half-hour, I'll go down the glen for the Macintyre boys. Not that they'll be able to do much,' and she stared out hopelessly at the tumbled commotion of the sky.

'I'll come with you,' said Jack.

'I'll be glad of your company, Mr Knight.'

It was then they saw big Hugh Maclean come stumbling up the brae, fighting against the storm. He was staggering, beaten, with his head bent down, and he carried one of his dogs in his great arms. The other crept weakly at his heels. He struggled across to the stable, and Mary moved quietly to the press.

Hugh groped his way into the kitchen, breathless and blinded, his face chalk-white and his big hands bleeding. His clothes were torn, and raw flesh showed where he had been dashed against the rocks. He brushed aside Jack, who had hurried to support him.

'You'll take a dram, father?' said Mary.

'To hell with a dram,' he whispered hoarsely. 'I'm needing hot milk for the dogs. Sheila's fair done.'

'Ye'll have your dram first, father.'

'Damn ye! Did ye no' hear what I said?' he gasped. '*Milk*—I'm needing milk for the dogs.'

Mary poured milk into the pan to heat. Hugh flung himself heavily into his chair, while Jack Knight, silent and aloof, hated the big man for his rough cruelty. Soon Hugh was snoring—he fell asleep at once when he lay down—and Mary, when the milk was warm, carried it out to the dogs.

Jack Knight sat idly before the fire listening to the wind outside and the loud breathing of the exhausted shepherd. The cheap American alarm-clock ticked harshly on the narrow mantelshelf above the polished range. The coals settled down noisily into the red heart of the fire. Mary returned from the stable, and stepping softly over to her father, pulled the boots from his feet and the

cap from his head. She did it all very tenderly so as not to waken him, as though he were a child fallen asleep after play.

' You'll be thinkin' him a rough man for swearing at me like that,' she whispered to Jack.

He nodded agreement.

' Och, Mr Knight ! ' she said, ' he was clean done after fighting all morning. If he hadn't sworn, it's crying he would have been. He'll take his dram all right when he wakes. You'll be wearying, Mr Knight ? '

' There's not much to do.'

Mary glanced at the clock. It was past one.

' I'll give you a bite of dinner in a minute,' she said, ' and the post'll no' be long now, and you can see the day's paper.'

It was after two when the post came, and Jack heard him talking to Mary at the door. ' Cold the day ! '

' Aye, post, it's cold. It's like to be snow.'

' Any letters ? '

' None the day.'

' I'll be getting back before the snow's on.'

' You'll take a cup of tea ? '

' I'll not wait for it the day, thanks.'

' Then, good-evening. I'll no' be keeping you.'

' Good-evening.'

The postman's footsteps were anxiously hurried as he went down the brae.

When Mary returned to the room, Hugh raised heavy lids from sleep-clouded eyes.

' What's it doing outside ? ' he asked.

' The wind's down, father.'

' Then the snow'll no' be long.'

The snow had come. A small powdery flake fell from the grey clouds. It drifted slowly down through the cold air, twisted gracefully in spirals to the eddies of the wind, turned, hesitated, fell again, down, down to the hushed waiting stillness of the glen.

V

All night long the white flakes drifted down on the brown hills, hiding the winding paths of the watercourses, filling the crevices between the strong stems of the heather.

In the morning, Hugh Maclean rose stiffly to a day of toil. When he opened the front door, snow fell softly to the lobby floor. He dug a path through the piled whiteness to the stable and the byre. The shuffling sound of his spade broke the infinite stillness that follows a storm. Behind him, as he worked, the snow fell, silently obliterating the shepherd's footprints. The clouds loomed low, stretching across the sky in dull unbroken grey. Darkness lightened to dawn, and the hills, like shrouded monsters, emerged from the black forest of night. The glen road was lost in the snow—only the tall wooden posts by its side pointed the long way to the valley.

Hugh judged the snow's depth too great to allow cars, vans, or even the postman's bicycle to break through. Glendarroch was snowed up, isolated from the world, left to the wild deer, the sheep, and the shepherd's small household until the thaw should come.

Through the hard days that followed, it was a battle for the life of sheep against the obstacles of

snow. Over the white hills Hugh Maclean and Jack Knight plodded to the rescue of ewes, carrying heavy roped bundles of hay on their backs to spread on the cold ground, searching for the yellowness on the snow's surface which showed where sheep were buried. Then back to the house they must hurry for spades to dig, while falling snow covered their footprints and blotted out all sight of the house, and a whisper of wind threatened the blizzard which, if it came, would kill all living things in its path.

In the hills' great loneliness, Jack Knight grew sometimes afraid. Tired from labour and dazed with the white monotony around him, he feared he might lose strength and never regain the warm comfort of the house. Then he would glance at the bearded, powerful figure at his side. The mere presence of Hugh meant security, his leadership voyaging in rough weather, but safe harbour at the journey's end. When the snow was cleared and the numbed sheep exposed, the two men would drive the stumbling beasts down the hill, Hugh carrying a weak or dead sheep on his broad back, grasping its fore-legs in his right hand, its hind-legs in his left. All the time he would be cursing the storm that had broken before tupping was over, so that lambs would be late and scarce when the spring came.

As the showers drifted in slow progress from the glen, Jack could see the cottage chimney throwing out a thread of smoke over the vast wilderness of white. Sometimes, in the yard, he saw Mary, a dark, animated speck in a world of death. Then she would move towards the door, pause, glance search-

ingly to the hills, disappear through the low entrance of the house. As dusk fell, the flickering lamplight shone out to the cold desolation beyond.

Three times a day the men stumbled in for warmth and food, great cakes of ice melting from their boot-heels. Tired and heavy-eyed, they would fain have slept after meat. But always Hugh Maclean would rouse himself and his pupil with, 'Well, Mr Knight, it's time we was moving.'

Jack would heave himself painfully from his chair, stagger a little when he stood erect, follow the shepherd to the hill. In the evenings the man and the boy who was turning a man lay in their arm-chairs at either side of a red fire, while Mary, on a hard chair between, sat knitting in the eerie company of those asleep. Outside was silence, save when a collie in the stable howled, or the cows rattled their chains in the byre. As the days went by and the snow still held, deer came snuffling around the outbuildings, searching for food. The herd left deep hoof-marks in the snow, and a tired old hind dying of starvation at the burn's side.

While she knitted in the long evenings, Mary's grave eyes would study the sleeping faces of the men, her father's rugged and red, the brown beard jutting out from his square jaw, Mr Knight's smooth and glowing, with red lips parted showing the white teeth. From time to time Hugh would rouse himself and glance at the alarm-clock to see whether bedtime was nigh.

One night Mary's gaze was resting on Jack Knight when, as though sensing her interest, his grey eyes opened. For an instant their glances met, then Mary blushed and busied herself with her

knitting. The red blood surged up the graceful column of the boy's neck, spread to his cheeks and brow. He feigned sleep, but, as he thought of the girl beside him, the colour came and went under the fine smoothness of his skin.

After that evening Mary felt uneasy when Jack was near. She knew that his eyes followed her eagerly as she moved about the room. She surprised him gazing at her as she bent low over her knitting, and at night when she slept, she dreamt of the redness of his lips which were like the ripe rowans, and of his neck white as the untrampled snow. As the year drifted on to the bleak coldness of its ending, as the nights grew longer and the days more short, Mary found herself restless and excited when the day's work drew to its close. The lonely drudgery of her tasks, the same things to be done and redone until she grew old, left her mind free to think of the tall handsome boy who would come smiling to her in the soft lamplight. Through the dusk of December afternoons she would keep looking at the clock, wondering whether all was well with her father and Mr Knight on the hill. She would whisper ' Jack ' as she bent over the glowing fire, then glance round in fear lest someone should be there. When she heard the shuffle of heavy boots in the loose snow she would tremble and feel weak, and turn down the lamp so that none could see her face.

' You're in darkness, Mary ! ' Jack Knight would cry, throwing back his head to jerk the brown hair clear of his eyes.

' Aye,' she would answer him, ' the lamp's been smoking.'

One night he must help her to put it right.

' I'll put it up for you, Mary.'

' You're turning it down, Mr Knight.'

' Is that right ? '

' No! you've got it too high now. I'll show you.'

They were laughing together when Hugh Maclean
came in, and they seemed not to notice his coming.
The shepherd's blue eyes puckered in suspicion.

' That's none of your work, Mr Knight,' he said
shortly, and noticed the flaming cheeks of the boy
and the downcast face of the girl.

' Aye,' he added sourly, ' it's time the snow went.'

For a week Hugh watched, and then his mistrust
was spent. The sheep and a shepherd's worries
claimed the monopoly of his mind. There was no
sign of a thaw, the hay was getting done, and the
ewes weak and lean with half the winter to come.
One clear evening, with a moon full up, he tramped
down the glen to the Macintyres, to see whether by
chance they had meat to spare.

When he had gone, Jack Knight followed Mary to
the milking in the byre. There was no gay laughter
in his eyes, only a restless seeking. He found Mary
milking by the dim light of the stable lantern. She
turned when she heard footsteps, and gasped with
wild fear when she saw who came. Jack stepped
forward, trying to smile, but the look on his face was
of hunger. He bent down over Mary as she sat on
her low stool, and when she looked up, kissed her on
her warm mouth.

Mary never moved. The tears ran down her
cheeks because she knew she should make Jack go,
and yet she was too weak to send him away. So
when she rose from the milking and he caught her

in his boy's arms, she buried her wet face in his smooth neck as she had been longing to do, and neither of them spoke.

At last Mary broke the long silence. 'If you'll take the lamp, Mr Knight, I'll be carrying in the pail.'

'Aren't you going to call me Jack now—after you've kissed me?'

'You'd best to forget about that, Mr Knight. We've been wicked.'

For answer he clasped her in his arms again. 'I'll *make* you call me Jack.'

She looked up at him, her blue eyes warm and soft in their surrender. 'Jack,' she whispered.

That evening, as they sat together waiting for Hugh to come home, Jack Knight blurted out all the confidences he had been aching to impart—his love of sheep, his hatred of confinement, his admiration of his teacher. He talked only of himself, and Mary, wide-eyed, sat worshipping the movements of his mouth.

It was late when Hugh came in. He flung himself down in his chair, grumbling. 'There's no' a bite of meat to be had in the glen. I'll need to be writing the laird to send hay, or the sheep'll starve.'

'Maybe the thaw'll come soon, father.'

'The thaw can wait if the wind keeps down— what was thon?'

'I heard nothing, father.'

'Was it no' the wind in the trees by the burn's side?'

As though in answer, the window rattled in its worn frame. A faint whispering breeze, like a sighing in sorrow, swept down from the hills. The

soft snow rose whirling to meet the wind, and dashed in pattering spray on the glass panes.

'My God!' gasped Hugh, 'it's here, Mr Knight, sir—it's time we was both bedded. We'll be needing all our strength the morn.'

Jack hurried to his room in joyous expectation of adventure. Mary, for the moment, was forgotten. He dreamt only of the white clouds of the blizzard rising in spiral smoke over the hill's crest, of the mad buffetings of the gale, and of men struggling bravely for the lives of sheep.

VI

Morning broke in scudding clouds of snow and with great trumpets of the gale sounding through the glen. The walls shivered when the high gusts clapped against them in their fury, and all down the corries and straths the blizzard hurled itself in the splendid frenzy of its unrestraint.

Hugh Maclean and Jack Knight sat anxiously before the fire, awaiting an interval of calm. Their preparation and early awakening were in vain, for none could face the hill that day and live. Mary knitted mechanically until the storm should pass.

Hugh Maclean pulled a crumpled envelope from his pocket. 'I've a letter for you, Mary,' he said. 'The post left it at the Macintyres two days past. It'll be from Johnnie Gillies, by the postmark.'

It was a pencil scrawl on a torn sheet.

'DEAR MARY,—Just a line to let you know I'm getting on fine. The boss here buys his tups himself and they're just bad beasts made bonnie with shears. He

likes them set low on their feet but they're high standing enough when the bellies go off them on the hill. Tell your father to drop me a line if he has a job at the lambing as I'm feed by the month here.

Hoping this finds you well as it leaves me.

JOHNNIE.'

It was all about the sheep, and Mary thought that in the hills they were of more account than women. That was all Johnnie had to write to her after a month away !

' What's Johnnie saying ? ' asked Hugh.

' You can read it, father,' Mary answered, and in saying so showed that the image of little Johnnie Gillies had faded from the secret places of her heart.

The afternoon brought quiet weather. The men went out to the hill, while Mary awaited their safe return. The wind was rising again by evening, its keen edge cutting away the white crests of the snow-wreaths.

Jack Knight came stumbling down the hill with the wet spray lashing his face. He lifted the cap from his brown head so that he could feel the long cold fingers of the wind in his overgrown hair. Far down, in the sheltered hollow beyond the snow-silenced burn, he could see the lamp's faint light.

He had been helping Hugh to drive the ewes off places where the soft drifts were blowing, and he was tired. The sheep had been stubborn and unwilling to move, the wind's force had sent him staggering against sharp rocks, and the clogged snow had made more perilous the steep descent. When he reached the stream's deep ravine, narrowed to a slit by the drifted snow, he felt too tired to cross.

' I'm just about done,' he murmured.

Hugh Maclean heard, but ignored the sense of the remark.

'Aye, Mr Knight, you're just about home,' he shouted. 'Take a grip of my cleek's end, and I'll give you a pull across.'

Jack accepted, and half stumbling, half pulled, struggled against the snow's passive resistance and the capturing clutch of buried trees. Across the burn he found hard ground bared of snow by the wind, easy going, and a gentle slope to the cottage door. His spirit revived at the nearness of sanctuary. He squared his shoulders, tossed back his hair, and swaggered through the door to the warm glow of the fire.

Tall and erect in his brown tweeds and leggings, the colour whipped by cold to his glowing cheeks, he seemed to Mary something splendidly alive come newly in from a world of death. The snow spray lightly powdered the long lashes over his grey eyes, and dusted the brown hair sweeping back from his smooth brow. His lips were the rich blue colour of ripe blaeberries, and between them his teeth flashed whiter than the corrie's snow. The smoothness of his skin was like the soft down on a pigeon's breast, and the curves of his throat had the graceful strength of trees. His smile to her seemed the warm brilliance of a summer sun, and his voice, when he spoke, held all the age-old music of the rivers and hills.

His eyes rested on her, followed her when she moved, caressed her with their soundless love-song. Mary knew that whatever Jack asked of her she must give.

That night the cold clouds melted to falling rain;

the snow grew suddenly soiled, and pitted by tumbling millions of pattering drops. The wind sighed in the trees by the stream's edge, and the heavy snow slid in thunder from the slated roof of the house.

Mary, in her narrow bed, lay listening to the rattling window, and the gentle movements of the world outside which told of thaw. She closed her eyes in the darkness, and pictured the brave lad with the snow on his dear hair, and the swift throbbing of the veins in his white throat. She stroked the softness of the pillow, imagining his smooth cheek, and whispered his name to comfort the yearning anguish of her heart. That he would come to her was her fervent wish, as it was also her most deadly fear. Every faint sound in the house might be Jack stealing to her, or only the dying embers of the fire settling quietly in the grate. The wind stealing over the bare floor seemed to whisper her name in his voice, and she moaned the loud beating of her heart that made it more difficult to hear.

When Jack opened the door and came to her, it seemed like an answer to her prayer.

VII

Hugh Maclean stood at the open door of his daughter's bedroom. He stood there for a long time, his grey flannel shirt sagging down to his knees, his brown beard resting on the bared expanse of his chest. His blue eyes had no kindness in them, only the flashing fury of his anger.

He had risen, as by custom, to waken Jack Knight before dressing himself. He had found the room

unoccupied, and at once the old suspicion was
reborn. He remembered the confusion over the
lamp-lighting, glances he had surprised in the
dozing relaxation of evening. Hugh went straight
to Mary's room. He opened the door, the candle
on the kitchen table throwing faint light into the
small room. He saw the dim outline of two heads
close together on the narrow pillow, and his ragged
nails drew blood in the palms of his hands.

' Ye whüre ! ' he hissed.   ' Ye damned whüre ! '
Then ' Mr Knight,' he shouted, ' come out o' that,
or, by God ! I'll pull ye out by the feet ! '

Jack sat up in the confusion of sudden awakening.
He wondered where he was and why the big shepherd was angry that morning. Then he remembered,
and threw a protecting arm across Mary by his side.

' Come out o' that, d'ye hear ! ' roared Hugh, as
though ordering his dogs. ' Come out o' that, or
there'll be murder ! '

' All right,' muttered Jack.   ' I'll go.'

He walked past the shepherd with head held high,
but when he saw Hugh's face he raised his left arm
instinctively in defence.

' No, I'll no' hit ye,' sneered Hugh.   ' You may
be thanking Heaven this day that you're a friend
to the laird. Get to your room, Mr Knight, and
be ready to leave here by daylight.'

The shepherd closed the door softly, turned the
rusty key on its inner side, advanced silently towards
the bed. Mary was frightened by the queer quietness, by the darkness, and by her father's stealthy
approach.

' What are you going to do, father ? ' she
screamed.

Hugh answered softly, as though reasoning out his course of action: 'You've disgraced the mother that bore ye,' he said. 'You've brought shame on this house and on those who live here. You should be punished for your sin.' Gradually his voice grew louder, his anger more intense. 'And punished ye'll be. I'll smash ye so that no man'll look ye in the face again.'

'Have mercy, father!'

'Aye, I'll have mercy. I'll no' kill ye.'

Hugh tore the blankets from the cringing girl.

Jack rushed back when he heard Mary's screams. He flung himself against the door, trying to break through to her aid. He heard the smashing blows of the enraged shepherd, and Mary's cries dying down as consciousness left her. He was trembling like a leaf when the key grated harshly and Hugh came out, with the spent fury dying down in his blue eyes.

'You damned murderer!' sobbed Jack.

Hugh answered in low, ashamed tones. 'Aye, I was too rough on her, but she'll no' dee. It was my duty to punish her. She's no mother to speak to her.'

'Duty!' sneered Jack. 'You dirty beast!'

'Mr Knight, I've done what I thought was my duty. Are ye going to do yours?'

'What do you mean, Maclean?'

'Are ye going to make an honest girl o' Mary? D'ye mean to marry her?'

'Well, I don't know. I'm hardly in a position to.'

'Then get to your room, ye damned rat.'

Jack Knight left Glendarroch soon after day-break, without his breakfast, and leaving his boxes

to be called for. He trudged down the road through the melting slush and in the cold rain, with the hill-tops hidden in drifting clouds. He had lingered in the kitchen, hoping that Mary would come to him. He had knocked at her door, quietly, when Hugh was outside, but she had not answered.

She could not bear him to see her with face swollen and discoloured by her father's blows. But when he had gone she crept across the kitchen to the little window, to gaze out sorrowfully on the glen. She prayed that Jack would turn, if only once, to wave to her, but he never looked back. He trudged on down the winding road, a tall graceful figure with bent head, trudged on through the wet slush and cold rain until the grey mist covered him.

VIII

The days dragged on in muddied wetness to the spring.

Through the long evenings rain beat on the cottage window, and Mary, with sad eyes, gazed into the redness of the fire. Always she knitted whilst her father slept, the sharp clicking of her needles breaking the stillness which the rain enhanced. Hugh lay dozing, half opening his eyes to see the time. But as the weeks crept by and February neared its close, he would stare for minutes on end at his daughter sitting by the fire. His eyes would be puzzled and narrowed in suspicion, then he would close them again and sink back into sleep.

Mary did the work which was her duty. She

cleaned, and baked, and milked through the bleak winter days. But she seldom talked, she never laughed ; her only interest was in the coming of the post. She would watch him clambering up the steep brae to the cottage, her heart beating painfully, hoping that that day there would be some message for her. The days went by, one after another, in the majestic monotony of the hills, but from Jack Knight there came no word. Gradually it dawned on Mary that none would ever come, that when Jack trudged into the grey mist he had passed out of her life.

It was an effort to rise on the cold, wet dawns, and to cook the morning's meal was sickening torture. She grew thin as the days lengthened, and always big Hugh watched her with blue eyes narrowed in suspicion. He never spoke of Jack, except once briefly, to say that Mr Knight had left the sheep and gone as an airman.

' And I'm hoping,' said Hugh, ' that he'll break his damn neck.'

For the rest, when he spoke at all, it was to grumble at the weather, at the leanness of the ewes, and of the poor lambing that must come. Sometimes, when they were sitting together, it seemed to Mary that much was on his mind, and many things that must be said. He would sit staring in front of him, instead of lying back in his chair as was his wont. Then he would sigh deeply, as in despair, and sink into accustomed slumber.

One night, quite suddenly, he spoke. It had been one of those bright February days which give encouragement to failing hearts by a dress rehearsal of spring's splendours. Light wisps of cloud had

blown buoyantly across a sunny sky, the larks had tried wings and song in a warm air, and the hazel catkins by the river-side had opened in golden sprays of fertile glory. The still evening held some of the sun's warmth, and with the rippling music of the burn outside, it seemed like summer in the cottage kitchen.

' I've been meaning to speak to you for a long time, Mary,' said Hugh. His voice was kindly and his eyes sad. ' I was speaking to the laird to-day and telling him of the hard lambing there's like to be this year. I was telling him I'd be needing help, and he says, says he, " Get what help you need, Maclean." '

' You'll be better of some help, father.'

' Aye, and I'm writing to Johnnie Gillies to come for the lambing.'

Mary gazed silently at the floor. Slowly the hot blood spread over her face and neck. She spoke no word.

' Johnnie had his eye on you before he left,' said Hugh.

' What do you mean, father ? '

' I thought you were taking up together before he went away.'

' Aye,' said Mary softly, ' I liked little Johnnie Gillies.'

' And he would be liking you, Mary ? '

' Aye, maybe he was.'

' I was thinking he had a mind to marry on you.'

' You were thinking that, father ? '

' Aye, I was.'

Hugh leant forwards in the green arm-chair. The flames of passion were beginning to blaze in his

blue eyes, turning them to grey steel. 'And I'm thinking, Mary,' he said, 'that he'll be of the same mind when he's back.'

'You think that, father?'

'Aye,' Hugh thundered, 'and if he's asking you, you'll say yes. D'ye hear me, Mary? you'll say yes.'

Mary looked up, with mild surprise on her patient face. 'Is it wanting to be rid of me you are, father?'

'No! I'm no' wanting to be rid of you, but I'm no' having you bring shame on this house.'

'I'll bring no more shame to you, father.'

'Will ye no'? There'll be more shame when there's a fatherless bairn in the place!'

'What do you mean, father?'

'What do I mean?' sneered Hugh. 'Are ye trying to tell me ye don't know what's come over ye? Well, I'll tell you now. There'll be a bairn here by the back-end of the year, and——'

'Am I going to have a bairn?' asked Mary.

'Aye! I've been watching you for the last month going about the house green as kale, no fit for your work in the mornings, nor yet for your breakfast. Aye, you're with bairn, Mary.'

'It'll be Jack's bairn, father!'

'It'll be nobody's bairn,' Hugh shouted, 'a nameless brat and a shame on us all, and if Johnnie Gillies is aye wanting to marry you, ye'll say yes. D'ye hear, Mary? ye'll say yes.'

She sprang up from her chair, shrinking away from her father, clutching her growing breasts with her worn hands. 'You're wanting me to cheat Johnnie Gillies!' she cried.

' Cheat or no' cheat,' stormed Hugh, ' I'm no' having a fatherless bairn here to shame us. It'll go down the glen road, and you with it.'

Mary stood defiant and erect.

' Ye can do what ye will do, father,' she said quietly, ' but I'm no' cheating little Johnnie Gillies.'

IX

It was a fine spring day when Johnnie Gillies came swaggering up the glen road. The little man aye seemed to bring the good weather with him. Whistling to make the long way lightsome, his bonnet cocked, the two dogs trotting at his heels, he found it good to be coming back to the fine hill country.

Clouds were blowing over the hills and out to sea, leaving ribbons of white in the pale washed blue of an April sky. The wind had some of the warmth of summer, yet with the stinging cold of snow from the mountain-tops. It would be bleak and bitter when the sun set. Rain had fallen through the night, bringing out the scent of peat from the bogs, and of dead bracken from the braes. The burns were full and swollen by the melting snow.

Far up at the glen's head the road grew thin, and died at the mountain's feet. From there a bridle track twisted, and sometimes lost itself, over the high watershed pass to the stretching arms of the hidden sea. At the road's end, a steep side-path led to the whitewashed cottage. From the squat chimney, grey smoke swept flat and westwards, in time to the wind's speed.

Mary was watching for Johnnie through the little

window. She hoped, in a way, that he would never come. She had pondered long over what her father had said, and her mind was made up : whether Johnnie asked her to marry him or not, he must learn the truth. She couldn't cheat Johnnie, who had never wished ill to her, or to any living thing in the world.

She shrank backwards to the room when she saw him first, a little black dot of a figure, with two specks of dogs at his heels. Then she returned to the window to see if he had changed. He came stepping along with the low stride that would carry him over the hills in all kinds of weather.

She could see him clearly now—a little stocky man in an old grey suit, with a stick in his right hand and a waterproof slung over his shoulder, tied up with string. His bonnet was down over his right ear, his step jaunty, and by the set of his mouth she could see he was whistling. She turned sadly from the window, and sat down with her back to the door, facing the fire. There she waited until footsteps on the path told her that Johnnie was nearing the cottage. She heard him bidding his dogs lie quiet outside, then the stamping of his tackety boots on the lobby floor. He was behind her now—Johnnie with his black hair and brown eyes with the laughter in them.

' Are you sleeping, Mary ? '

' Is that you, Johnnie ? '

He strode over to her, laid his soiled hand gently on her shoulder. ' Are ye no' well, Mary ? You're surely thinner ! '

' I'm fine, Johnnie.'

He pulled a hard chair forwards from the table,

sat down opposite her. 'What's the do with you, Mary?' he asked. 'There's something no' right.'

'I'm sorry you ever went away, Johnnie.'

'Well, there's no harm done. I'm back again.'

'Aye, Johnnie, there's harm done.'

The little man's eyes flashed angrily. 'There's been somebody telling lees about me,' he cried. 'I'll tell you right now, Mary, I've been no more than ceevil to a lassie since I left Glendarroch.'

'I believe that, Johnnie.'

'Then what's wrong wi' you, Mary?'

'I can't say what you've said.'

There was a long silence, broken only by the ticking of the alarm-clock on the mantelpiece, and by the whining of the young dog at the door.

'Are ye going with one of the Macintyre boys?' Johnnie asked. 'Or maybe that's no' a fair question, Mary?'

'I've never seen them since you left.'

'Then is it—? No, it canna be—the young gentleman that was stopping here?'

'Aye—him,' she whispered.

'My, Mary!' he gasped. 'So you're going to marry into the gentry.'

She turned away her face, so that he would not see her crying.

'There's to be no marrying in it, Johnnie.'

Johnnie stepped over to her, putting his arm round her shoulders, comforting her. 'Dinna cry, Mary, dinna cry, lassie,' he said. 'There's many a long day before you yet, and you'll forget about him.'

She sprang up, forcing away his hands. She hurried over to the window, leaning her forehead against the cool glass.

' Can ye no' *see* what's wrong ? ' she sobbed.

He saw that her face was thinner, and her hair grown long, but what with the hard winter and the work she had to do there was nothing strange in that. He saw that she was sad and the love of life gone out of her eyes, but that would be because of the young gentleman and his fine words and smiles meaning nothing.

' It's hard weather that's done it, Mary,' he cheered her. ' You'll be your old self again by clipping.'

' Johnnie,' she said brokenly, ' you've got to know soon, so I'll tell you now. There's a bairn coming in the back-end of the year.'

The clock ticked on and on, the young dog scratched and whined to come in to its master, the peewees tumbled and called in the glen below the house. The brightness of the day came and went as the light clouds blew across the face of the sun. From the yard came the mirthless cackling of hens.

Johnnie sat down in the green arm-chair, covering his face with his brown hands. It seemed to Mary that he would never speak. Then he sprang up. ' Where is this fine gentleman ? ' he sneered, ' that I may get at him and make him marry you.'

' He's away in England, Johnnie, and I wouldna have you touch him.'

' Is that the way you feel about him, Mary ? '

' Aye, Johnnie, that way.'

He strode over to her at the window, stroked her fair hair with his rough hands. ' My poor lassie,' he whispered. ' Johnnie's here to look after you now.'

Their talk together was rudely broken by Hugh's entrance.

'Well, Johnnie,' he cried, 'and what kind of a winter have ye had about Cranok?'

'Better nor ye've had here, by what Mary tells me.'

'Och, she!' Hugh laughed. 'The lassie's aye girning.'

'She'll be taking after her father, maybe. How are the sheep doing?'

Hugh flung himself down wearily in his arm-chair. 'They're no' doing at all, Johnnie,' he said. 'There's a ewe to bury every day.'

'Are you through with the udder-locking?'

'Aye, and I did the whole lot mysel'! The Macintyre boys couldn't get over because of the cow calving, and a bad job they had.'

'Did they save the calf?'

But Hugh had lost interest in the Macintyres' troubles; he had too many of his own. He had been tired out by the udder-locking, where every ewe has to be turned on its back, felt for its lamb, and the rough wool pulled off its udder so that a weak lamb might suck.

'There'll be a lot of yeld beasts the year,' he continued; 'Mackenzie was telling me they're no better off in Strathord. There'll be more ewes going without lambs in Glendarroch than ever I can mind of.'

'Well,' said Johnnie, 'if lambs are scarce, it's likely they'll be a good price, and the fewer there are the better they'll be.'

'Your tea's ready,' said Mary.

The men drew their chairs to the table.

After tea, the men sat talking together, while Mary washed up. The talk was all of the sheep and

' Why not, Mary ? '

' Because the bairn's no' yours.'

' I'll be a good father to it.'

' There's more than that, Johnnie.'

' You're maybe no' caring for me ? '

' Aye, Johnnie, I care for you. But it's thon other lad I'm thinking on most.'

' I'll make you forget him, Mary.'

' I wish you could.'

' You'll marry Johnnie Gillies ? ' he pleaded.

' Well, I'm no' cheating you, Johnnie,' she said. ' You can have me if you're aye wanting me after what I've told you.'

She wept, the bitter racking sobs of misery and fear. He put his arms round her, and she nestled to the comfort of his strength. Then she smiled wanly into the kind brown eyes that were wet.

' I'll make a good wife to you, little Johnnie Gillies,' she whispered, ' for I'm thinking you must be Christ Himself.'

X

They were married a week later in the minister's house at the foot of the glen, quietly before witnesses, and without any ceremony.

Johnnie was kind to Mary. In the mornings, when she felt sick, he would rise early to make her tea, and bring it slopping into its saucer to the bedside. He would milk the cows for her in the evenings, when she got easily tired. Hugh stifled a father's shame in a stockman's sense. He would call to her to take things easy, and carry in wood and coals lest the weight should bring her harm.

Mary had never liked the lambing. There was no knowing what time of the day the men would come in hungry, or asking warm milk for a lamb. The hard work and the worry told on their tempers, and at the back of their minds there was always the fear of storm.

But this lambing brought her a personal dread. She would see Johnnie driving a bleating ewe slowly downhill to the buchts. Hugh would go out to him, and the two men be busy over the groaning sheep. They would come in with bared arms, sometimes carrying a weak and unwashed lamb to heat before the fire.

' Is the ewe all right ? ' Mary would ask.

' God knows ! ' Hugh would answer sourly. ' They're that weak the year, they'll no' stand a handling.'

And Mary would think of what lay before her.

One evening she sat knitting while Hugh and Johnnie slept. Before the fire a young lamb struggled dreadfully with pneumonia. It writhed its head up to the air, its nostrils dilated and its eyes closed, beating its feet weakly on the floor. Its head fell back with a thump, its limbs were still, and Mary thought that it had died. Then its mouth sagged loosely and it tried to bleat, but the sound that came was like the weak cry of a tortured child. Very slowly it lifted its agonised swaying head, its suffering not yet past. Mary tried to forget about the sick lamb, to concentrate on her knitting, which required no concentration, yet she kept waiting for the pitiful cry to be repeated. Despite herself, she must look downwards, and the swaying head had a bubble of blood at its nostrils, expanding and

The widow returned to her mental calculations. 'Was Johnnie up the glen in December, Mary?'

'No, he wasna.'

'Then I canna understand how the bairn's to be here in September. It's against nature, Mary, my dear.'

Mrs Macintyre looked sharply at the tired girl before her. Mary's dates would be right, by the look of her.

'Have you felt life in you yet, Mary?' she asked.

'Aye, by June.'

'Well, well, Mary,' the widow concluded, 'we must get on with our work. I doubt Johnnie *must* have been here in December.'

There were so many things to be knitted and sewn, pilches, barrows, socks and shawls.

'You'll be hoping it'll be a boy,' said Mrs Macintyre.

'Aye, I'd like it a boy.'

'A lassie's more help in the house, Mary.'

'I'm no' needing any help.'

The widow laughed. 'Wait till you've got three or four, my dear. You'll be thinking different about it then.'

The burn whispered and burbled outside, trickling lazily from pool to pool. Mary went on sewing. She wondered what story about her would be carried down the glen. It would be unkind, she knew, but not so much so as were the whole truth known. She thought of what would have been said had Johnnie not married her, and she was determined there should be no gossip about him.

'Johnnie wasn't here in December,' she repeated.

'Maybe no',' replied Mrs Macintyre. 'It may have been after the New Year.'

Immediately the men returned from shooting, the widow became knowingly sedate. 'I've got Mary well started,' she said to Hugh, as she prepared to leave.

'We'll be seeing you later in the year,' he joked, for Mrs Macintyre was the midwife of the glen.

Johnnie saw her down the brae to the road. 'It's a fine evening the night,' he remarked.

'Aye, Johnnie, but we're needing rain.'

'No' till the clipping's by. Thanks for giving Mary a hand.'

'And thanks to *you*, Johnnie Gillies,' laughed Mrs Macintyre. 'I'd sooner spend a fortnight up here in September than in the middle of winter.'

She went down the glen road, the midges swarming round her black hat. Johnnie wondered what she had meant, then realising, spat savagely on the roadside.

That night, in bed, Mary demanded that they leave Glendarroch.

'I canna stay here and have the neighbours laughing and saying I'm months before my time.'

Johnnie rolled over to comfort her. He found it as difficult to keep awake, as she to sleep with the movements of the bairn and the hot weather. 'And where would you have us go?' he asked. 'A steady job among sheep's no' easy to come by with so many of the stocks being cleared.'

'I'm no' caring, Johnnie, but we must go.'

'We canna shift between terms, Mary. I'll look for a married herd's place at the term.'

'I must go before September, Johnnie. I don't want to have my bairn here. Father's laughing at me ; Mrs Macintyre was laughing at me the night ; everybody's laughing at me.'

'Let them laugh and talk, Mary, my dear. What's there in a bairn coming before its time? How many of the country folk wait for the minister? No' the half o' them!'

'But Mrs Macintyre was counting all night in her head.'

'She, the old butch! She was wondering how I got through thon snow to come to you.'

XI

In the cooler days of September Mary's labour began. Johnnie and Hugh were out in the buchts drawing ewe lambs for sale when, in the late afternoon, she felt the first sharp twinge of pain. She struggled down the brae to tell Johnnie. Her first thought was to go to him for help. The dogs sprang over the grey stone walls of the buchts to meet her, yelping at first, then wagging their tails when they saw who came.

Johnnie lifted his tousled black head to the level of the dyke's top. 'Aye, Mary,' he cried. 'Are ye needing me?'

She walked slowly across to him, staring with frightened and piteous eyes. 'Johnnie,' she whispered, 'it's begun.'

'I'll come the now, Mary.'

The black head bobbed backwards out of sight, then there came the voice of unseen Hugh—'We'll finish the job we're at, Johnnie. The bairn'll no' be here till morning.'

'I'll be along in a minute, Mary,' Johnnie called. 'Away you back to the house.'

She went, walking very slowly, wondering

whether she'd have the strength to climb the steep brae to the cottage. She was crying quietly, because she thought Johnnie would have come to her at once. But then the sheep—always the sheep—must have first consideration in Glendarroch!

When Johnnie followed her a few minutes later, she lay deathly white in Hugh's arm-chair. She did not seem to see him until he spoke.

'Are ye pained, Mary?' he asked.

'It just comes and goes.'

Johnnie changed quickly into the worn blue suit which was his best. Then he wheeled Hugh's rattling bicycle from the woodshed. 'I'll go down the glen for Mrs Macintyre,' he said. 'And then I'll go on to Lochend for the doctor.'

Hugh came in and gave a quick glance at his daughter. 'You'll no' need to be long, Johnnie,' he muttered.

Mary overheard what was said. 'Dinna ride too fast, Johnnie,' she urged. 'Mind the rough bits in the road.'

He sped away without speaking again. There was a lump in his throat because Mary had thought of his safety in her own danger. The bicycle bumped and clattered over the ruts and holes, Johnnie bending over the handle-bars, forcing round the pedals in their rusty revolutions. Down the glen he flew with a west wind behind him, between the banks of bracken, brown and dying with the year.

His legs were aching and his breathing agony by the time the Macintyres' farm was in sight. He flung himself from his bike at the door of the rambling whitewashed house. He thundered with his fist at the front door and then round at the

back. The chained dogs howled in fury from the stables. There was a sound of shuffling footsteps coming from the kitchen, the latch rattled, and young Jenny Macintyre blinked stupidly to see who was there.

'It's *you*, Johnnie Gillies!' she exclaimed. 'I didn't know who it was at the door.'

'You'd have seen soon enough if you'd taken a look. Where's your mother?'

'I'm no' just sure where she'll be the now.'

Johnnie stared impatiently at the pale sharp features and straggling fair hair of the girl, at her red nose and watery blue eyes with the cast in them.

'Your mother'll be knowing where you are, all right!' he grunted.

'Come in, Johnnie,' invited Jenny. 'You'll take a cup of tea before you go.'

'I'm no' coming in. Where's your mother?'

'She's gone into Lochend this afternoon.'

'Could ye no' have told me that before? It's her I'm looking for.'

'She shouldna be long, Johnnie.'

Jenny stared down the road, as though that would bring Mrs Macintyre more quickly. 'You'll stay for a cup?'

'No, thanks,' said Johnnie, 'I'm away in to look for your mother. If I was to miss her, you tell her that Mrs Gillies is needing her up at Glendarroch.'

'Oh! *that's* it,' murmured Jenny.

'Aye, *that's* it,' yelled Johnnie, springing again to his shaking saddle.

He sped on until he passed between the steep shoulders of the hills which formed the entrance to the glen. He left the rough track for the smooth

valley road leading down to the town. He scanned
the lumbering blue buses that he met, to see whether
Mrs Macintyre was in any of them. But they flashed
by so quickly that it was difficult to distinguish one
black hat from another. Then he turned a corner,
and the street of the town lay before him.

Lochend nestles snugly at the foot of the hills.
It lies at the top of a stretch of salt water that comes
twisting in from the western sea, until, as though
homesick, it turns in its tracks, to splash small waves
in the face of the setting sun. A straggling row of
buildings runs towards the south, the older houses
grey, substantial and slated, the bright new bunga-
lows crouching close to the ground lest the wind
should sweep them away. Yachts ride smoothly at
anchor on the rippling waters of the loch, and when
old men meet in the street they talk sometimes of
the hills, and sometimes of the sea.

The doctor's house stood sedately back from the
street, in a garden so neat that little was left to grow.
The green iron gate clanged noisily as Johnnie went
through, to follow the gravel path winding among
the smooth lawns and prim beds of flowers. As he
passed the big bay windows of the house he caught
sight of the doctor's bald head bending over his
soup. Johnnie went up the three stone steps to
ring, hoping that no one would steal his bicycle
leaning up against the spiked iron railings. An
elderly maid came in answer to the door, and Johnnie
lifted his cap. ' Can I see the doctor ? ' he inquired.

' Dr Brown consults from six to seven. It's after
that now.'

' Is it, though?' gasped Johnnie. 'I'd no notion
I'd been so long on the road.'

' Do you wish Dr Brown to call ? '

' Aye, tell him he'll need to come at once. I'm under-shepherd up in Glendarroch, and my wife's taken to her bed.'

' Come this way, please,' said the maid, leading the way to the waiting-room.

Johnnie found himself shut into a dreary emptiness of polished linoleum and flowers. He sat down on the edge of a leather-backed chair and dangled his cap in his shaking hands. He grew wildly impatient while the doctor finished his meal.

Dr Brown walked briskly in, wiping the remains of his dinner from his grey moustache. He was a spare, elderly man in a dark blue suit, and his brown eyes twinkled shrewdly on either side of an aquiline nose. ' Well, what can I do for you ? ' he asked.

' Hurry ! ' pleaded Johnnie. ' For God's sake, hurry. My wife's taken to her bed more than two hours ago, and she was that white when I left.'

' Well, you don't expect her to look rosy about it, do you ? Is it her first ? '

' Aye, doctor; there's more danger in the first, isn't there ? '

' There is certainly less hurry, but I shall come at once.'

' Can I come with you, doctor ? You'll be motoring ? '

' How did you come in, shepherd ? '

' On the bike.'

' Well, you'll have to get it back somehow, won't you ? Take your time about it too. You're much better out of the way.'

Dr Brown's swift Bentley passed Johnnie at the

end of the town. The doctor waved encouragement to the toiling figure on the wrong side of the
road. But Johnnie was praying as he pedalled,
' Oh, God ! give the poor lassie an easy time.'

It was growing dark when Johnnie reached the
Macintyres' farm, but he had no time to struggle
with the rusty lamp. He flung himself off at the
door, and now Jenny stood ready to greet him.
' Mother's away up the glen an hour ago.'

' Thank God ! ' Johnnie mumbled, and flung himself onto his bike again.

He saw lights moving in the little cottage as he
fought against the wind, and shadows crossing and
recrossing the kitchen window. The doctor's car
stood at the foot of the hill, and Johnnie wheeled
his bike past it and up the steep brae. He heard an
inhuman groan and dashed through the doorway to
the lobby. There Mrs Macintyre met him.

' Away into the byre with you, Johnnie, out of
the way ! You'll find Mr Maclean there with a lamp,
and we'll give you a call when we're through.'

' How's Mary ? '

' She's doing fine, poor lassie, and the doctor's
with her. Now, away with you ! '

Johnnie drifted aimlessly across to the byre,
where Hugh, squatting on a milk-stool, chewed at a
strand of hay. There, in solemn silence, the two
men waited for news. It was long in coming, and
the cold greyness crept under the byre door to make
the lamp seem pale.

At last Mrs Macintyre came bouncing over the
yard. ' Come away in, Johnnie,' she called.
' You're a father '; and Johnnie had to bite his lip
to behave himself like a man.

He crossed to the cottage alone, for Mrs Macintyre was already back inside, and Hugh sat solemnly in the byre, steadily munching hay. There was nobody in the kitchen. Two kettles and a pan were heating by the fire, and there was a strange sweet sickening smell in the house. Only a guttering candle on the mantelshelf lighted the room; both the lamp and the table had been carried away. Johnnie sat down in disconsolate solitude. He heard the weak wailing of the newborn child, and the voice of Mrs Macintyre grown suddenly maternal. Dr Brown came bustling through.

'Well, Gillies,' he said, 'you should be a proud man. Your wife's splendid, and you've got a fine boy.'

'Mary's well?'

'Couldn't be better. You don't seem very interested in the boy. Did you want a girl?'

'I wasna caring.'

'Would you like to see him? Mrs Macintyre has him in the parlour.'

'I'm no' just caring the now.'

'Goodness, man, what's wrong with you? You should be proud of the boy.'

'I'll be a good father to him.'

'Well,' said the doctor, 'I must go. I'll be up soon again to see that everything's all right. Mrs Macintyre is a good nurse.'

'Can I see the wife, doctor?'

'In a few minutes. Good-bye, Gillies.'

'Good-bye, doctor, and thank you.'

Johnnie listened to the doctor's footsteps growing fainter in the distance, then to the drone of the big car going down the glen.

'Mary's asking for you, Johnnie,' called Mrs Macintyre.

Johnnie walked slowly through to his wife. He scarcely glanced at the red and writhing baby in the pulled-out drawer of the kitchen dresser. He went straight past it to Mary, lying pale and faintly smiling in the double bed.

'Aye, Mary,' he whispered, 'was it bad?'

'It's past, Johnnie. You'll be good to the wee bairn?'

'I'll be a good father to it, Mary.'

She pulled his dark head down to her, stroking his hair. 'Poor Johnnie!' she whispered.

'You'll maybe give me a boy of my own some day, Mary?'

Mrs Macintyre in the next room listened hard.

'There'll *never* be another, Johnnie,' said Mary.

Mrs Macintyre smiled.

"Mary's asking for you, Tobias," called Mrs.
Simmons.

Tobias walked slowly through to the side. He
never glanced at the red and glowing baby in the
published figure of the swaddled drapery. He went
straight past it to where Mary, pale and faintly
smiling, in the bed he laid.

"We haven't got stopped?... Was it bad?"

"It's past, Tobias... You'll be good to the wee
lamb?"

"I'll be a good father to it, Mary."

She rolled the dark head down to her, smiling
his part. "I've learned," she whispered.

"You'll maybe give me a kiss of my own now,
then, Mary?"

Her likeness in the cross-roads before him.

"I shall never be keeping faithful," said Mary.

His blood to smiled.

PART TWO

MARY'S SON

THE wee boy's breeks were wet. He had seen a fish gliding in and out of the weed-covered stones in a deep pool of the burn. It had stayed still for a moment with its questioning nose upstream, and its tail fin waving gently from side to side. Leaning forward to catch it with his grimy hands, little Duncan Gillies had slipped on a stone and gone in to his waist, and now his breeks were wet.

He struggled up the brae, crying for his mother, the water dripping down his legs, his bare feet feeling their way carefully on the gritty path. Mary, hearing his sobbing, left her work to go to the door. ' What's wrong, Duncan ? ' she called.

' Mother, I'm wet.'

He had been called Duncan because Mary liked the sound of the name, and Duncan Gillies he had been registered and baptized. At three years old he had to look after himself a good deal, since his mother was busy with the house, and with his brother, wee Johnnie, who wasn't yet two.'

' I'm wet,' Duncan sobbed.

' Then take down your breeks till I fetch a clout to dry you, and dinna come into the house and make a mess.'

Without his trousers, and with only a jersey to keep him from the early morning chill, Duncan shivered at the cottage door. His mother came out

to rub the wet and the green slime from his body and legs. Then she gave him a gentle pat on the bare buttocks, and sent him toddling down the brae again until his porridge was cooked. He ran to the burn to see if the fish was still there.

Dunçan couldn't see the fish at all. The pool was all muddied and stirred with the splash he had made in falling in. He lay down flat on the ground, damp with morning dew, and watched the grass turn from silver to green where he laid his hands. Under the palm-like fronds of the bracken he could see the rippling expanse of the pool, with a winding trickle of water flowing in at the top, and the thin ghost of a waterfall passing out at its foot. Faint clouds of yellow dust still floated up from the shingle bed, and all the fish and water-worms were hidden under stones.

Duncan wriggled forwards so that his face was close to the ripples on the water's surface. He lay there a little time until all was again quiet, while the sunlight streamed through the bracken's tracery to warm the back of his sun-browned neck. He stared intently into the water and saw his own reflection— the fringe of brown hair falling forwards over his freckled forehead, the clear grey eyes and finely chiselled nose, the wide red mouth and strong teeth, white as ivory. He gently lowered his head until he touched the image of his chin, and the reflection shivered and vanished in ever-widening rings.

Something silver and swift as lightning flashed across the shingle—the fish again !

'Duncan ! Duncan ! ' His mother's voice rang clearly, echoing back from the hills' recesses.

Duncan knew that his porridge was made, and felt hungry. He wriggled backwards from the burn. Out on the brae it was warm. The August sun rose late, but had warmth in it, the close thundery heat of summer at its close, heavy with the humming of bees and the bleating of ewes new-weaned.

Duncan hurried up the brae, careless of the stones, because his porridge was poured. He did not see Johnnie Gillies climbing up behind him, the dogs at his heels.

'Here, boy,' shouted Johnnie, 'what did I tell you?' Duncan, turning, stared blankly at the little man overtaking him. 'Did I no' tell you that if I saw you without your breeks again I'd give you a skelp?'

'I fell in the burn.'

'I'll no' skelp you for that, boy. I've done the same mysel'. Give me your hand, or your porridge'll be cold.'

Duncan hurried over his breakfast because he wanted outside again. The blue-bottles were buzzing round the kitchen and flying with soft bumps against the window-panes, the fire was red and hot, and wee Johnnie was crying because his mother had put him down. But outside there was the cool trickling of the burn, the shade of bracken and alder leaves, the heavy humming of bees on their way to the heather. The sunlight streamed in at the open door of the house, and with it came scents of warm earth and greenery. The air over the peat mosses rose in shimmering waves.

'It'll be a hot day the day,' said Hugh.

His shirt sleeves were rolled up, showing the knotted muscles of his arms. The brown beard and hair were flecked with grey.

'Aye,' said Johnnie, ' it'll be hot.'

The flies buzzed, the fire glowed, and wee Johnnie went on crying. Duncan slid from his chair and ran to the door.

'Here, Duncan,' cried Mary, 'wait till I put on your breeks.'

They had been drying on the warm shelf of the range. Duncan waited until he was clothed again, then bounded out to the glory of an autumn day.

Mountains rose sharp and splendid against a deep blue sky. The glen lay in still serenity, surrounded by mounting waves of majestic purple. Curlews, flying high, called their sorrowful singing as they drifted gently westwards from the silent hills. They cried with the magical low clear whistle they croon to the sands when winter waves come tumbling in to the wet expanse of a lonely shore. Duncan looked up as they passed overhead, seven long-billed birds in a straggling lazy line, calling more to themselves than to each other, in gentle sorrow at a summer's passing, yet full of restless heartache for the sea. He watched them float over the distant hills, their song growing fainter and fainter as they drifted away.

Duncan wandered up the steep sides of the burn. On either side sprang the gnarled brown trunks of the alders and the silvery whiteness of birch. Under the cool shade of their leaves grew tall bracken, erect and luscious green, spreading broad fronds to the filtered light. Delicate mauve of willow-herb painted the rocks' recesses, and challenging spikes of purple bugle stood sentinel by the stream. The clear water trickled gently over the rounded stones, spreading in shallow pools, falling almost lazily over

scarred bed of the pool. He had carried small stones with great effort and had laid them in the wrong places. But he had kept close beside Johnnie, who was patient and cheery and never tired of showing him a shepherd's ways. When it was dinner-time the child followed the men up the brae, forcing his legs to a long hill-stride like theirs, and Mary, watching from the window, smiled when she saw what he was at.

At high noon the men went out to the hill to search for maggoted sheep. The fly was striking badly in the hot weather. Duncan ran down the brae, the sun, beating on his back, warming him through and through. He hurried because there was a big job of work before him that afternoon. He was going to carry more stones to the dam to make a bigger and deeper pool. He found the water still and unrippled in the calm air, clear and unsullied as a mountain spring. He could see the spade-marks on the bottom, scratches and grooves on the hard red moor pan which lies under the peat. He ran over the heather to fetch a big white stone with sparkling bits in it that shone like silver. He struggled and pushed until he was tired, but the big stone would not budge. So he carried a smaller one and dropped it in the pool. He watched it sink to the bottom and slowly settle, and saw the thin eddies of dust rising up through the water from the place it had struck. He carried another stone and then another, until he could not see the pool's depths because of floating sand. Then he forgot about the big job of work he had set out to do, and threw in gravel and sand to see the great splashes they made. He was laughing to himself at the fun

he was having, when he heard his mother calling from the top of the brae.

' Duncan, you're to stop that this minute ! '

The boy looked up at the familiar figure in the print dress. He dropped the stone he was carrying and strode up the brae with his long hill-stride.

' What were you doing, Duncan ? '

' Working—working hard.'

' Your grandfather'll be angered at you if you've made a mess in the dam. Away down the brae and play yourself, and don't get into more mischief.'

Duncan strolled away, hanging his head a little, hurt at being spoken to as though he were wee Johnnie. But when he saw the dirt still rising in the pool, he was afraid—afraid of what Hugh might do to him. He waited by the dam through the drowsy afternoon, hoping that the water would clear before the men came home.

Midges and flies swarmed in hazy clouds about his head ; the water trickled rhythmically ; the afternoon sun drew warm scents from the earth. From far away came the faint whistling of Johnnie coming home, the sound rising and falling as the whistler stepped down into hollows or crested the ridge. Hugh's black-and-white collie came racing on ahead of its master, scrambling down to the burn's side with panting breath and quivering tongue to quench its thirst. Duncan heard the rustle of boots on the dried heather—the men were coming down to the burn to look at the dam.

Duncan ran up the brae to seek safety in the house. He was less than half-way there when he heard Hugh roaring to him to stop, and redoubled his speed in a wild dash for sanctuary. But Hugh

was following; Duncan could hear his muttered
curses as he came nearer, gaining with every yard.
Duncan knew that he would be caught. He turned
like a cornered hare and dashed past Hugh, down
the hill, to hurl himself in trembling terror against
Johnnie Gillies's legs. He buried his face in the
rough breeches smelling of sheep.

'Dinna let him, father! Dinna let him,' he cried.

'Hold him, Johnnie!' Hugh shouted. 'I'll
learn the brat to keep out of more mischief.'

'Dinna let him,' Duncan moaned.

He felt a rough hand stroking his head, and rough
fingers twisting tenderly in his tangled hair.

'Keep your distance, Hugh Maclean!' yelled
Johnnie Gillies. 'You'll no' skelp the bairn.'

'Will I no', John Gillies?'

'You'll no' touch him, man; you're daft.'

'My God! I'll show you what I'll do.'

Duncan felt himself pitched bodily behind his
father, and scrambled out from the bracken, dazed
and sobbing in fear. He saw the two men facing
each other, the big bearded man with his stick
raised in menace, and the little dark man backing
slowly, a stone held poised in his right hand, a very
David before Goliath. They were shouting furi-
ously at each other.

'Keep your distance, Hugh Maclean!'

'Fight fair, Johnnie Gillies!'

'Will you leave the bairn alone?'

'I'll skelp him till he's sore.'

Duncan saw his mother hurrying down the brae,
anxious because of the noise, holding wee Johnnie
in her arms.

'My!' she shouted, when she saw the men

quarrelling, 'is it no' enough to have the bairns aye fighting, without the men starting too? Put down your sticks and stones and come in to your tea!'

Her presence put an end to the disorder, but the storms of wrath still rumbled.

'I'm waiting for you to apologise, Johnnie Gillies.'

'Indeed, and I'm thinking it's you should do that.'

'Then I'll ask you no' to speak to me.'

'And that'll no' be ill to do, Hugh Maclean.'

There was silence that evening at tea. Neither of the men would speak first; they sat stolidly munching their scones and bread, glaring at Mary as though she were to blame.

When tea was ended, Johnnie rose. 'I'm away out to put the dam right for the morning. Are you coming, Duncan?'

The boy raced out to sunset and shadows of evening. Johnnie broke the dam, allowing the fouled waters to escape. Then he scraped out the mud and shingle and replaced the big stones. The clear water spread softly over the pool. 'That'll be fine by morning,' he said. 'It's time you were bedded, Duncan boy.'

By late evening Duncan lay secure beside wee Johnnie in bed. They slept in the room where Jack Knight had stayed. Duncan listened to the swallows settling to rest. There was a nest just above the window under the sheltering slope of the eaves, which could not be disturbed because of the bad luck that would surely follow. The birds were out of the nest through the day, fluttering and twitter-

ing about the yard and sheds, but in the evening they returned to the nest's warm shelter. There was unspeakable peace in the faint chirping, the low rustling, the ultimate stillness of the birds. Duncan listened until the only sounds were the distant hum of voices from the kitchen and the dreamy murmurs of the stream. Then he slept.

II

Duncan went to school when he was five years old, in the back-end of the year, when the early lamb sales were by. An old man drove an old Ford car to the foot of the brae, and tooted his horn for the bairns to come down.

Old Jimmy Macfarlane was seventy-two, and he ran his car up and down the glen to transport young scholars at the Education Authority's expense. He had never had to go farther than the Macintyres' before Duncan was of age, and he disliked the boy at once because he added four miles of rough road to his journey each day.

Duncan was crying because he had to go to school on a day when the wool was dispatched. He liked to see the men straining and tugging at the huge and bulging wool-sacks, tight laced with twine. The motor lorry always looked like some weird monster animal, swaying and lurching down the glen road with its towering burden swinging from side to side, and to-day he was to miss it all.

He scrambled into the palpitating car. Old Macfarlane wiped the dribbles from his hanging grey moustache and leant out to bang the swinging door. 'Mind your fingers, boy,' he snapped when

the door was safely closed, ' and don't you keep me waiting another day ! '

The old man turned to a laboured manipulation of controls. The car bounded into motion. Duncan snivelled in the back seat, and Mary was waving to him through the wee window.

The car stopped at the Macintyres' for the shepherd's children, a sandy-haired squat boy of seven and a pale studious lassie of twelve. ' Aye, Duncan,' they said as they sat down beside him.

' Mind your fingers ! ' mumbled Macfarlane, slamming the door.

It was a cool autumn morning when the car clattered into Lochend, and Duncan had his first view of the town and of the sea. A stiff wind was blowing, rustling the first fallen leaves in the cobbled gutters of the street. The loch was whipped into millions of white-crested waves, and feathers of foam drifted over the low pier, to lie like quivering jelly-fish on the uneven pavement. A yacht leapt through the water, spinning before the wind, drenched with sun and spray, its white sails heeling over to the waves. Men in blue jerseys tramped the pier with their hands deep buried in their pockets, sucking idly at pipes which the wind had emptied. Across the loch were deep wooded hills, the light green of the larches and the deep green of the firs. White gulls in a blue sky followed the seething wake of the yacht. Duncan thought he would like to be on a boat, but he was bound for school.

The yellow benches were hard and the desks initialled by pupils, some old, some dead, all forgotten except two. There were the letters A.M. on a corner desk, said to have been carved by Angus

Maclean, who had become a director of companies and Lord Strathgroam. There were the letters J.C. on half a dozen desks. They were said to be those of Johnnie Campbell, who had won the V.C. in France for playing the pipes on the trenches' tops. There was a window in the schoolroom which looked on to the street. Between two of the houses opposite was a blink of the sea.

Duncan stuck firmly to his companions in travel. He felt safer with them than with the boys and girls of the town. He thought of the wool lorry and of the boats on the sea, and stared at the teacher he was to know for seven years.

She was called Miss Gray, and the children called her 'Pock' because she had pimples on her face. She might have been a kind woman, but she knew what her pupils called her. When one of them stared or laughed she thought it could only be because of her face. She found Duncan's eyes fixed, as she thought, on her spots. She stamped her foot.

'What are you staring at, boy? Yes—*you*. Can't you answer?—Are you dumb? You country children are hopeless. Are *you* Duncan Gillies?'

'Aye.'

'*Don't* say "aye." Say "yes, mum."'

'Yes, mum.'

'And *don't* stare.'

Clouds skimmed across the blueness of a sun-kissed sky, gulls swooped down to touch the laughing whiteness of the waves, the wind sang and whistled up the streets and burst roaring round the corners. Ropes span out from boats to waiting hands on the pier, straining and tightening as the ships came bumping gently against the piles. The

wind rushed up the glen, bringing the waves of
the sea to the heather on the hills, sweeping the
mists from the mountain's face. Across the sea
sounded the echoing hail of the sailor, and over the
hills the far-carrying whistle of the herd. But
Duncan sat on the hard bench of the dust-filled
room, listening to the harsh, complaining voice of
a tired woman. For seven years, for the greater
part of the day, he must hear her talk.

At the dinner-hour Duncan went out to the
playground, a square of beaten earth with weedy
grass straggling from the corners. A bicycle shed,
roofed with corrugated iron, was near the gate,
and in the very centre stood a flagpole, where the
Union Jack fluttered on Empire Day. The children clustered round the new boy. He stood, slim,
erect, and shy, while they asked him his name and
what his father did. A little girl offered him some
of her piece, and smiled when he took it. The boys
kicked stones about because they had no football.
Then Miss Gray straggled up again from her dreary
lodgings, took off her dreary hat, and formed the
children into line. She clapped her thin hands
together while they marched in some semblance of
step into the dust-filled class-room. Duncan sat on
the hard bench until it was time to go home.

Old Macfarlane was half an hour late. He had
had trouble in starting the car, and was in the worst
of tempers. He was tired, and in dread of the dark
nights and ice-bound roads that were coming with
the winter months. He grudged the extra two
miles to the head of the glen. 'Get in,' he grumbled.
'Did I no' tell ye to mind your fingers?'

He drove stiffly and very slowly, hazy eyes glued

on the road ahead. Sometimes he would dream and his attention wander, when the car would drift towards the ditch. Then he would jerk himself upright, sound his horn at nothingness, and stare straight ahead at the white ribbon of the road.

'Cheerio, Duncan,' said the shepherd's children when they stepped off before the Macintyres' white-washed house.

Old Macfarlane half-turned the car from habit before he recalled the extension of his duties. The Ford lurched and staggered to the foot of the brae. Mary had been watching the road a full hour. She had been getting anxious about the car, although it was said old Macfarlane was a safe driver and had never had an accident. She ran down the brae to meet Duncan, who came plodding up to meet her. She thought he looked so small with the new school satchel on his back.

'Aye, Duncan boy, so you're home,' she said.

'Aye, mother.'

'And do you like the school?'

'No!'

They were all asking questions of him that night.

'And who do you like best at the school?' asked Mary when they were at their tea.

'There was a wee lassie that gave me a piece.'

Hugh Maclean thumped his great fist on the table and roared with laughter. 'Breeding aye comes out!' he cried.

Mary and Johnnie were silent and uncomfortable. Hugh saw that he had made a mistake and grumbled sulkily to himself.

Duncan felt as though he had been stuck in the hen-house all day. He wandered out after tea to

watch the sheep clambering up the braes. To the west the clouds were silver and gold above the black masses of the hills. The wind had dropped, and the stillness of evening held the glen motionless as in prayer. The track running over the hills to the western sea caught the sun's rays. For a moment it shone white and glistening against the dark shadows of the heather. Duncan thought of the sea on the other side where the track led, of boats rocking gently beside piers that smelt of tar, of big men in jerseys smoking pipes in the evening, and the thin smoke drifting over their heads as they spoke. He thought of the green waters swelling gently to a wave, then breaking in a sheet of white, and of gulls flashing down out of a blue sky. He thought of sweating men struggling with sacks of wool, and of lambs new gathered for a sale. He thought of speckled trout in the cool deep pools of the burn, and of the splashing sound they made when they jumped for flies. He thought of all this, but remembered nothing of what Miss Gray had told him that day.

III

Duncan got more fun out of school as the months went by. It was fun to make banging noises in the back of the car to keep old Macfarlane from dozing. The old man had a fear of the Ford taking fire, and would jerk up in his seat at any noise. If the banging went on he would stop altogether and give the car time to cool down. That made the scholars late for school.

It was great fun staring at Miss Gray until she

blushed. Sometimes the whole class would do it together, so that whenever she lifted her head she would meet eighty bright eyes assessing the more recent ravages of her disease. Then she would seize on some trifling excuse to thrash a boy or a girl with the leather strap called the tawse, and the girl would blubber and turn to the wall, or the boy snatch away his hand so that the tawse came slashing down on Miss Gray's own knees. Duncan didn't mind the plunking, as the children called it, because the skin of his hands was hard through exposure to cold and rough weather. He didn't think much of Miss Gray. Once a week she gave a nature lesson, and she got all muddled up between peewees and grouse, and between rooks and crows. She would clear her tired voice and arrange her straw-coloured hair, and proceed to the expounding of the Scriptures.

Miss Gray was an unbeliever; she could not conceive that a beneficent God had created spots. She reduced Revelation to a series of rather absurd fables, and was happier when she turned to arithmetic and spelling.

In the dinner-hour Duncan wandered down to the pier, munching his piece. Mary spent great trouble in making his sandwiches different from day to day, and sometimes she would put in a slice of gingerbread to surprise him.

There was always something doing at the pier, a boat being loaded or a yacht coming in. On rough days the waves slapped up against the green slime on the wooden piles, and the spray dashed over to the street like a shower of rain. Then the sea would sink back with a regretful roar, and the wet ropes strain and crack as the tied boats followed the wave.

When the mail-boat steamed in the postman came running down with his rattling hurley, the pier-master put on his official hat, and the long ropes came singing to shore like uncoiling snakes, to be caught by leathery hands and tied to the iron stanchions. There was always a smell of salt-water and tar, of rotting seaweed and smoke-cured fish, of strong tobacco smoked in well-seasoned pipes. Duncan would tear himself away from the place where men were working to take up position in a straggling line, to march into school while Miss Gray clapped her hands in time.

It was an eerie business going home in the late autumn nights. The lights of the Ford were a feeble compliance with the Law. They flickered like candles in the dense darkness of the glen road. The deer were rutting, and stags called to each other from hill to hill—a mad, infuriated roar, starting in a shrill bellow and dying down to muttering thunder. They were tame and stupid in their sexual orgy. Sometimes fleeting shadows of the herd flitted across the road before the dim head-lights of the car, and old Macfarlane would jerk to attention and tread on the clutch instead of the brake. The Ford would rock madly from side to side, while the stags bellowed out of the darkness.

Mary was always waiting anxiously for the sound of the car. She felt frightened of what might happen, with the black night falling so early and the deer coming right down to the road. But there was no other way for Duncan to get to the school, and no chance of such a healthy boy being excused until he was six. So she waited, as she had done so often in her life, with the lamp lit and set close to the

window, a signal and a welcome to those who were out in the night. As soon as she saw the lights of the car creeping up the glen, she hastened down to meet Duncan, to take his hand up the brae for fear he was frightened of the dark. She was thankful when the snow came and the roads drifted, so that old Macfarlane could not venture to Glendarroch and Duncan could bide at home. He was glad too, shooting down the snow-covered brae on the sledge Johnnie had nailed together from old wooden planks, carrying hay from the shed to the byre, or sitting by the warm fire when the blizzards blew. But the snow soon went, except for the piled smudged drifts at the sides of the road, and the Ford came rattling and clattering up the glen. Duncan felt it was like going again for the first time to school. He was shy as ever of the others in his class, and had forgotten the little he had learnt. Miss Gray made it no easier for him.

' Have you done nothing at home, Duncan ? '

' No, mum.'

' Doesn't your mother help you with your lessons ? '

' No, mum.'

' What on earth *does* she do ? '

' Works, mum.'

The class tittered and stared, uncertain whether to make pupil or teacher their prey.

' Are you being impudent, Duncan ? '

' No, mum.'

' Well, I can hardly expect you to do your lessons if you get no encouragement at home. You must tell your mother to help you. Do you think she will ? '

'No, mum.'

'Then I'm afraid she's as lazy as yourself, Duncan.'

The class laughed openly because the teacher was getting the better of five-years-old. Duncan was very angry because they were all laughing at his mother. He glared at the smiling face of Miss Gray. She was happy because the children were on her side. Duncan hated her. He wondered dumbly why she had been put in authority over him. But he knew how to hurt her.

'My mother's got a clean face,' he murmured.

Miss Gray heard. It had never been openly said before. She lost control of herself. She snatched the tawse from her desk and rushed across the room. She slashed Duncan across the face again and again with the hard handle of the strap. 'I'll send *you* home with a *nice* face,' she panted, while Duncan screamed and tried to shelter his head. He went home that night with blue weals on his face.

'That'll learn you, boy,' growled old Macfarlane when he saw what had been done.

But there was wild fury in Glendarroch that night.

'She *did*, did she, the butch!' Hugh bellowed, when he heard the sobbed-out tale. 'Away out for my bike, Johnnie. I'm away in to make a pro*test*.' The steel-grey glitter of battle was in his eyes.

'I was going in myself,' Johnnie shouted.

'Get my bike, John Gillies! I'll see to this mysel'.'

Mary was bathing Duncan's face. She was content to leave the fighting to her men, knowing that it would be well done, and Duncan smiled through his tears because everyone was on his side.

It was late when Hugh came home, and Duncan was long in bed. Mary and Johnnie sat on either side of the fire—waiting.

'Did you give her a good skelping?' Mary asked savagely.

Hugh poured himself out a dram. 'The boy's health,' he muttered, tossing it off neat. He wiped his grey-flecked beard with his red hand. 'I didna skelp her,' he said. 'The lassie's fair scared to death that she'll lose her job over the head of it all. She was saying that if I'd no' tell she'd never put hands on Duncan again. I saw what she was feared for, so it's straight down to the Loch Arms I went and told the story to them there.'

'And what were they saying to it?' Johnnie asked.

'Ach!' Hugh answered. 'That she would be the better o' the tawse hersel'! They were saying that she's gey stuck-up like, and never comes out o' her lodgings till after dark. She's no' popular at all.'

'And little wonder at that,' Mary agreed.

The next day Duncan was a hero at school. It was soon rumoured that Miss Gray was applying for posts all over the country, and that no one would have her. It was said, with truth, that a sailor had found her wandering at night on the pier, and had had to prevent her from jumping into the sea. But she never touched Duncan again or spoke against his mother.

Duncan did what he liked in school. He drew faces on his books instead of doing his sums, and painted red blotches on the faces with his coloured crayon. He learned to say 'Cheerio,' and to use

foul words unknown in the glen. He did not grow as he should have done, because he spent all day on a hard bench in a dust-filled room. He lived for the day he would be done with the school. He got colds and sore throats, and infected wee Johnnie at home. It was Saturdays and Sundays and the snow that kept him going until the spring. At Easter he got ten days' holiday and freedom on the hills.

'No school to-day, mother,' he grinned.

'Well, don't get into any mischief, Duncan boy.'

Mary would find work lighter and the days more short because he was home.

IV

Spring came to the glen that year with the thrilling glory of migrating birds. Peewits tumbled above the dead bracken and grey grass, curlews with outstretched wings floated down wind in a passion of song. Wild-geese straggled in V-shaped formation across the face of the sun, and black-cock, their splendid tail feathers curving outwards, sailed down the valley in all the pomp and circumstance of polygamy.

Duncan drew in great gulps of the snow-smelling air, tossed the fair hair back from his eyes, and bounded over the dead brown heather to the high moors. The wind had swept the sky clear of everything but bird-song, the sun had melted the white snow in the corries to send the hill burns thundering down. Saxifrages, white, purple, and yellow, covered the cold wet rocks in coloured mist.

Duncan had been told not to wander too far, but

set his face towards the Craig and the Corriemore. He went farther up the hill that day than he had ever done, following the banks of the swirling streams. The hazel trees were a golden mist of yellow catkins, and the first willow was opening in honeyed fertility. Over the wide moors the little plover were piping, and in the thickness of bare rowan branches fieldfares and redwings sang together in their migrating thousands.

Duncan heard them from afar—the tumult of their singing like the rush of water. When he came on them he saw the branches sagging with their weight, speckle-throated thrushes singing together, facing the north. They sang together until the hill air lived with the magical melody of birds. Duncan watched and listened and felt afraid. It was uncanny to find wild things lost in the music they made, never heeding the boy who watched them. A light cloud crossed the sun, and all grew still.

The silence and the cold when the sun was hid made Duncan feel that the world had suddenly died. The wind came sighing through the passes of the hills, stirring the dead heather and the bare branches by the stream. A hail-shower blustered over the bleak ridge, and the sky was hidden in flying pebbles of ice. A rabbit, caught by a hunting stoat, screamed in its impotent pain. Loneliness and terror fell like a cloak over the cold moors.

Duncan ran down the stream, seeking the shelter of the house. He was trembling and crying from fear. But the shower swept by, and with it his mountain panic. He turned to face the life of the unclouded sun, and watched the tail of the shower,

like myriad diamonds, sink gently to earth from a
sky of blue. He slowed down and paced towards
the edge of a wide bog.

The ewes were gathered there in numbers. The
bog was on the Pot heft, so called from the great
marsh lying in a cup of the hills, and it was the
best spring grazing in Glendarroch. Duncan heard
a dog bark, and there, not far distant, was Johnnie
Gillies, standing with his two hands and chin resting on his stick, watching the sheep. Duncan ran
shouting across to him.

' Quietly, boy,' said Johnnie. ' Always move
quietly among the sheep. I'm no' wanting them
shifted from here.'

' What are they eating, father ? '

The ewes were browsing on fresh green cotton-
sedge, tugging out the pale succulent stems from
the sheltering leaves.

' Draw-moss,' Johnnie answered. ' The best
meat in the world for putting milk on a ewe. If
ewes get a good bite of draw-moss in the spring,
there's no fear of them at lambing, unless they've
more milk than a weak lamb can stand.'

' What's wrong with that one ? ' Duncan asked,
pointing to a thin, ill-thriven beast with blood on
its tail.

' She's slipped her lamb, boy, cast her lamb. She
did the same last year, and she'll need to be sold
herself this back-end.'

' Cast her lamb, cast her lamb,' Duncan murmured, committing the phrase to memory.

' Aye,' said Johnnie. ' That means she's put out
her lamb before it's fit to live. I've seen them bad
with it some years.'

'Can they no' have another lamb, father?'

'Not the same year, boy. They need the tup for that.'

'They need the tup. They need the tup. What for do they need a tup?'

'There's no lamb can grow inside a ewe, Duncan, till a tup's jumped on her and put his seed in her.'

'Father,' said Duncan suddenly, 'can I no' leave the school? I'd sooner be a herd.'

Johnnie smiled, and his eyes saw visions in the blue distance, visions of a great shepherd, wise in sheep-lore. 'You'll need to bide at the school, Duncan, though it's a real pity. They'll keep you there till you're fourteen, and you could have been learning a lot about sheep by then.'

'What's the use of school, father?'

Johnnie Gillies spat far into the bog. 'None—for a herd.'

Duncan thought of the ships and the tarry piers. 'Is the school any use to a sailor, father?'

Johnnie pondered long before he answered. 'I've never heard tell that Noah could read,' he said.

The two dogs were fawning round Duncan, trying to lick his face. Johnnie's old black bitch had been sold to a low-ground farmer. She had become too slow for the hill. The big black dog, her son, was grizzled about the nose. Her daughter, a black puppy bitch, was learning her life's trade. Duncan rubbed his head on the puppy's smooth coat until Johnnie intervened.

'Never pet a working dog, boy,' he said. 'They're no manner of use when they're spoilt.'

Duncan went on rubbing his head.

' Did ye no' hear what I said ? ' Johnnie snapped.
' You'll do what I tell ye, boy ! '

Duncan looked up in hurt astonishment, but kept
his face from the dogs.

' I'm away across to the Corrie,' said Johnnie.
' D'ye think ye'll manage that far, Duncan ? '

' Aye, fine ! '

Duncan set his face to the hills again, to the
steep shoulder which sheltered the Corriemore,
where he had never been. As he followed Johnnie's
long stride over the heather, he imagined he was
grown to a man and done with the school. He
walked like a herd with the dogs behind him, and
Johnnie cut him a long stem of heather to use as
a stick. There was no fear in his heart with his
father before him, and he set his face with a stout
heart to the long climb. There was one thing he
must ask.

' Do you see the sea from the Corriemore,
father ? '

' No, boy ; you'd need to be climbing up the hill
at its top.'

' Can we do that the day ? '

' It's too far for you yet.'

Duncan remembered that he was still at school.

They tramped on over the broken surface of the
moor. Patches of hard snow lay in the corners of
the peat-hags, and the mountain hares, still winter-
white, leapt up in startled fear before the dogs.

Round the shoulder of the Craig Johnnie Gillies
tramped, with Duncan struggling gamely at his
heels ; round the Craig's shoulder to the sheltered
wildness of the Corriemore. There, in the green
marsh ground in its centre, grazed the deer.

' Look ! ' Johnnie cried.

Duncan scanned the steep mountains of the Corrie's sides, and the sheer precipice rising at its end. He saw the stream winding through the green rushes from the unmelted patches of snow. Then, one by one, he distinguished the silent, motionless deer. They stood as though carved in rock, their faces turned towards danger, their dun-coloured bodies blending with the background of the rocks. As though at a signal, they trotted up the hill, turned to gaze backwards, then galloped away.

' They're bonnie,' said Duncan.

' Useless brutes,' Johnnie grunted, ' and far too many of them, eating up good sheep's meat.'

' What are they for, father ? '

' To be shot at by idle bodies from London in the back-end, that have nothing better to do with their time.'

' What do they shoot them for ? '

Johnnie Gillies halted to lean on his stick. ' What for ? ' he repeated. ' To give them some walking on the hill. They eat that much in London, that if they didn't come crawling on their bellies for a month in the year, they'd get too fat to move.'

' Where's London, father ? '

' Do they no' learn ye that at the school ? It's a long way off, but no' long enough. Come on, boy, I'm wanting to see if the moss's through here yet.'

They tramped on to the stream's side.

It was fine weather all the way home, with the wind at their backs and the warmth of the sun to face. Johnnie was whistling all the time, tunes with a lilt and a spring in them that made the way seem short. His old shabby cap was tilted to the side, his

eyes laughing at the fine day, his brown face twisted as he whistled. Behind him ran Duncan, whistling too, his heather stick over his shoulder and the long hair straggling over his brow. The puppy rolled and gambolled at will because there were no sheep at hand. Down the brae they went, the man, the boy, and the two dogs, amid sunlight, heather, and the wind.

Far below them was the whitewashed cottage above the thin grey ribbon of the road, the smoke from the chimney, and the washing blowing on the line.

Johnnie turned his head, laughing. 'You'll be ready for your dinner, Duncan boy?'

'Aye, father.'

But Duncan had no thought of food. He had formed a resolution. He ran down to the cottage ahead of Johnnie.

'Where have you been all morning, Duncan?' his mother asked.

'Learning to be a herd,' he answered.

V

The days of freedom soon passed. Duncan was back at school.

Miss Gray had spent her holiday with a married sister in Westown, without enjoyment. Her sister had never tried to get on as she had, had never worked so hard at school, had wasted her time at the University, dancing, playing, and flirting. But she had achieved a clear complexion and marriage to a newly qualified doctor with a future in noses and throats. Miss Gray grudged good fortune to her sister, and how she *hated* the Lochend school!

' Duncan Gillies,' she complained, ' you're hope-less ! What on earth do you expect to do in the world ? '

' Be a herd, mum.'

Miss Gray thought of hard things to say, re-membered an unfortunate incident in the past, and refrained. ' That's not much of an ambition,' she grumbled.

Duncan was silent, but he stared. The boy beside him saw what he was at and stared too. Soon all the class was staring. The teacher blushed. How she detested those children and that school !

It was still bright when Duncan was free at the end of the day, and Jimmy Macfarlane could safely allow the batteries of his old car to go down. It was a fine run up the glen in the May days, past the small waves of the loch, where the white gulls flashed before the low sun, by the arable farms where the early lambs were already grown big, through the young larch plantations with pigeons calling from the sprays of tender green, up the narrow road with rain-pools silvered by the evening light.

The men were busy when Duncan got home, for the hill-lambing was at its height. Bodies of skinned lambs would be lying on the tops of the bucht walls, and the sheds and byres be loud with the bleating of ewes brought in from the hill. Johnnie would be walking across the yard with the slow mechanical walk of a dog-tired man, carrying the milk-bottles with rubber teats to give suck to the motherless lambs. Duncan must hurry over his tea to get outside again, to help his father in the byres, to work with him as the light failed, bedding up the sheep with the moulded hay, tying up the ewes that refused

their lambs. In the kitchen there would be the weakest lambs, the premature lambs, and the dying lambs, and Mary stepping carefully across the floor to the range. She made supper with the feebly bleating beasts about her feet.

On Saturdays and Sundays, the days of release, Duncan followed Johnnie on his round of the hill. The weather was kindly that May, with mild airs and the young green shoots thrusting through the mat of dead winter grass. The wind was in the west, the sun gaining strength, the young lambs rising quickly to their feet. The man, and the boy in his outworn ill-fitting clothes, climbed the steep braes, keeping to the ridges where the view was wide.

On the second Saturday of the month, when he was six years old, Duncan lambed his first ewe. He had watched Johnnie so often that he knew, as by instinct, what was to be done. They had watched this sheep from a grey lichen-covered rock, saw her black head twisting upwards as in supplication when the pains were on her, then laying it quietly down on the trampled heather. Johnnie gazed at her with his chin resting on the top of his cleek. ' She's not making much of it, Duncan boy,' he said. Duncan looked up at the brown humorous face, which to him expressed all the deep wisdom of the world.

' We'll give her just a wee whiley longer,' said the man.

' Aye,' echoed the boy in loyal agreement.

The black head rose again, and a dreary moan sounded over the lonely hills.

' Aye,' Johnnie decided, ' she'll be needing help,

poor beast. Bide you here, Duncan, and I'll be
getting a hold of her.'

Johnnie made a sign, and his black dog, making
a wide cast, slid slowly on its belly downhill, hind-
legs tucked well in, head well down between softly
padding paws. It moved stealthily round to face
the sheep, which lurched to its feet when the dog
was in view. Then Johnnie, bent almost double,
his cleek clutched ready in his right hand, crept
silently to the rear. The sickened ewe, watching
the dog, allowed the man to approach unnoticed.
Johnnie drew his cap more firmly over the right
eye, crouched lower, made ready to spring. He
whistled softly, and the dog rushed forwards on
the ewe, which swung clumsily round into Johnnie's
arms.

'Will ye sit *doon*?' he roared to the dog, in all
the excitement of successful capture. 'Duncan boy,
come you down here!'

Duncan ran as fast as he was able. His father
had turned the ewe on her side, thrown his left
knee over her neck to keep her down, and was
busily examining the lamb's presentation.

'We can manage her fine here, boy,' he said.
'There's only the one leg showing, but the other
shouldn't be far back. Man, she's a tight one!
Here, Duncan boy, you've a smaller hand than me.
Take that lysol bottle from my jacket pocket and
put some on your fingers. Fine, boy! Now put
your hand in like a man and see if you'll find a foot.
Canny, boy, canny; you'll tear the poor beastie to
bits. D'ye feel anything?'

'Aye,' said Duncan doubtfully, 'I feel something.'

' What is it, boy ? '

' I'm no' sure, father.'

' Hut, man,' exclaimed Johnnie in impatient irritation. ' Can ye no' tell a fut from an airse by the feel o' it ? '

' It's no' an airse, father.'

' It's maybe the head, boy.'

' Aye, father, it's a head. I can feel the teeth.'

' Then you'll need your two hands, boy. Put your left hand—man, do you no' know your right from your left yet ?—put your left hand over the snout and push back, and see if you'll get your right hand past it. Fine, boy, fine, that's it—you'll make a herd.'

' I've got the foot, father. It's slipping.'

' Get a grip above the joint, boy—fine ! Now pull down towards her feet. Canny—now—canny. Let her help hersel' ! *Fine*, boy.'

With a spurt of liquid the twisted leg straightened alongside the lamb's head.

' Now take the two legs together, boy, and pull with her pains,' Johnnie instructed. ' Keep pulling down ! Hold your left hand over the head to keep her from tearing. Fine, boy, you'll make a lamber yet.'

The lamb's head and shoulders slipped out, followed by its body, like a slimy slithering fish. The lamb spluttered, wriggled, and the cord broke.

' Clean its nose and mouth with your fingers, boy,' Johnnie shouted.

' Right or left, father ? '

' What in hell does it matter ? That's the way, boy. Now give me a hold of it. Never let a ewe rise after she's been handled until she's licked her lamb.'

'Suck—suck—poor beastie,' Johnnie encouraged, holding the lamb at the sheep's nose.

The ewe lay quite still, her head stretched, in the peaceful reaction of release from labour. Slowly she turned to the lamb, licked it, then gave the soft muttering grunt of the motherly sheep.

'Plenty of milk,' said Johnnie, drawing off a spurt of thick yellow fluid from the leathery teats. 'Now, Duncan, get you quietly up the hill, and I'll hold her down till she's settled.'

Duncan crept away like a stealthy shadow. He turned round when curiosity compelled, to see Johnnie wave his dog away, then rise gently and sneak quietly backwards. The ewe staggered up, and turned to the cleaning of her lamb. Johnnie joined Duncan on the lichen-covered rock. They waited until the lamb, after some clumsy lurches, was safely on its feet and making tentative pokes at its mother's flanks in search of milk.

'She'll do, boy,' said Johnnie. 'We can be leaving her now. Wash your hands in the burn to take the smell off, or you'll be putting the next ewe off her lamb.'

They climbed again, the red grouse rising with whirring wings from their very feet. Here and there among the heather a ewe stood on guard over her lamb, new-born in the night. One, with lowered head, was motionless beside a still small patch of white.

'That lamb's dead,' said Johnnie. 'We'll bring her down on our way home. I've a spare lamb in the byre.'

They passed on to the foot of the Craig, towards the high ground where the little brown dotterel,

with their piping whistle, flew swiftly over the ridge's crest.

In the far distance they saw a high-stepping ewe, with her head in the air, trotting quickly away from a tired-looking lamb, that bleated most pitifully as it ran. At every few yards the ewe turned to butt the lamb savagely with her curved horns, and roll the little beast downhill on its back. Then off she would go again, and the lamb kick and struggle and rise to its feet to follow.

' The damn butch ! ' Johnnie exclaimed. ' She's done that the last three years, since ever she was a gimmer. I'll be giving her a taste of the dog, and that'll maybe learn her !—Go for her, lad ! ' he called to his dog.

The black collie gave three excited bounds in the air to get a clear view over the tops of the heather, then sped like an arrow on the ewe. ' Go for her, lad ! Go for her ! ' Johnnie yelled, and the dog barked and snapped and yapped in front of the menacing horns.

Instinctively protective, the ewe kept her quivering body between the dog and her lamb. Then she showed fight, chasing the dog backwards over the heather and rocks until Johnnie called it off. The ewe halted, gave a loud whistling snort and a stamp of her forefeet, then ran anxiously back to her bleating lamb. She smelt it, licked it, gave it suck, and its white tail wagged and wriggled and quivered in expression of satisfied ecstasy.

' She'll do,' said Johnnie. ' There's nothing like a bit danger, Duncan, for making a ewe mind her lamb.'

' We'll take a sit here a minute, boy, before we go

down. Your mother put a piece gingerbread in my pocket for us. Here's your piece, boy. I'll be keeping a bit for mysel'. I'm not too old for a bite of cake.'

Duncan was happy. He wanted days like this to go on and on until he was a great strong man like his grandfather, but kind and laughing like his father, until he was wise and skilled in all sheep lore and the ways of the hills.

'I like the lambing,' he murmured, half to himself.

'It's a grand job, Duncan, when the weather's fine,' said Johnnie, 'but it's no' aye that way. We'll manage away fine if it bides warm and the wind in the west, but a cold east wind would be killing a lot of the lambs.'

They set off together again, down the steep braes.

The ewe still stood with lowered head by her cold dead lamb. Johnnie lifted up the stiffening body and threw it on ahead. The ewe ran bleating to where it fell. Thus, lifting and throwing the lamb, they coaxed the ewe downhill to the buchts. There they shut her in until Johnnie should have time to skin her lamb and put the skin on the motherless lamb in the byres.

Johnnie and Duncan went up the brae to their dinner. They saw wee Johnnie marching around the house, drilling his short fat legs to a long hill-stride. A very old cap of his father's was cocked on the side of his dark head, he carried a crook much taller than himself, and he was whistling to an imaginary dog to come in to his heel.

Johnnie laughed when he saw what the boy was

at. 'See him, Duncan, see him,' he cried. 'Wee Johnnie's for being a herd too.'

But Duncan was jealous.

VI

One fine August day, when Duncan was eight and wee Johnnie six, they waited at the foot of the brae for the laird's shooting-party to arrive. Duncan had grown slender and tall, not so broad as he should have been, because of the school. His fine grey eyes stared solemnly down the road from under his rough fair hair, and there was something supercilious in the set of his mouth and his straight nose as he waited to stare at the strange bodies come newly from London. Beside him, wee Johnnie, dark and squat, gazed at nothing in particular with his slanting gipsy-like eyes. He clutched Duncan's hand, because he had heard rumours of strangers about to arrive and was shy. The boys were alone that day, for Hugh and Johnnie were away with the keepers and ponies to help drive the grouse to the guns, and Mary was busy in the house with the baby-girl Jean, who had come in the dark days of winter.

Duncan saw a cloud of dust on the road as a line of cars rolled up the glen. He gripped wee Johnnie's hand and pulled him to the roadside. The cars glided smoothly to rest, and the loud-talking, tweed-clad men sprang out to the road.

There were six sportsmen, all tall and bronzed, with small clipped moustaches and flashing teeth. The laird was known to Duncan, although only by sight, the big elderly man with the limp and the greying hair. He knew the head-keeper too, burly

Jock MacCulloch, who, like big Hugh Maclean, was always so civil when gentry were about. The keeper glared at the children as though nothing but grouse and the shooters had a right to the glen that day, then he hurried away with the laird to talk over the posting of the guns. Duncan and Johnnie stared silently as the party passed, the gentry talking too loudly for the laird's liking. He nodded in answer to his keeper's remarks, and turned quickly round.

' We are only a few hundred yards from the first butts,' he said.

There was immediate silence. The loaders and gillies followed the gentlemen, carrying the guns. They winked and grinned at the boys as they passed up the hill.

Soon the first shot was fired, and Mary looked anxiously through the window to see that the boys were safe. She had warned Duncan not on any account to go out of sight that day. The shooting had been a terror to her since ever the boys could walk, for the gentlemen got so excited they would shoot anywhere after a bird.

Duncan wished his father had taken him beating, but Johnnie had such a contempt for the business that he had never even suggested such a thing. Still, it would be a dull day hanging about the house seeing that wee Johnnie came to no harm.

The shooting grew faster and faster, the double shots coming almost together. It was a good place for grouse, a dry year for the chicks, and the laird's friends could shoot. Something fell like a rocket from the sky past wee Johnnie's head, to land, flapping helpless wings, in the heather. Duncan ran to see what had fallen. It was a fine cock grouse,

with bright red crescents above the eyes, and the brown feathers of its breast all battered and broken and stained with blood. The flapping of its wing grew ever more feeble, its beak opened widely as it gasped for air. Then it lay still.

Duncan caught up the dead bird and ran up the hill with it to show to his mother. He thought it would make a fine supper to them all, for Hugh and Johnnie were not above shooting or netting a bird for the pot. Mary was suckling wee Jean when he rushed into the kitchen. Her blue blouse was open, and she bent crooning over the baby.

'See what I've got for you,' cried Duncan with pride.

The noise disturbed Jean, who ceased to suck and began to cry. Mary looked up with impatient anger. 'You're not to shout like that when I'm feeding wee Jean. And what have you got there, and where's wee Johnnie?'

'It's a grouse that's been shot, mother, and Johnnie's playing by the buchts.'

'You should have more sense at your age, Duncan,' Mary cried in alarm. 'Away back with the bird and put it where you got it, and don't be telling anybody you've ever seen a grouse in this house before.'

'Why not, mother?'

'Ach, boy, you're aye asking questions! Because the grouse all belong to the gentlemen, and are only for them to shoot. Away now, like a man, and see wee Johnnie's no' in mischief.'

Duncan did as he was bid, but his heart was sore. It was all wee Jean now with his mother, ever since the doctor's big car had come up the glen on a cold

February night. It was all very well being a man, but looking after wee Johnnie was a lassie's job.

He laid the bird down on the bloody spot where it had fallen, and walked to the buchts, to find wee Johnnie busy with imaginary sheep. Duncan strolled away with hands in the pockets of his shabby shorts, and sat down beside the cars at the roadside. There were three of them, a big blue car, a big grey car, and one that was all flashing silver and glittering glass.

A brown pony was toiling downhill, led by a gillie. Big wicker baskets were swung on either side of its broad back, and the baskets were full of the grouse that the gentry had shot. Away in the distance Duncan could see the tiny figures of men waving white flags as they advanced in a line, driving the game towards the silent butts. Then the shooting started again, a crackle of fire from butt to butt as the birds flew over. A frightened hare ran right across the road, not knowing where to seek sanctuary on a hill gone mad. Yet the little grey and white wheatears flitted from stone to stone as though nothing were wrong.

Duncan sat quietly for a long time, until another grey car came bumping along the glen road, to draw up smoothly behind the others. Four talkative, tweed-clad ladies got out; they had come up to lunch with the men among heather and stone. Duncan wondered what they found to talk about, and laugh about, for they never stopped talking or laughing. He rose to his feet as they came, and stared solemnly while they passed.

Then one of the ladies stopped. ' What a good-looking boy ! ' she exclaimed. ' He's the image of Jack Knight ! '

Duncan gazed dumbly at the four gentlewomen, who seemed to be laughing at him in a way he did not understand. He fixed his eyes on her who had spoken about him first, a tall dark smiling lady in grey tweeds, a lady who looked as if nothing would turn her back when she meant to go on.

' What is your name, boy ? ' she asked.

Duncan blushed, but did not answer; he had a vague feeling that his name was none of this lady's business.

' Don't be frightened,' she said more gently, seeing his confusion, and Duncan began to thaw.

' Duncan Gillies,' he whispered shyly.

' What a nice name, Duncan ; and where do you live ? '

Duncan pointed dumbly to the cottage.

' And who is your father ? '

' Johnnie Gillies. He's under-shepherd to the laird.'

' There, you see, Anne,' cried one of the other three ladies, a perky thing like a bright cock chaffinch, ' another of your mare's nests. The boy's ancestry is perfectly respectable.'

' I'm not so sure,' the dark lady laughed. ' I must ask Jack about it.'

Then they all moved away, and Duncan felt that they had lost all interest in him and were talking of something else. They went talking and laughing, laughing and talking, up the quiet glen road.

That evening Johnnie and Hugh returned tired from their day on the hill. They had done much tramping through long heather in the service of the laird and his guests, but it was big Jock MacCulloch that got the rough end of their tongues that night.

'Man,' said Hugh, sitting down to his welcome tea, 'did ye ever see a body so puffed up wi' himself?'

'A fair disgust,' Johnnie grumbled.

'Who is?' asked Mary, standing between the table and the range with the already emptied tea-pot in her hands.

'*Lord* MacCulloch,' Hugh growled, his eyes flashing fire. 'Ordering the whole party about like a parcel o' bairns, with his " Maclean, keep your line with the rest," and his " Gillies, this is no' a sheep-gathering ye're at." '

'Impudence!' said Mary, filling the tea-pot from the steaming kettle.

'Aye, impudence enough for a dozen head-keepers, and the whole of them's tarred wi' the same damn brush. " You were too long over that beat," says he to me. " Aye," says I, " and no' much wonder at that, wi' the heather coming near up to a body's neck. It'll maybe learn ye to burn next year," says I. " I want none of your impudence, Hugh Maclean," says he, with his whiskers wag-wagging like a lambie's tail.'

'Aye,' Johnnie broke in as he munched a scone, 'but I had a better one on him nor that. " There's too many birds breaking back on you, Gillies," says he to me. " An' is that so, Jock?" says I to him. " I'm thinking I'll be too wee for this job; the birds are no' feared o' me. But I'll be telling you what I'll do, Jock," says I. " The next beat I'll stick a whin-bush in my bonnet, an' the birds'll be thinking it's your whiskers that's in it, an' that'll scare the beasts if there's anything will." '

'And what did he say, Johnnie?' Mary laughed.

'He didna speak, he just wagged.'

Duncan and wee Johnnie ate and stared while the men were talking, and wee Jean slept in the tumble-down pram in the kitchen's corner. Mary moved across to the window to light the lamp.

There came a heavy rap on the door, and Hugh, being nearest, went to open it. ' Come in, come in,' he cried genially. ' Man, we've just been talking of ye.—Mary, if it's no' Jock MacCulloch himself.'

' Make yourself at home, Mr MacCulloch,' said Mary. ' Duncan, fetch a chair for Mr MacCulloch to sit on ! You'll stay to your tea, Mr Mac-Culloch ? '

The keeper was the strongest man for miles around, and much respected because of his physical strength. He had been a police-sergeant in Westown, and was reputed to have broken ten Irish heads on a night of riot. He had once thrown a savage stirk with a swing of his mighty arms, and in a time long past had sat on three incendiary suffragettes throughout a hysterical night. He was six feet three in his socks, yet his breadth made him seem like a man of but average height. His eyes were fierce blue, like Hugh Maclean's, and his hawk-like nose rested on the fringe of a huge moustache. His brown tweeds were faded with weather and smelt of peat-reek.

' Well, boys,' he said, sitting down to a full plate and cup, ' it's been a grand day and the best bag for years in Glendarroch.'

' Man, and it's me that's pleased to hear that, Jock,' cried Hugh, striding across to the press. ' An' you'll take a dram in your tea at the end of it all.'

' Canny, Hugh boy, canny ! ' Jock expostulated as the tea was laced. ' That's enough now, that's enough.'

' An' what was the bag, Jock ? ' Johnnie inquired.

MacCulloch sipped his tea appreciatively as he answered : ' Eighty-three brace grouse — seven brace blackgame—ten snipe—three duck—seventeen hares—and twelve rabbits.'

' An' what would it be last year ? ' asked Hugh.

' Fifty-four and a half brace.'

' Man, the laird will be pleased.'

' Aye, Hugh boy, he's fair delighted.'

' I was thinking, Jock,' said Johnnie, ' that the heather would be the better of a bit burning. The birds would do better. If it hadna been a dry summer there's a lot of the chicks would have drowned in that long stuff.'

' Aye,' Jock agreed, with his mouth half full, ' we'll do a fair bit of burning next year.' Nothing could have better expressed the keeper's contentment than such a promise made in a shepherd's house.

MacCulloch munched and drank away, and his eyes lighted on silent Duncan. ' You'll need to watch that boy of yours, Mrs Gillies,' he laughed. ' The ladies were all talking about him at the lunch.'

' And what were they saying about Duncan ? ' Mary asked.

' That he was the bonniest boy that they'd seen for a while, and the living image of some lad that I canna mind the name of, some actor chap in London, likely.'

' Aye, it was Jack Knight, they were saying,' said Duncan shyly, speaking for the first time.

There was a sudden, dead silence around the table, broken only by the ticking clock, the crackling fire, sounds which made silence worse.

Then Jean cried fretfully from the pram, and Mary hurried across to bend over the baby and hide her flaming face. Big Hugh glared at Duncan, and Johnnie stared at the floor.

MacCulloch drew the back of his hand across his moustache and rose to go.

' I'll no' be keeping you longer from your work, Mrs Gillies. It's no' little you'll have to do, with three bairns about the place.'

He strode heavily to the door, and the two men followed him. Wee Johnnie ran out to play beside the burn. Duncan sat still in his place at the table—crying. He knew he had spoken words that should never have been said, although why he did not know.

Mary slipped over to him, and drew her arms round his neck. ' Dinna cry like that, Duncan boy,' she said, sobbing too. ' What's been done wrong has no' been done by you. Wheesht, my bairnie, dinna cry. Wheesht, now, wheesht ! '

When Duncan was asleep that night, Mary came in to kiss him as he slept, while little Johnnie Gillies watched gravely from the door.

VII

The next day a little red sporting car drove up the glen at a perilous speed and with popping exhaust. Mary looked through the window to see what all the noise was about. She was alone that morning with baby Jean, for the men were waging

their seasonal war with the maggot, and Duncan and wee Johnnie were down by the burn at play. Mary watched the car stop at the brae foot and a gentleman get out. He came swiftly up the brae towards the house.

There was something familiar in the set of his shoulders. There was something in the way he walked that brought back a picture to Mary's mind, a picture of a tall figure with bent head trudging through slush and rain until the cold mist covered him.

The man was tall and finely made, with the grace of good health and the poise of authority, and the cut of his tweeds was that of a gentleman clothed in town. His head was bent under the deer-stalker's cap, and Mary at first was unsure whether or not it was he.

When he raised his head and she saw it was Jack, she knew she had been dead for more than eight years. As she stared through the window into his grey adventurous eyes, she felt that it was only his smile could bring life to the world. She opened the door to his knock, and he raised his cap from his brown hair.

' Will you come in, Mr Knight ? ' she whispered.

' Thank you, Mary.'

They went through to the kitchen, and stood there awkwardly and in silence. Mary, with one worn hand stretched out behind her, rocked the shabby pram to keep Jean asleep.

' You must wonder why I have dared to come here, Mary ? '

' Yes, Mr Knight.'

' You must think me an awful cad ? '

'No, Mr Knight,' Mary whispered, scarcely hearing what he said.

She was thinking how little he had changed, how much the boy he still looked in spite of the assurance that manhood gave him. She thrilled to every vibration of his voice, and to every movement of his lips. Then she wondered what he could be thinking of her after her eight years of child-bearing and work. In sudden absurd panic she thought of her untidy hair and toil-worn hands. She remembered that her blouse was loose after feeding Jean, and made fumbling efforts to close it.

Jack Knight couldn't think of a word to say. He found it difficult to believe that the drab little farm woman before him was the same Mary he had once held in his arms. She was so terribly aged and changed.

'My cousin, Anne Winterton, was up here at the shoot yesterday,' he stammered. 'She told me there was a boy lived here—is he ours, Mary?'

'Aye, Mr Knight; there was a bairn.'

'That was very bad luck, Mary.'

'Oh no, Mr Knight,' she smiled. 'There's no bad luck about Duncan; he's the life of the place.'

'Who looks after him?' he asked. 'Who pays for his clothes and things—your father?'

'No, Mr Knight—Johnnie Gillies, my good-man, has been a father to him all these years.'

'And does your husband know?—I'm sorry, Mary, I shouldn't have asked you that.'

'Aye, he knew everything before we were married.'

'Then there's nothing for me to do. I mean to

say, I had thought I'd better help about school or something.'

'Duncan's just like the rest, Mr Knight. We've never let him think himself different.'

Jack thought of the boy who was said to be so like himself, living lonely and uneducated among the hills, guarding the blackfaced sheep or the red grouse in the heather. He would rather have him like that than in office, or factory, or shop. 'Could I see Duncan?' he asked.

Mary was silent for a time. 'Maybe that would no' be fair to the boy,' she said. 'I'd no' like him to think he wasn't Johnnie's bairn.'

'Of course, if you think that way about it, Mary——'

'Oh, it's the boy I'm thinking of.' She smiled quietly, as though to her inner self. '*I'm* pleased and proud that you left me Duncan.'

'Mary!' he cried in horrified amazement, 'you haven't cared for me all these years?'

'It would be a sin to say so, Mr Knight.'

'I'm so sorry, Mary.'

'There's no need to be sorry, Jack,' she answered. She raised her head proudly, and he saw how bright and fine her blue eyes still were. 'I'm no' ashamed of what I did,' she declared, 'though you may be. I'm proud to have had a bairn to a man like you, and there's no' a finer boy than Duncan in the countryside.'

'Well,' he said, 'if I can ever be of any use to you or our—our—boy, please let me know.'

'I'll do that, Mr. Knight, but he's set his heart on being a herd.'

'Well, there's no better life, is there?'

' It's fine for the men, Mr Knight.'

Jack was miserably confused. He wanted so much to be easy and natural with this odd little woman, so much a stranger to him. He wanted to make up to her for what she must have suffered, and saw no way in which he could help. So he held out his hand in farewell. ' Good-bye, Mary,' he smiled. ' Good luck.'

' Good-bye, Mr Knight.'

She watched him go down the brae to the road. She saw him turn the car and drive away. She waited until there was only a cloud of distant dust to show where he had gone.

Then she broke down. She flung herself, sobbing, into the worn arm-chair and lay there for a long time, her head on the hard green cloth. When she had wept to exhaustion, she sat up, dabbing her eyes with the sleeve of her blouse. She turned round, hoping that by some magical means Jack had heard her and returned. In imagination she saw him coming through the door to her with outstretched arms, snow powdering the long lashes over his grey eyes, and his smooth skin soft as a pigeon's breast.

Then Jean stirred in the pram, and Mary hastened to her. She glanced at the clock and saw that it was past the baby's feed-time. Drying her eyes again, she went to the small cracked mirror in the bed-room. Her face looked so strange that at first she thought she must be ill. One cheek was dead white, and all patterned and impressed with the hard green cloth of the chair.

VIII

As the years went by, Duncan saw less and less of the school. He had grown a strong, active boy, and was so useful among the sheep that there were weeks together when old Macfarlane's car took wee Johnnie alone down the glen. Letters came from the Education Authority, typed official letters strongly worded, and after one of these threatening communications Duncan would have to pack up his books in his dilapidated satchel and be regular in attendance for a week or two. But in the holidays and in truant time he was third shepherd in Glendarroch.

He had a dog of his own, a little black bitch called Meg, and she was always waiting and whining at the end of her chain when he went tramping out to the stable and a morning's work. Duncan and Meg were out on the big days, the sheep-gatherings at Glendarroch, or the neighbouring farms, when shepherds in communal labour herded the sheep from the outlying hills for dipping, clipping, marking, or branding.

Great days indeed at Glendarroch, when red-headed Mackenzie came over the Craig from Strathord, when the Macintyre sons, wrestlers and hammer-throwers both, tramped up the glen with their dogs, when little tippling Alicky Mag from Glendruid was always a good hour late, and even Jock MacCulloch, head-keeper to the laird, vouchsafed assistance in superior way.

There were two clippings on the hill-farms, the eild clipping in June, when the young ewe hoggs and the barren ewes were shorn, and the milk clipping

in July, when the white young wool of the nursing ewes was ready for shears. The days were arranged between the neighbouring herds ; on the Monday they would all be at Strathord, on the Wednesday in Glendruid, and on Friday, if the day was fair, in Glendarroch. Duncan had missed the gatherings at Glendruid and Strathord, but he was out early with Meg at his heels on the day they were clipping at home.

It was five o'clock of a fine July morning, with the dew still wet on the heather. Duncan pulled on his heavy boots in the chill darkness, then tramped across the yard for Meg. A late-nesting mavis sang from the willows by the burn, and a blanket of mist lay over the glen road.

Duncan could see Hugh striding out towards the valley to gather the sheep in the East-end heft. There the Macintyres would meet him with the ewes that had straggled across the fenceless march. Johnnie was away to the big Glendarroch heft to wait for Alicky Mag coming whistling over the hills from Glendruid, and Duncan himself was to gather the Pot and stay there until Mackenzie gathered the Corrie and rounded the Craig.

The sheep were already grazing when Duncan was out on the edge of the bog, where dried-up peat-hags scarred the hill. The ewes and their well-grown lambs came down the twisting sheep-paths from the high places where they slept, ambling along in single file, pulling mouthfuls of fresh green grass, which grows so sweet near the beaten ground.

Duncan set Meg away on a wide cast, and the little black bitch went off with a will. She was soon out of sight over the ridge's brow, but Duncan

could tell the progress she made by the scuttling ewes and lambs, which came bounding over the crest of the hill. Then Meg came in view, paused expectantly with head on one side, taking her bearings and awaiting commands. Duncan signalled to her to clap flat on the ground, then walked to where she lay. From there he could scan the ground right up to the bare rock of the Craig, where no sheep were likely to be found. Meg had done her work well, and had left no ewe or lamb ungathered in her circling run.

Duncan sat down beside her on the damp heather. He would have liked to test the cunning of the little bitch, to have made her cut off two or three, perhaps even a single ewe, and hold them separate from their lambs and flock. It was the sort of thing the great masters made their dogs do at the sheep-dog trials, the men who earned hundreds of pounds with dogs trained perfectly as circus animals. But that was a trade in itself. Johnnie and Hugh would allow no unnecessary dogging of ewes, so that Duncan was forced to idle until Mackenzie would have gathered the Corrie and come round the Craig.

Distant bleating showed that the Corrie heft was disturbed. Soon the first slow moving dots were in view, then the flock came streaming downhill, with the deep baaing of ewes and the answering call of their lambs. Behind them strode Mackenzie, his shoulders hunched and his chest hollowed by the chronic indigestion which cursed his life. The ewes of the Corrie bleated and sniffed at their neighbours of the Pot.

' Aye, Duncan,' cried Mackenzie, pulling off his ragged cap and clawing his red head, ' you're no' at the school the day ? '

Duncan grinned.

'Man,' said Mackenzie, casting an eye on Meg, 'thon's a good bitch. You should get her lined by a good dog.'

'It'll no' be in Strathord that I'll be looking for one,' Duncan laughed, pointing his stick at Mackenzie's couple of black-and-white ordinary dogs.

The shepherd aimed a friendly cuff at Duncan, who ducked out of the way, while Meg gave an ominous growl.

'See thon,' Duncan cheeked. 'She'll tear the breeks off ye, Mac.'

'Come away, boy,' said the shepherd; 'we've no time for waiting here, or we'll be behind Alicky Mag.'

They drove the sheep down towards the road, Duncan stretching his supple legs to Mackenzie's stride. The dogs ran out to the flanks of the flock, and then back to the heels of the men. They were fussily busy, panting quickly, with their tongues lolling out. The sheep bleated and baaed in a medley of pastoral sound, and from the east, the west, and the south rose the sharp shouts of men, the shrill barking of dogs, and the noise of sheep gathering in to the buchts.

Mackenzie belched forth wind, which seemed both to relieve his pain and release his tongue. 'Man, you're growing a big lad, Duncan,' he remarked, leering out of his red-lidded eyes. 'Have you got a lassie yet?'

Duncan grinned, and hoped Mackenzie would think that he had.

Then they had to concentrate on sheep as the buchts were neared, for the Macintyres and Hugh,

a gigantic trio, were making simultaneous approach with the East-end heft.

' Canny, man, canny ! ' Hugh roared, raising his stick in alarm, and pulling anxiously at his brindled beard. ' *D'ye hear?* '

' Way by ! ' Duncan whispered, and Meg flew to the head of the flock—' Sit ! ' and she clapped to the ground, creeping stealthily in the direction of a big bold ewe that threatened a break. She crouched like a boxer awaiting his chance, or a wrestler planning a strangle-hold, and Duncan was full of an owner's pride as he leant on his stick. The sheep from the East-end heft streamed through the alley-way to be safely penned.

' Now, boy ! ' yelled Hugh. ' Are ye asleep ? '

' No ! and we're no' daft,' Mackenzie muttered.

' Morning, Duncan. Morning, Mac,' the Macintyres greeted. They were all rippling muscle and jutting features, and could scarcely walk for pride in their strength.

' By God, Hugh,' Mackenzie sneered, ' and the ewes are thin the year.'

' They're no' that bad if it wasna for the Corrie heft,' retorted Hugh ; ' and a body canna be expecting them to be fat wi' a damn cheat-the-wind like yoursel' keek-keeking at them each day to see how many beasts will be dead.'

' Canny, now, canny,' implored Bob, the younger and bigger of the Macintyre men. ' Can ye no' be thegither for ten meenutes wi'out fighting ? '

' An' where in the name o' hell's Johnnie and Alicky Mag ? ' Hugh roared, lashing himself to a fury. ' Was there ever a clipping but that Glendruid puddock was an hour late ? '

'Man, you should wash your ears, Hugh,' Mackenzie growled, thrusting forwards his long red nose. 'Can you no' hear them coming?'

Bleating sounded from the thinning mist, then the Glendarroch heft streamed across the road to the buchts. Johnnie brought up the rear with his dogs, whistling away as he always did. Hugh herded in the oncoming sheep in a dour silence. 'An' where's that daft old bodach of an Alicky Mag?' he growled.

'He's brought his pipes wi' him,' grinned Johnnie, 'and he's washing his chaunter in the burn. He's got a dram in already.'

Hugh was wild with rage. 'Is he thinking this is the Cowal Games?' he roared.

'Canny, Hugh, canny,' soothed the Macintyre men. 'He'll likely have minded his shears as well,' said Bob.

Then Alicky Mag came up the brae with his pipes well cleaned and under his arm. He grinned toothlessly from his brown wrinkled face, and raised his bonnet to display a bald old head.

'Aye, boys,' he squeaked in a far-carrying voice, 'an' how are we all the day? Man, did you ever see a bonnier day for a clipping? There's no more than a dampness on the wool the day.—Aye, Mac,' he called to Mackenzie, 'is your belly aye burning? —Aye, Hugh, was it sour milk you had to your porridge this morning?—Aye, Duncan boy, you'll soon be the height o' Bob Macintyre.'

'Come on,' Hugh grumbled, stretching to the wall for his shears. 'We're no' here for a clack.'

Duncan was sorry when Alicky stopped, for Alicky was a wit and the district's mysterious man.

Some said he had once been coming out for a doctor, but couldn't stand the sight of the blood, others that he had tried for divinity, but couldn't keep fun from his sermons. His knowledge was certainly wider than the average herd's, and he certainly drank much more. There was a smell of whisky wherever he moved.

The men were soon busy on their triangular clipping-stools, all except Duncan and Alicky Mag, who caught the sheep and rolled the fleeces on the kitchen table, put ready in the buchts. The clicking of shears, loud breathing of men, and smothered imprecations when a ewe kicked free broke the mild quietness of that morning in July. The mist had melted away as the sun rose, and there was no cloud to threaten rain and the work of the day.

Duncan seemed even more slim with his jacket off and his shirt-sleeves rolled. He spat in a manly way when he laid fine hands on a struggling sheep. He took pride in rolling the fleeces tightly, with the straggling weathered ends outwards and a soft inner heart of clean white wool.

'Put that one in your pocket, boy,' laughed Alicky Mag, when a pining ewe was shorn. 'The beast or its wool, boy, there's no' much in it.— Hugh, you should give capsules to your ewes.'

'Aye,' said Hugh, glowering at the corrugated ribs of the sheep, 'she'd be the better of one.'

Carbon tetrachloride capsules were a sure remedy for fluke in the liver, but were used by the shepherds as a universal and sovereign remedy for all the diseases of sheep.

'And give Mac one while you're at it,' Alicky squeaked.

Duncan grinned at the fun and spat again. The sweat ran down unruly locks of his hair into his grey eyes, making them smart, and his hands and arms were soft with wool grease and bleeding where they had struck the bucht's stone walls. Hugh and the Macintyres solemnly clipped, Mackenzie blinked over his shining nose, Johnnie whistled as he worked, and Duncan smiled at the monotonous humour of Alicky Mag.

Jock MacCulloch, the keeper, came striding majestically to lend a hand. There was something of condescension in the very manner he rolled a fleece.

'Keep your face well off o' the table or you'll tie up thon hair on your face,' screeched Alicky Mag.

This sally met with the herds' approval. Even Jim, the elder and more silent Macintyre, laughed.

When Johnnie had finished the ewe he was at, he stepped from his stool. 'Come away wi' me, Duncan boy,' he whispered, 'an' we'll get a stool from the shed for you. It's time you were learning to clip.'

Duncan was proud to be asked, but afraid he would make some dreadful mistake. But Johnnie kept him right. 'Always clip well down the neck for a start, boy,' he instructed, when Duncan was beside him. 'Now the side! Fine, boy! You'll make a clipper yet. Canny, boy,' he cried, when Duncan cut through the soft pink skin. 'The best of us whiles does that.'

'Here!' yelled Alicky Mag, dragging out an old done ewe that had cast her wool, 'here's a beast with less wool on her than Jock MacCulloch.'

The keeper glared and the shepherds laughed.

All through the hot day Duncan sweated and worked beside little Johnnie Gillies, who taught him to clip. His right wrist ached and burned as though fire was in it, but he stuck to his job. At twelve the men went in to dinner, carrying the table with them. They sat or stood round the stifling kitchen, while Mary laid out places for them. It was difficult to find crockery for so many, and the very dogs' bowls had been scoured and scrubbed for the occasion. The vapours of broth and stew mingled with the reek of sweat and wool. When the men sat down with a clatter of chairs there was scarcely space to pass a plate between one man's head and his neighbour's. Duncan ate his meat between Johnnie and Alicky Mag, and was proud of the wool on his trousers, and the dirt and blood on his arms.

' Just the smallest piece for me, Mistress Gillies,' Mackenzie implored.

' Do you no' care for stew, Mister Mackenzie ? '

' Aye, fine that, but it doesna like me.'

' You should try raw meat,' piped Alicky Mag.

' Is that a good thing ? ' Mary asked.

' It should be good for Mac. He says his stomach's aye burning inside, and that would be cooking the meat for him.'

Nobody laughed. They were too busy getting through their dinner.

Hugh was the first to rise. ' We've got work before us, boys,' he said.

The men clattered outside, and Mary was left to the washing of a mountain of dishes.

All through the hot afternoon the men sweated

and worked until the Corrie and Pot sheep were branded and ready to go back to the hill, until half the Glendarroch heft was clipped, and the rest of Glendarroch and East-end hefts were left to be clipped in the morning. Mackenzie was to take the Corrie and Pot sheep with him on his way to Strathord, and leave them at the Pot to spread to their grounds.

' You'll have a dram before you go, Mac,' said Hugh.

' It's been poison to me this last year, Hugh. I daren't touch it.'

' Well, thank you for your help, Mac.'

' You're welcome, boy.'

When Mackenzie had departed with the new-shorn sheep, the bottle came out.

' Come on to the hay-shed,' cried Hugh. ' There's no' room to swing a cat in the house. Come on, and Alicky'll give us a tune on his pipes.'

' We'll have our tea first,' said Johnnie.

After their tea, and scones, and eggs, the men crossed to the hay-shed. It was a fine mild evening, with the sun slow sinking. Duncan sat down in the sweet-smelling hay with the rest, with Johnnie and Hugh and the Macintyre men, with Jock MacCulloch and Alicky Mag.

' Give us a tune, Alicky,' roared Hugh, and none could be more jovial at the end of a day.

' Aye, a tune, boy,' they echoed together.

' Then I'll need to wash down my tea,' squeaked Alicky Mag, and Hugh passed the bottle with a laugh in his eyes.

Alicky drank until the men cried halt, lest he should empty the bottle and leave none for the

rest. He licked his lips, showing edentulous gums, then laughed in his high-pitched laugh till the hay-shed rang with it. He told a story of red-headed Mackenzie and his bonnie wife, a story that should never have been told had that wife held her tongue.

Hugh Maclean roared until the tears streamed down, but little Johnnie Gillies was vexed. ' Put your pipes in your mouth, Alicky,' he bawled. ' They've been in the clean burn. You'll mind there's a boy with us.'

' And whose boy——? '

' Put your pipes in your mouth, ye damn Glen-druid puddock,' Hugh thundered, ' or I'll stuff them down your throat.'

' Steady, boys, steady,' pleaded the Macintyre men.

Alicky played a lament, and the sob of the notes drifted over the roofs of the sheds and the house, over the heather and the evening shadows under the Craig, stealing down the winding road of Glen-darroch, echoing in the Glendruid hills. The brown eyes of the Macintyre men were filled with dreams, MacCulloch leant his elbows on his knees and his head on his hands, keeping time with his feet. Johnnie played the notes on his thick ash stick, and Mackenzie, far out on the distant Corrie, caught a whisper of the playing and forgot his pain.

' An' how did ye like thon, Duncan boy? ' Alicky asked.

' Fine, Alicky.'

' An' what did it make ye think on, boy? '

' I'd like to play mysel'.'

' My God, an' it's the fiddle you should be learn-ing, boy. Men like the pipes, but it's the fiddler the lassies run after.'

'Give us another tune, Alicky,' said Johnnie.

'I'll play ye a march, boy, and it's mysel' that made it.'

Then the glen echoed and thrilled to the sounds of war, and strange atavistic ecstasy brought blood to the brows of Macintyres, MacCullochs, and Macleans.

Alicky Mag paraded the shed, backwards and forwards in the small space clear of hay, then he marched outside to salute Mary Gillies. He played before the windows of the whitewashed cottage, and Mary hoped Jean would sleep through the noise. She knew there would soon be more of it when Hugh came, laughing but shamefaced, for the very last bottle that was left in the house.

'You'd best go in, Duncan boy,' said Johnnie, who saw a wild night ahead, but Duncan implored with his eyes and was allowed to stay.

'A reel!' Hugh demanded, and Alicky played while the Macintyres, Macleans, and MacCullochs danced on the cobbles of the yard as the late moon rose. They hooched, and kicked, and birled about, while Duncan, sitting beside Johnnie in the hay, laughed to see grown men make fools of themselves.

It was late when they stopped. When the pipes were out of Alicky's mouth he began to talk. 'You'd no' know by the look o' me I was an eddicated man,' he giggled, 'and ye'd never guess what I've been in my day.'

'You were aye a drunken tinker at bottom,' laughed MacCulloch, 'I'll swear to that.'

'I was not talking to you, Mr Hairy Face,' said Alicky in a well-bred mincing voice, 'and you may be unaware that my knowledge of Latin is pro-

found. I shall teach Duncan to talk in the Roman tongue. Stand up, Duncan ! '

Duncan grinned sheepishly and felt very foolish. He struggled stiffly to his feet.

' Now, repeat after me—*unus, duo, tres, quatuor, quinque, sex, septem, octo, novem, decem, undecim, duo- decim, tredecim, quatuordecim, quindecim, quinque— quinque—quinque—viginti !* Now, repeat that, boy ! You can't ? You're an ignorant rustic.—Johnnie, fetch me my pipes, and like the very good fellow you are, just point me the way to Glendruid.'

Alicky Mag lurched into the gathering dusk.

' He'll go down a bog-hole one of these nights,' said MacCulloch.

' Ach ! ' Hugh laughed, ' I'm thinking the wee bodach turns into a weasel when he's out of sight.'

He seemed to ponder over what he had said and grew grave. The other men were silent and uneasy. Superstition still lived in Glendarroch. ' Good- night, boys—good-night, boy,' they said to one another, and tramped down the brae towards their homes.

Duncan stood at the door after Johnnie and Hugh had gone in. He listened to the few sounds that broke the quietness of a summer night—the cease- less drumming of snipe over the bog, the muttered bleating of the penned sheep, footsteps growing faint on the glen road. Then, from over the moor that stretched towards Glendruid, came a curious chant, half sung, half said :

> ' *A, ab, absque, coram, de,*
> *Palam, clam, cum, ex, or e*
> *Sine, tenus, pro, and pre.*'

Duncan shivered and went in.

IX

Next day Macfarlane was at the brae-foot, and Duncan slammed his satchel down on the worn seat of the car.

' Careful of the cushions, boy,' Macfarlane muttered.

Wee Johnnie came scampering from the house, and Mary, with Jean by her side, waved farewell.

' Are ye right ? ' asked Macfarlane, and the old Ford shook.

Duncan gazed longingly at the buchts as the car drove past. Johnnie and Hugh were busy with the sheep unclipped on the day before, and Johnnie waved his shears above the high wall when he heard the loud clatter of the ' School Express.' Duncan thought of Meg, chained and unhappy in the stable, of the eager bustle of yesterday's work, and the humour and piping of Alicky Mag. He wondered whether the little man had got safely home. Then wee Johnnie poked him in the ribs, made giggling suggestions with his gipsy lips, and silently laughed with his great sloe eyes. Duncan nodded, and the two boys together made dreadful popping noises with their mouths, and banged their satchels at the rear of the car.

Old Jimmy Macfarlane jerked to attention, and stopped his engine and stepped on his clutch. The popping ceased as the car swerved perilously to rest.

' Do you no' smell burning, Jimmy ? ' roared Duncan in the ear of the deaf old man.

Wee Johnnie was out of sight on the floor of the car, hiding his laughing face.

' What's that, boy ? ' asked Macfarlane.

' Are ye deaf, Jimmy ? Do you no' hear the smell ? '

Wee Johnnie could stand it no longer; he shouted with glee.

' I'll put in a pro*test* about you boys,' Macfarlane growled. ' I'll report you at the school.'

The Ford clattered off with a rattle of stones. There was no stop to be made at the Macintyres' now, for with the bad sheep times they were doing without a herd.

' Hi, Jimmy,' Duncan shouted, ' there's a car coming.'

The old man jerked the car to the left and slowed down to a crawl.

' But it's no' here yet,' yelled Duncan, and wee Johnnie held his sides.

' I'll report ye this time, boys. I'll have no more of it,' stormed Macfarlane, and held to the middle of the road.

A butcher's van, new painted scarlet and gold, honked loudly to pass. Old Jimmy Macfarlane took no notice at all.

' There's a car right enough this time,' bawled Duncan.

' Aye, Jimmy, there's a——' began Johnnie, and lay back on the cushions in helpless delight.

' I'll report the two of yous.'

The van hooted again and made frantic efforts to pass. Old Jimmy Macfarlane held on his way. They drove like that all the way to Lochend, and when old Jimmy stopped to let the boys down, the butcher's van stopped as well.

The driver got out, purple with rage and his life amongst meat, and strode to the side of the rocking

Ford. 'Here, you old fool!' he hoarsely bellowed, and uttered a string of foul names, 'I've seen you do that before, and I'm having no more of it, see? I'll report you, that's what I'll do, I'll report you.'

Wee Johnnie laughed to see the tables thus turned, and the butcher gave him a cuff on the ear, a thumping blow that sent the boy flying against the side of the car, to lie in a sobbing heap, with blood on his nose.

'That'll learn *you*,' growled the butcher.

'And that *you*!' screamed Duncan, and swung his full satchel in the butcher's face. 'Come on, Johnnie,' he shouted, and the boys tore off to the school.

'Late again!' exclaimed Miss Gray, glaring viciously out of her watery eyes.

'Please, mum,' said Duncan, 'the car broke down.'

'Is that why Johnnie is crying?'

'Aye, mum, he was feared to be late.'

'Well, it doesn't seem to have upset you, Duncan Gillies!'

'Please, mum, I'm too old to cry.'

'In*deed*!' said Miss Gray, wondering how many strokes of the tawse would bring hot tears to those insolent eyes. 'And where were you yesterday?'

'Please, mum, I was seek.'

Johnnie, recovering quickly as an April sky, bubbled and laughed.

'And what are *you* laughing at, boy?' asked Miss Gray.

'Please, mum, Duncan's aye seek—he's a fair piner,' and Johnnie laughed helplessly and long.

'I'll make you laugh on the other side of your face,' said Miss Gray, and she opened her desk to

feel for the tawse.   Then she remembered a terrible
time when a sailor had pulled her back from the
pier, when life seemed hopeless, and one other day
in that school was not to be borne.   She gently
closed her desk.   'Go to your places, boys,' she
said.   'You're wasting our time.   Now, children,'
she continued brightly, when the class was quiet,
'I want you to look at that sentence on the board.
Will you read it out, Jeannie?'

A small, wizened, tow-headed lassie rose in the
front row of desks.   'I know thaat thaat thaat in
thaat sentence is a noun.'

'Quite right, Jeannie.   Now I want you to parse
that first "that."'

But Jeannie had no time to parse.   The purple-
faced butcher burst into the room.

'Well?' said Miss Gray in surprise.

'There's a pair of boys here that I've come to
report on.   Those two—sitting over in the corner
yonder,' and he pointed to Duncan and Johnnie.

'What have they done, Mr Wilson?' asked Miss
Gray timorously, for the butcher was prominent in
the town, and had influence with all sorts of people.

'They're nothing but a couple of savages, and
if that's all they learn at the school I'd like to know
what we ratepayers is paying for.'

Miss Gray disliked the fat red man with his
greasy hands and dirty teeth, but her anger turned
on the Gillies boys, who had brought this horrible
scene upon her.   'They're the most ill-mannered,
rowdy children I've ever had in the school, Mr
Wilson.'

'It's the tawse they're needing, Miss Gray!
That china-faced brat clouted me over the face

with his bag, and thon young tinker's no' a bit better.'

There was an excited hum among the forty scholars at this sensational piece of news. A titter sprang up, to the butcher's discomfort. He turned on the teacher. 'I'm thinking it's maybe the way they're taught that's the do with them,' he sneered.

Miss Gray could no longer tolerate his unpleasant proximity. 'Get out, *please* !' she hissed. 'You've no right here.'

'Oh! I haven't?' he blustered. 'We'll see about that, my fine lady,' and he slammed his way out.

Miss Gray rubbed her eyes. Their watering was only partially due to conjunctivitis. She blew her nose.

'Please, mum,' piped Jeannie, distressed for her darling's sake, 'your face is bleeding, mum.'

Miss Gray glanced at the little round mirror she kept open on her desk beside her damp handker-chief. Yes, it was true ! That little spot she had thought quite healed had opened again. That was too much for her. 'You will have half-an-hour's silent reading,' she sobbed, and dashed from the room.

The closing of the door was a signal for a babel of tongues. 'What did you hit him for, Duncan boy?' 'Was it an in*sult*?' 'You'll have the *po*lice after you now, boy !'

Wee Johnnie crept to the blackboard, licked a grimy finger, rubbed one word out and added two more. The class tittered as he crept to his desk. 'My, boy, you'll catch it when she comes in !' they gloated.

It took Miss Gray a full ten minutes to wash her

face, dry her eyes, and compose herself. There was sudden expectant silence when she returned. 'Now, children,' she began, 'we'll continue our parsing'; and she turned to the board. '*Who did that?*' she screamed, for the sentence read, 'I know that that that in that sentence is Miss Gray.'

'Please, mum,' cried loyal Jeannie, 'it was Johnnie Gillies.'

Miss Gray decided that something *must* be done. 'Go out!' she gasped. 'Both of you, out of my room this minute, and don't *dare* come back until you've both apologised. Yes, you, Duncan and Johnnie Gillies, I'm speaking to *you*.'

For one terrible moment she feared that they might stay. But the boys were too glad to go out to the sun. They marched out together, Johnnie rather frightened, with downcast eyes, but Duncan with upright carriage and scornful face.

'Duncan,' said Johnnie in the trampled playground, 'where'll we go now?'

Duncan puckered his brow in anxious planning. 'We can't go home,' he said.

'No!' agreed Johnnie, 'we can't go home.'

'I'll tell you what we'll do,' said Duncan. 'We'll away up Glendruid and see Alicky Mag. It's no' that far if we get going the now, and Alicky'll no' tell on us.'

They set off stoutly on their ten-mile tramp, on the fine July day, with the breeze at their backs and the sea-loch white and blue. Duncan had the longer legs, but Johnnie's were stout, and they made good speed on the long straight road.

'An' will the *po*lice be after us?' Johnnie asked in a voice of awe.

' Away, man ! ' laughed Duncan, ' there's nobody will be telling them, for it's thon butcher body that hit you first. If it's anybody the *po*lice'll be after, it's him.'

' An' will ye apologise, Duncan ? '

' Aye, on the first weet day.'

The boys tramped on by the side of the loch, with the sea-birds rising from the tangle and crying about their heads. They left the main road where it curved to the north, to take the rough hill-road of Glendruid.

Bare hills shut the road in from the sun and the wind. It was cold there, and still, with the hush of evening in it, although it was day. Bare earthen scars showed where the waters rushed down in the winter's floods, and the river that ran by the hill-road's side was silent, inky, and deep. A salmon splashed lazily in its summer pool, and black crows flapped singly or in pairs from hill to hill.

' This is no' canny,' whispered Johnnie. ' Have you been here before, Duncan ? '

' Never.'

' An' where's Glendarroch from here, Duncan ? '

' Just over the hill to the right of us, Johnnie, an' we're no' that far from home. I wouldna like to be herd here. They say it's a deathly place for sheep. They lost fourscore o' ewes from trembling in the spring o' the year.'

Johnnie shivered, then plodded ahead.

They turned a shoulder of the hill, and there to the left of the road was the tumbledown two-roomed cottage where Alicky dwelt alone. No smoke came from the chimneys ; there was no barking of dogs ; but the door stood open.

' He's no' in,' said Duncan. ' We'll go and wait for him.'

He opened the wicket-gate, which tumbled on its side when the latch was off, and the boys crept uneasily through the nettles and weeds where a garden had been. They entered the lobby and looked into the room on either side. The one was filled with sacks of potatoes, and coal, and wood, with a rusty bicycle propped at an angle against the wall. The other room was where Alicky lived, for there were the embers of a fire in the grate, a pot and a kettle were by its side, the table was spread with dirty plates, and a straw mattress, covered with tattered rugs, was where Alicky slept. A shelf above the range was filled with old books, and Johnnie stepped forwards to see what they were.

' That's no' manners,' said Duncan firmly, and Johnnie sat down on the dusty chair.

Hung on the wall were two sets of pipes ; and two fiddles lay on a shelf by the bed.

' I wonder where he keeps his whisky,' whispered Johnnie.

' That's likely out of sight,' said Duncan.

A grey long-haired dog dashed into the room and stood snarling at the boys with its fangs laid bare. It growled very quietly at the back of its throat, then drew in its breath with an ominous snort.

' Dinna move, Johnnie,' said Duncan. ' Down, Gyp boy,' he called to the dog, for they had met before.

The dog recognised the smell and the voice, wagged its shaggy tail, and jumped on the table to lick the plates. A young black dog ran in, snuffed

at the boys, and flopped down on the bed. It was followed by Alicky Mag.

'Well, Duncan boy,' he squeaked in welcome, 'an' what's brought you round to Glendruid, an' wee Johnnie wi' you? Is the school burnt?'

'No, Alicky,' laughed Duncan, 'I'm wishing it was. Johnnie and me was put out the day.'

'Now, isn't that fine?' cried Alicky Mag. 'And me with nothing to do till evening. I'll tell you what I'll do, Duncan boy,' and he clapped his hands together. 'I'll give you your first lesson on the fiddle.'

'I'd rather the pipes,' Duncan protested.

'An' spoil the shape o' thon bonnie mouth? No, boy, it's the fiddle you'll learn.' He laughed his high-pitched laugh and showed his toothless gums, and his little pig eyes were twinkling all the time. 'No, Duncan boy,' he went on, 'it's the fiddle for you. I'll teach wee Johnnie the pipes one of these days. He's only a damned wee tinker, anyway.'

'I'd rather you learnt me the pipes,' persisted Duncan.

'That's because you've heard me play them,' cried Alicky, and grinned with conceit. 'Wait till you've heard me fiddle, boy, and then you can speak. But first, boys—our dinner!'

'We've got our pieces wi' us,' said Duncan, unpacking his satchel.

'It's no' pieces you'll have when you come to see Alicky Mag. Away through for some sticks, Johnnie. Duncan, get them plates into sort o' order, an' we'll have some trout, boy, all clean and bonnie from the burn the day. I caught them wi' my bare hand under the stones. Get you the plates ready!'

' The dog's been licking them, Alicky.'

' An' what o' that, boy ? It's a poor herd that wouldna eat with his dog ! '

' They'd be the better o' a wash, Alicky.'

' Hut, boy, the well's near dry.'

So Duncan set the places, Johnnie brought the sticks, and Alicky opened the oven to bring out the trout. He fried six fish, black like the river they came from, with red and yellow spots on their glistening sides.

Alicky muttered away whilst he cooked, ' Bonnie and clean, bonnie and clean,' and Duncan and Johnnie made faces at each other when the flies settled buzzing on his lined, bald head.

' Now, sit ye down, boys,' grinned Alicky, when the fish were fried, ' if ye can find anywhere to sit when there's only one chair. Duncan, be a man and sit down on the bed, and Johnnie, ye wee tinker, clap ye down on the floor ! '

' Now,' said Alicky, ' I'll give ye something you've never had. Do ye have a grace said at home ? '

' No,' said Duncan.

' Well, it's time ye learnt, ye wee heathens. Alicky'll say a Latin grace to ye—" *Panem et circenses.*" And now ye can start.'

The boys ate the trout and their pieces, then went out to the edge of the nearest burn to slake their thirst.

Alicky smelt of whisky when they returned. ' Now, Johnnie boy,' he cried, ' fetch me that fiddle, like a man ! I'll play to you boys, and when you see how it's done I'll give Duncan his lesson.'

The little old man held his fiddle to tune. At the

very first note the two dogs slunk whining from the room. Alicky laughed till his gaping red throat was visible, a high-pitched laugh that made the dogs run faster. 'The brutes won't listen, the foul beasts,' he shouted, 'but the birds, Duncan,' and he bent forward in his chair, 'they come flocking to the playing o' Alicky Mag, the daft old bodach that he is. Now, watch my fingers, Duncan boy.'

The old man played, a slow sad tune with the sigh of the waves in it, like the tide lapping up over tangle and sand, with the croon of the sea and the wailing of birds. Duncan gazed through the window into the face of the hill, and three long-billed curlews floating over the glen called out together, as though they had heard. 'You like that, Duncan boy?' asked Alicky Mag.

Duncan trembled. 'It's no' canny, Alicky,' he said.

'An' it's no' meant to be that,' laughed Alicky Mag.

Next he played a gay country-dance tune with a swing and a birl and a haunting lilt, keeping time with the upturned toe of his thick hill-boot. 'Aye!' he screeched when he had done, 'an' that one will make the lassies skirl. Man, if I'd a drink in I could play ye that. Ye'll need to learn thon tune, Duncan. D'ye like it, boy?'

'Fine!'

'Now, listen to me and I'll play a tune for wee Johnnie. Can ye dance, ye wee black deil, eh? Can ye dance?'

'No,' Johnnie giggled.

'And what are they learning ye both in Glen-

darroch that ye can neither dance nor pray ? Are ye all deid ? '

' Work,' answered Duncan loyally.

' Fine ! ' laughed Alicky Mag, and he tucked his fiddle beneath his chin. ' Work in Glendarroch and play in Glendruid. Listen to me, boys ; I'll play ye a *reel* ! '

His wrist flashed up and down, his small eyes twinkled, and his foot kept time on the floor. Duncan and Johnnie winked at each other and kept time too.

' Now away, Johnnie, and fish for puddocks,' said Alicky when his playing was done. ' I'm going to teach Duncan, and you'd keep him from learning by making him laugh.'

Johnnie went out to the back of the house, where he could hear the daft noises his brother made.

Duncan's right wrist was sore and stiff from the clipping of the previous day, but his fingers were long and supple and his ear was good. He got much encouragement from Alicky Mag. ' Eh ! ' the old man gloated when they made a pause. ' It's a grand thing to be a fiddler. You're sitting on a wee platform at one end of the hall, and all the lassies smile at ye when they swing past, and it's easy to make any of the creatures think that you're playing a tune for her, and no' bothering about any other living thing in the world. An' you make them dance slow when it's your mind to do it, and make them birl and skirl when you just feel like it. An' they'll look at ye, Duncan boy, an' say what a bonnie fiddler, I'd like to give him a kiss. Would you like to be kissed by a lassie, Duncan boy ? ' And the old man smirked and leered.

' No ! ' said Duncan, ' an' it's time we was going.'

Glendruid had grown darker as the sun sank, the fire had flickered to dust, and the room felt damp and dismal with its litter of dirt. Duncan shivered, and wondered where wee Johnnie had gone.

' An' you'll no' go yet ? ' protested Alicky Mag.

' Aye, I'm going.'

' Well, Duncan boy, and you'll no' be long before you're back. I'll make a fine fiddler of ye yet.'

' Aye, I'll be back, Alicky.'

Johnnie came running round the house when he heard the others come out. Duncan felt cheerful again with Johnnie and the clean air.

' You know your way, boys ? ' asked Alicky. ' You'll be going over the hill ? '

' Aye,' Duncan answered. ' We'll manage fine.'

' Ye'll come back, boy ? '

' Aye, I'll come back, Alicky.'

' An' I'll teach you to fiddle and pipe ? '

' Thanks, Alicky.'

' An' tinker Johnnie to dance ? '

' Aye ! '

' I'd teach ye Latin, Duncan, but I'm forgetting it, boy. It's that long now since I was at the College.'

' You mind it fine when you've a dram in, Alicky.'

The old man laughed his high-pitched laugh, and the bare hills echoed it back. ' Aye, when I've a dram in,' he cackled, ' I can mind *anything*.'

' Good-evening, Alicky.'

' Good-evening, boys.'

They set out over the rocky ridge between Glen-

druid and Glendarroch. They crossed the Druid river over a high-arched bridge with a broken causeway and moss-grown parapet. They followed a winding hill track, which often lost itself among pools and bog, deep pits in the peat full of stagnant water and fragrant myrtle. The Glendruid sheep, small and sickly, scampered away at the sound of steps.

' What time will it be ? ' asked Johnnie.

' I canna tell,' said Duncan. ' It's late.'

He looked back, and far below, in the shadowed depths of the glen, the cottage of Alicky Mag looked small as a box, and the lamp in its room a lighted, flickering match. There was the sound of the river and a barking dog, otherwise all was still.

' It's no' a canny place,' breathed Johnnie, and his lips trembled.

' Come on,' said Duncan. ' We'll soon be in Glendarroch, Johnnie ; it'll be light enough there. It's the hills being so near thegither that makes Glendruid dark. Here, boy, you're no' going to cry ? Ye'll need to be hardier nor that if you're to make a herd.' But wee Johnnie was blubbering by the time the chill in the wind proved that the top was reached. ' See ! ' cried Duncan, ' we're near home now.'

The hill sloped steeply to the flat moor, stretching unbroken to the Glendarroch road. The sun was well up after all ; it was only in Glendruid that dusk was come. The whitewashed cottage in the distance looked solid and square, with the comforting smoke drifting up from the chimney and the washing hung out to dry. Wee Johnnie was glad to be safely home, and dried his dark eyes. They

plodded together across the moor, and as the house
drew nigh they wondered what story they should
tell. But they knew there could be no deceit when
they saw their father striding to meet them.

'Where have ye been?' he hailed. 'Old Jimmy
waited an hour for ye in Lochend, and came all the
way up the glen to say that ye were lost.'

'We've been at Glendruid,' said Duncan stoutly,
but wee Johnnie hung his head.

'In Glendruid, have ye, boy?' cried Johnnie.
'And what were ye doing in Glendruid?'

'We got put out of school,' said Duncan, 'and
we went up to the glen to see Alicky Mag.'

'And what for?'

'To learn the fiddle from him.'

'And what for did ye no' come home?'

'We was feared.'

'Here,' said Johnnie to his younger son, 'away
you home to your mother and tell her you're both
safe home. Run, now, like a man.'

Wee Johnnie hobbled away to the house.

'It wasna his fault,' said Duncan.

'And fine I know that, Duncan boy,' Johnnie
agreed, 'and it's time you and me had a talk. Take
your time, boy, for I've a lot to say to ye.'

They walked slowly together across the sour-
smelling moor. 'You'll need to mind, boy,'
Johnnie began, 'that you're no longer a bairn, and
it's no' fair o' ye to be tormenting old folks like
Jimmy Macfarlane, and weak folks like thon lassie,
Miss Gray. Thon sort of thing's all right for wee
Johnnie, but no' for you. You'll mind that?'

'Aye, father.'

'An' then there's this fiddling wi' Alicky Mag,'

continued Johnnie. 'Ye may think him fine fun, Duncan, but he's nothing but a damned old rascal. He'll have asked ye back?'

'Aye, father.'

'What for?'

'To learn the fiddle.'

'An' ye think he means that?'

'Aye, father; that's what he said.'

'But it's not what he meant, Duncan boy. He's too old a man now to bother much wi' the lassies, though he's done them enough harm in his time. But he'd like fine to pit you on the road that he's gone himsel', wi' his drams, and his skirts, and his ranting fiddle.'

'Then ye'll no' let me learn?' asked Duncan sadly.

'Aye, ye can learn,' said Johnnie, 'but Alicky Mag will come *here* to learn ye. Now tell me, boy, how you came to be put out o' the school.'

Duncan told the whole story, while Johnnie's eyes twinkled and his mouth twisted up. 'Well, boy,' he said, when Duncan had finished, 'ye were right wi' the butcher and wrong wi' all else. You and wee Johnnie will need to apologise to Miss Gray.'

It was lucky for the boys that Hugh had gone with a headache to bed, and that only Mary awaited them with their supper cooking and the table spread. She looked at Johnnie's face to see that all was settled and right, and was thankful to see there would be no harsh words. 'Sit in and eat, boys,' she said, 'and then ye'll go to your beds. It's no' much of a dinner ye'll have had at that daft old Alicky Mag's.'

Duncan thought of the little man away back in Glendruid with only the dogs to speak to, and of the dark hills closing in upon the loneliness of his light. He thought of the trout and of the slow sad tune. 'We had a good dinner,' he said.

That night, beside wee Johnnie in bed, warm and safely home, he felt the pillow shake. 'What's the do wi' ye, Johnnie?' he asked.

Wee Johnnie spluttered and laughed. 'I never tell't ye, Duncan,' he giggled.

'Tell't me what?'

'What I was doing when you was making thon daft noise on the fiddle.'

'What was it, Johnnie?'

'I did what Alicky tell't me to do. I looked for puddocks.'

'Aye?'

'I found ten, an' I put them down his well.'

The whole bed shook as they laughed together.

X

The effect of his father's talk reformed Duncan for ten days at most; after that he had as good fun as ever with Jimmy Macfarlane and poor Miss Gray. But he didn't go to Glendruid again. He waited until his father should see Alicky Mag and ask him across to Glendarroch. There had been something repellent in that lonely neglected cottage, in the glen's sombre gloom, and in the old man laughing in his queer cracked voice. Alicky Mag was fine fun among the other herds at a gathering or clipping, but there was something uncanny about him when alone. So Duncan lost interest in the fiddle

and the pipes, and counted the days until the school was closed and he free.

On the first day of holidays Duncan and wee Johnnie went mad with the joy of release. They fooled about in the yard and by the burn, until their mother tired of their noise and sent them to chop sticks. There Johnnie found them when he came down from the hill. 'Here, boys,' he said, 'you'll come with me and pack the wool. All you're doing there will no' help your mother much.'

They followed their father to the shed, where a big empty wool-sack hung suspended from the rafters. 'In you get, the two of yous,' cried Johnnie, and hoisted them into the bag.

Wee Johnnie went right out of sight when his father tossed him in. Then Johnnie threw up the tight-rolled fleeces for Duncan to pack, and he and wee Johnnie tramped them down with their feet. The sack swayed wildly from side to side as they tramped, and the dusty rafters creaked.

It was warm, exhilarating exercise, with the spring of wool under their stamping feet, and the swing and roll of the stretching sack. Duncan laughed when the soft fleeces struck wee Johnnie on the head, and rolled between his clutching arms to be trampled down. Soon the boys' legs were level with the sack's edge, and they had to cling to the creaking cords to keep balance. 'Now ye can come down,' cried Johnnie.

Duncan swung himself out with a pull on the ropes, and hung in mid-air, with his thin legs dangling down. 'Drop!' Johnnie commanded, 'I'll catch ye,' and Duncan let himself go, to be caught in stout arms and landed safely on the floor.

'Now, ye wee deil,' cried Johnnie, and his younger son sprang laughing down.

'I'll have to wait on Hugh,' said Johnnie, scratching his black curls. 'Man, Duncan, we're no' strong enough between us to sew that up,' and he ruefully regarded the swaying sack. 'Away out, Johnnie, and see if ye'll see your grandfather. He should be back off the hill by now.'

Wee Johnnie raced out and was back like lightning. 'He's coming up the brae sweering,' he announced.

'And what's wrong now?' Johnnie grumbled. 'There'll be a sheep dead, like as not.'

Then Hugh's voice bellowed from the yard: 'Are ye there, John Gillies?'

'Aye.'

Tramp — tramp — tramp — the tackety boots rang over the yard. Hugh's bulk, like a thundercloud, filled the doorway and cut off the sun. 'See *thon*!' he roared, and hurled a bloody sheep's head to the floor. It rolled absurdly over the cobbles, its horns rattling, and came to rest in the shadow of the sack, leaving a sprinkled trail of blood behind it from the door.

'Ah!' growled Johnnie, 'they've started *here* now, have they? Sheep-stealers, Duncan boy; that's what's been in it. I'll get your bike out, Hugh, and go down for the *po*lice.'

'*Police!*' sneered Hugh, 'and would you be going to Lochend for the *po*lice! An' do you know what they're calling the new sergeant in Lochend? *East*, they call him, because that's where he goes when there's a fight on west. We'll do our own *po*licing in Glendarroch, John Gillies.'

'But the damage is done, is it no'?' asked Johnnie.

'No' much, boy, no' much. They didna get much in Glendarroch last night. I doubt the daylight came on them before they were finished. There'll be no more than a three or four sheep off the place *last* night. But they've had a taste, John Gillies, they've had a taste.'

'Will they be back, d'ye think?' asked Duncan in huge excitement. He had heard of the new sheep-raiders, the Westown roughs in their motor-vans, who prowled the hill roads in the stillness of night.

'*Back*, did ye say, boy? Aye, they'll be back when they've seen the flesh that's on a Glendarroch eild ewe in the month o' August.'

'You wait,' cried Duncan, feeling six feet tall with this taste of adventure. 'Wee Johnnie and me'll give them a fright.'

'Well said, boy,' yelled Hugh, diving a hand into his trouser-pocket. 'There's a sixpence to ye for saying that. There's no fears of the country if we aye breed boys that can fight.'

'Aye,' said Johnnie, twisting up his face to hide its laughter, 'but we'll maybe give the two of yous a bit hand.'

'Come on,' Hugh cried, 'we'll away and see how many more heads have been left in the ditch.'

Duncan spent the rest of the morning searching in the drains at the side of the road, puddling among the damp peat, pulling back the overgrown sprets and purple masses of bell-heather. He found nothing but a puddock and a couple of nuts off Macfarlane's car. But Hugh, farther down the road, had had more luck. With a scream of rage

he lifted up a lamb's head, and held it aloft to the desolate glen with all the solemnity of an executioner proclaiming the death of a king. Duncan ran down the road, thrilled to the marrow as though gold had been struck. ' Let's see it,' he cried.

It was the head of a distinguished and sweet ewe-lamb that followed a brock-faced ewe with the tip off one horn. Duncan recalled the face as though it were that of an old acquaintance. His excitement died and his anger grew. ' What for do they hack off the heads ? ' he inquired.

' What for ? ' repeated Hugh. ' What for ? So that the *po*lice can no' tell the lug-marks and the place the sheep come off. When the head's off a sheep there's no telling where it comes from, nor how it was come by.'

They found ten heads that day, and all was stormy planning when they gathered together for their tea. Hugh thumped the bare table with his great fist, expounding his points, whilst the crockery jumped. ' They'll maybe no' be back the night, or the next night, or the night after. But, sooner or later, it's back they'll come.'

' Wheesht, father,' urged Mary. ' You'll waken Jean.'

Hugh was further roused by her interruption. ' Aye,' he sneered, ' it's maybe nothing to you supposing every beast in Glendarroch was stolen—aye, the sheep, and the stirks, and the hens ? It's maybe nothing to you supposing the blame's put on John Gillies and Hugh Maclean ? '

' Havers ! ' said Mary. ' Shouting will no' help, anyway.'

' Aye,' agreed Johnnie, laying bare arms on the

table, ' Mary's right. We'll need to watch each night from now till sale. I'll take a turn down the glen on the bike to the Macintyre boys. If they was to keep a watch there and us here, we'd catch the deils atween them and oursels.'

' Fine, Johnnie,' grinned Hugh, who liked the plan. ' We'll take turn about at the sitting up.'

' An' me too ? ' pleaded Duncan.

' No ! ' Johnnie answered. ' Boys need their sleep.'

It was late that night before Duncan could close his eyes. He saw Johnnie rattle down the glen on Hugh's old bike in the dusk, and heard him come home in the dark. He listened to the fire being banked up for the night in the kitchen range, and to the flop of Johnnie's boots as he cast them off to ease tired feet. His eyes grew heavy, but he dreaded to close them, lest the cry of ' Thief ! ' should ring its wild challenge through the night and he asleep.

Wee Johnnie was just the same. ' Are ye wakened, Duncan ? ' he whispered.

' Go to sleep,' grunted Duncan. ' *You're* no' coming, anyway.' Then he slept himself and dreamt of Homeric conflicts, wherein, like the tailor of fable, he killed nine men with a blow.

Four nights and four days passed, and Duncan was beginning to despair. Then, on the fifth night, he awakened with thumping heart in the pitch-black darkness of a moonless night. There was a curious prickly coldness in his scalp, which ran in shivering waves down his neck and spine. He heard the chair in the kitchen pushed suddenly back, as though Johnnie had risen in excited hurry, then urgent

tapping and hoarse whispering at Hugh's closed door. There came the creaking of Hugh's bed and the thud of bare feet on the plank floor. Duncan crept over to the chair and slipped on his clothes, very quietly, so as to leave wee Johnnie asleep.

The men had gone out when he tiptoed through the house. He could hear the crunch of their boots as they ran down the brae. The night was still and cold for summer, with myriad stars glittering like jewels in the black roof of the world. Duncan crept back to the kitchen to arm himself with the twisted poker; then, with his hair still ruffled from sleep, he dashed out to fight for the fun of the thing.

There was no mistaking where the battle must begin. The brilliant head-lights of a stationary car lit up the side of the glen where the moor sloped down to a V-shaped bend in the burn. Duncan thought he could see the scurrying shadows of harried sheep dashing across the beam of light. He clenched the poker in his right hand and set off down the glen as fast as he could go. As he got nearer the car he heard the yapping of a dog, and the dunt of something thrown down on the resounding floor of the lorry. He saw a man running, and quite suddenly felt lonely and afraid. He caught sight of a crouching figure almost at his side and trembled with fright. Then Johnnie's comforting voice hissed through the darkness—' What the hell are ye doing here, boy?'

' Come to help!' whispered Duncan.

' Away home wi' ye, then. My God! boy, what have you there? A poker?'

' Aye, father.'

'Here, Hugh,' signalled Johnnie to a second black creeping shape. 'Here's Duncan wi' a poker!'

'Fine,' grunted Hugh. 'Give it me!'

'Indeed no, Hugh,' said Johnnie firmly. 'We're no' wanting murder done the night.—Away home, Duncan!'

'Let the boy stay,' Hugh whispered. 'He can hold my jacket for me.'

Duncan caught the coat, while Hugh rolled up his sleeves above the knotted biceps muscles.

'Wheesht!' said Hugh.

A long low whistle sounded from down the glen, and Johnnie, sticking his fingers in his wide-stretched mouth, sent it echoing back. 'Bide here!' he called to Duncan, and dashed through the swishing heather with Hugh by his side.

But Duncan could not bide. If a fight there was to be, then he must be in it; so he picked up a stone and ran straight for the light. He heard a man shout and the roar of the lorry as it started up, then all was a confusion of swaying and wrestling figures, muttered curses, thumps of blows, and the pitiful whining yelp of an injured dog.

Duncan felt sick. He saw what looked like big Bob Macintyre smash two men's heads together like a couple of eggs, then a little man run up behind and whack with a long pliable thing that made no sound. Bob Macintyre went down, and the little man went on hitting and hitting. He heard little Johnnie Gillies give a scream of what sounded like pain, and the injured dog went on yelping, yelping. The lorry lurched into motion with roaring engine, swayed on the road, and smashed right into the ditch. It lay like a wounded

thing with its engine still, and one head-light burning, sending a search-light into the sky. Two figures, clinched and sobbing, staggered across the road. It was Hugh at death-grips with the little man.

' Let go ! ' Hugh screamed. ' Let go, I say !—Ah ! Got ye, ye Irish rat.'

Then the little man was babbling stupid, apologetic, incoherent words, babbling away in a Westown accent. ' I didna mean to hurt ye, shepherd, and I'm no' Irish ; I'm a Campbell, that's what I am.'

' *Campbell* ! ' roared Hugh. ' And would ye tell *that* to a Maclean ! '

The little man screeched to the stars like a strangled hare. Duncan watched the shadow of his head go back, and back, and back ; heard Johnnie yell, ' Dinna kill him, Hugh ! '

The dog whined weakly, as though dying. Duncan turned away, crying, and was sick. He felt better after that, and was thankful to see the first faint streamers of dawn dim the brilliance of the stars. He ran down to the road, where shadows were moving about and his grandfather laughing away as he always did when a job was done.

' Here's the boy,' Hugh shouted. ' I'd clean forgot him. Hi, Duncan, have you aye the poker, boy ? Away up to the house for a lantern and let's see what we've got. Thon wee Irish rat's no' come to his senses yet.'

Duncan hurried away up the road, his legs so weak that they scarcely seemed to belong to him. Still, he was thankful to have something to do. The house was brightly lit when he got in, the fire crackling, and the bottle and tea-things on the table.

Mary was dressed and busy, but she rushed to

the door when Duncan came in. ' My wee lamb ! '
she cried. ' Why did they no' send you home ?
Are they all right ? '

' Aye, they've won,' stammered Duncan, then
flung himself sobbing against his mother's skirts.

She bent down to comfort him, sobbing herself.
' Oh, Duncan laddie,' she said, ' ye canna aye be
the big man yet, can ye, boy ? '

Then he remembered his errand. ' They're
needing the lamp,' he muttered.

' The lantern, ye mean, Duncan ? Sit ye down,
boy, and I'll fetch it to you. There ! Take a wee
dram while I'm lighting it.'

Duncan felt the whisky run like fire down his
throat, and spread with tingling comfort to his feet
and hands. It took the sickness from him. He
hurried down the road with the lantern turned low,
and handed it to his grandfather.

' Aye, Duncan,' Hugh beamed, ' we've brought
down six men and a dog. The dog's dead and the
wee Irish rat no' far off it.'

' And Bob Macintyre ? ' asked Duncan.

' *Him !* ' Hugh laughed. ' It would take a lot
to kill *him*. He's been on his feet these ten minutes.'

' Duncan,' called Johnnie, ' away home now and
get your porridge. Tell your mother we'll no' be
home for a whiley. We're taking this Westown
rubbish down to the Macintyres'.'

' Aye,' Hugh bellowed for the prisoners' benefit,
' and we'll lock them in wi' the black bull till the
*po*lice come.'

Duncan crept sadly home as the sun rose. The
redness in the east reminded him of blood, and the
whine of the dying dog rang in his ears.

Wee Johnnie was waiting for him half-way up the brae, with black eyes round with admiration. ' Did ye see the fight, Duncan ? ' he asked eagerly.

' Aye.'

' Boy, I wish it was me that had been there ! '

Duncan sighed wearily. ' Ye wouldna have liked it, Johnnie,' he said.

Slowly he walked up the brae, with wee Johnnie asking questions which he would not answer. He was shivering from fright and cold, and in no mood for talk. The warmth of the kitchen and his mother's welcome were the haven that he longed for after sordid storm. Mary fussed about him as she had not done for many a long day, and it reminded Duncan of the time when he was still a bairn, when there was no Jean to occupy his mother's attention, and when wee Johnnie could only cry. Seeing that Duncan was tired out, Mary asked no questions. She just coaxed him to his porridge and milk and ran her hand through his dew-damp hair. She said nothing of how he had clung crying to her skirts, nor did she ever mention it again. Duncan was grateful for that.

The men were home by nine o'clock. They were tired, battered and bruised. Johnnie's right eye was swollen and closed, and beginning to turn to blue. Hugh's lower lip was torn down at the corner, and a trickle of blood had dried on his greying beard. Johnnie was trying to laugh about it all, but Hugh's temper was frayed and his head was sore.

' You're tired, father,' said Mary.

' Aye,' Hugh answered, and he staggered a little, ' I'm for my bed.'

' Indeed, and you look as if you need it, father.
Are the men away with the *poli*ce ? '

' Aye ! the six wee rats will be in the jail by
now. These Westown trash are like wee weasels,
no' easy to get a hold of, but no great strength in
them when they're caught. I'll away to my bed.'

Mary looked anxiously after him. ' He's no' weel,
Johnnie,' she said. ' It's no' like him to give in
like that.'

' He took a lot out of himsel',' Johnnie replied.
' He's an awful one to fight. He near killed the
wee rabbit o' a mannie that tore his lip.'

Wee Johnnie had been staring at his father. ' Tell
us how ye got yer eye blackened ! ' he demanded.

' Away wi' you,' said Mary, ' and don't bother
your father.'

Johnnie laughed, and his swollen eye bulged
when he wrinkled his face. ' It's coming out,' wee
Johnnie whispered in awed tones.

' It'll no' be a bonnie sight for a day or two,' his
father said. ' An' you were asking who gave it
me ? Well, I don't rightly know, boy. It was just
dark, and things fleeing about, and something hit
me. But whoever or whatever it was, it fair roused
Johnnie Gillies, I'm telling ye that.'

Then Johnnie looked at Duncan, who was staring
moodily into the fire. Duncan wasn't well pleased
with the part he had played that night. He hadn't
done what he had meant to do when he went
galloping into the dark. He wished everything
would happen all over again. Then he would dash
out when he saw Bob Macintyre fall, and he would
throw a stone full in the face of the Westown rat.
He would pull away the wee man's legs when he

fastened on big Hugh's beard. He would do all manner of gallant and daring things if only it would happen all over again. Yet, when he'd had his chance, he'd just gone and been sick, then cried about his mother's skirts.

Johnnie saw what was to do with the boy. ' It was fine to think last night,' he said, ' that you was there behind us if we'd needed your help.' Duncan looked up from the fire with grateful eyes. ' An' if ye felt a wee bit seek, boy,' Johnnie went on, ' I felt just the same when I saw my first fight, an' it wasn't a fight like thon. It's easier to be in the thick of a thing like that than to sit holding jackets. Will ye give us a hand the day ? Wi' Hugh in bed and the sheep upset wi' yon shindy last night, there'll be a lot to do on the hill.'

Duncan thought of Meg and the fine weather outside, and though tired, he rose with a will.

' The boy had better rest the day,' said Mary.

' Huts ! ' answered Johnnie. ' The boy's hardy. Aren't ye, Duncan ? '

' Aye ! ' agreed Duncan, and went swaggering out to show just how hardy he was.

XI

The sheep-stealers were talked of for many a long day. Then they were forgotten, for Cranok sales drew nigh—the sales where the top wether and the second ewe lambs were sold ; when the annual harvest of the hills was scattered to all the hay stubble and clover fields of southern Scotland and the English north.

Duncan had always wanted to go to Cranok, ever

since, as a wee boy, he had seen the big double-decked lorries rumble down the glen with their cargoes of bleating lambs.   Johnnie had told him of the old days when the lambs were driven all the way down to Lochend pier, but now the lorries came right up to the buchts at the brae-foot.   They were huge monsters of things, like sheep-pens on wheels, and the road was cut up for weeks after they had gone by the deep-rutted pattern of their double tyres.   One lorry could take a hundred lambs, and Hugh and Johnnie, anxious and excited, would climb up beside the silent, big-muscled men who drove.

It seemed too good to be true when Johnnie said, on the night before the sale, 'Duncan boy, we're thinking of taking you to Cranok with us to-morrow.   You've never seen a sale, boy?'

'No, father.'

'Well, it's a fine thing to see other folk's sheep. It makes you think less of your own.'

'Will we be staying the night in Cranok, father?'

'Aye, boy, we'll need to do that.'

'Eh!' Mary intervened.   'Cranok will be a rough place, by what I've heard, for a young boy like Duncan.'

'I'll look after him, Mary.   He'll have that much to see of the sheep that he'll never heed what the men are doing.   There's some herds carry on as though they went to the sales to amuse themselves, but it's a grand place to see sheep.'

'Will grandfather be going too?' asked Duncan.

'Aye,' said Johnnie, 'if he's fit.'   For Hugh had not been well.

'Well, Duncan,' Mary smiled, 'if you're going,

you'll need to be away to your bed now, for it's an early start.'

'Can I take Meg wi' me?' asked Duncan.

'Aye, boy,' said Johnnie, 'ye'll need her.'

Duncan went to bed thinking of the lambs safely penned in the buchts against the morrow, and of the lumbering lorries that would come lurching up the glen road, their lights paled by the grey dawn. He was all excited and longing to be up and doing, and he feared he might sleep in. As he lay listening to the burn's music and the distant muttering of resting sheep, wee Johnnie stirred beside him.

'Will you be going to-morrow, Duncan?'

'Aye.'

'Man, but it's you that's lucky!'

There was something like a sob when wee Johnnie turned over to sleep.

Duncan was awake before morning and the light had come. He lay still, listening to the sleeping hush of the house, and the stirring of dawn in the hills. He didn't know what the time was—it might still be the middle of the night. Yet there was something in the movement of the wind, some quality of the darkness, that told him he had not long to wait.

Then he heard the alarm go off in his father's room, the burring of the bell against rusty metal, and the dull resonance of the mantelshelf. He heard Johnnie jump from bed, and pad across the floor. The alarm was stilled. There came the sound of knocking at Hugh's room, the grunted response, the crackling of the kitchen fire, and then the creaky opening of the door.

'Are ye wakened yet, Duncan?' Johnnie whispered.

'Aye.'

'Well, here's a candle to you, boy, and there's milk put out for you on the kitchen table.'

Duncan hurried into his clothes by dim candle-light. Wee Johnnie's head was tossing about on the pillow, but he did not waken. Duncan ran through to the kitchen, to the warm fire, the smell of paraffin, and his glass of milk. Johnnie and Hugh were struggling into their boots. They were silent and purposeful, as though great work lay before them that day.

'Take a keek out an' see if the lorries are coming, boy,' Hugh ordered.

Duncan ran out to a cold, fine morning with dew on the grass, and the darkness lifting in the east. He gazed and listened, but there was no sign of the lorries. 'They're no' here yet,' he called.

'Damn!' Hugh grumbled. 'They're aye late! We'll away out for the dogs, an' go down to the buchts and wait them there.'

'Will we no' be having our breakfast first?' asked Johnnie.

'Man,' Hugh grumbled, 'you're aye thinking on your belly. It's no' meat we need on Cranok sale day, it's punctuality.'

'The boy'll need *his*, anyway, Hugh.'

'Ach!' Hugh growled, 'you're aye thinking on him too. Bellies and bairns—that's you, John Gillies.'

'The lorries!' Duncan shouted, and ran off down the brae, just as Mary came in to get the breakfast ready. Duncan was like Hugh, he had no thought of food on this day of all days.

It was the lorries, all right! There was a dim

yellow glow moving across the sky beyond the glen's defile. They turned the corner, and the glen road was lit. They came much more slowly now that they were on the narrow road with the unguarded ditches, and the dogs, feeling the vibrant tremors of the shaking earth, howled their warning and alarm.

There was the crunching of boots as Hugh and Johnnie came striding down. 'What's this?' Hugh yelled. 'There's only the one!'

'The other'll be behind,' Johnnie soothed.

'Aye! behind its mate and behind its time, John Gillies. Where's the boy got to now? There's no light to see a thing by.'

'I'm here,' Duncan cried, wishing his grandfather had been unwell enough to bide at home.

'Have you yon bitch of yours?'

'No.'

'An' what the hell's the use of you without your dog? Away up for her, an' let the others out.'

Duncan raced up the brae.

Mary put her head round the door. 'You're not to go without your breakfast, Duncan.'

Duncan scowled. It was going to be a difficult day. He unchained the dogs and ran back to the road with the yapping, tumbling pack at his heels. Hugh was in fierce altercation with the driver of the lorry. He laid his stick about him to quieten the dogs.

'My God!' bawled the driver, a big burly man with arms like trees, 'and are ye meaning tae tak a' these?' He pointed contemptuously at the whining curs.

'Aye!' Hugh stormed. 'I've taken my dogs

with me to Cranok these twenty years an' more, and aye in the lorry.'

'It's no use wagging your beard at me,' said the driver, descending to the road like a human mountain. 'I cam here tae lift sheep and no' a bloody menagerie. You're no' thinking of flitting the day too, are ye, shepherd?'

Johnnie Gillies stepped forward. 'Come away up to the house for a cup of tea, boy,' he said to the driver. 'You'll be cold after sitting up there all night. Have you a mate with you?'

'Aye.'

'Then bring him along too.'

'Fine!' grinned the driver, rubbing his oil-stained hands. 'Come on, Jack; we're all right. There's a ceevilised body in this God-forsaken place aifter a'. They're no' a' like faither Abraham here.'

The driver's help climbed down, a sturdy smiling youth with a dirty face, a cap at the back of his head, and a red rag round his neck.

Hugh fumed and fretted by the roadside, while Duncan crept round the lorry and its trailer, examining its huge bulk. It was the biggest vehicle that had ever come up the glen, and looked as though it could easily hold the three hundred and odd top lambs bound that day for Cranok sale.

'Is there no' another coming?' he asked, curiosity having conquered his timidity.

'No,' Hugh answered, 'there's no' to be another in it. Thon big ox o' a man says he can take all the lambs in that chariot o' his, but he's not for taking us nor our dogs.'

'Then how are we to get in in time?' Duncan asked.

'God knows!' growled Hugh, and led the way up the brae to breakfast and the house.

Johnnie Gillies had the lorrymen in great form by the time Hugh and Duncan came in. They were sitting over bacon and eggs, and oatcakes and tea, their greasy caps flung carelessly down on the bare table beyond their plates. Their cold hands had thawed and their stiff limbs loosened. They were telling Mary how it was a parcel of yabbling monkeys they thought they had fallen amongst, and how old father Abraham had wagged his beard near off, when Hugh came in.

'This is my father,' she said.

'My God!' stared the big driver with his mouth full of scone. 'Look what the wind's blown in!'

'Sit down and have your breakfast, father,' Mary said.

'Aye, and tuck in, shepherd,' the driver encouraged. 'It's a good feed, and we'll squeeze you and your men and your dogs in wi' us.' He winked slyly at Mary with a knowing eye. 'And we'll tak' the mistress atween us, if she'll come.'

'Indeed,' Mary laughed, 'an' that's the first time I've been asked to Cranok sale.'

Hugh looked downwards at the floor.

Duncan was too excited to eat much, but he stuffed something down inside him. He wanted to shout to the men to hurry and not be late. They were all so *slow*!

Then Hugh shuffled his feet and brushed his beard with the back of his hand. 'It's time we werena here,' he said, pushing his chair back.

The men all stumbled up, and Duncan was first

out, whistling the dogs to heel. The drivers climbed into the lorry, started the roaring engine, and reversed backwards towards the buchts. The soft earth sank and churned beneath gigantic wheels. Hugh and Johnnie shouted conflicting directions. The driver stared solemnly backwards, thrusting his big face out. It looked like a large impassive cheese in the morning light. A cock crowed from the hen-house and a flash of scarlet flame shot over the hills. It was dawn.

The driver's mate climbed to the top of the trailer, and let down the slatted gangway and erected its hinged sides. Hugh and Johnnie opened the bucht gate to drive up the lambs. Duncan watched them come bounding out, clean black legs springing clear of the heather, sharp ears cocked forwards from white wooled heads, eyes bright hazel and full of alarm. They hesitated before the sloping race leading to a shadowed unknown.

'How many does the top deck hold?' yelled Hugh.

'Seventy-five—same above as below,' the driver answered.

'Hup! Hup!' bawled Johnnie, clattering his stick along the rail.

Hugh counted the leaping lambs with his bobbing stick. 'Right!' he called, cutting in before the rest of the flock. 'There's seventy-five there.'

'Burr-r-r-r,' Johnnie shouted, chasing up the last of the lambs.

The driver's mate climbed up again to close off the upper deck with little wicket-gates, then he pulled on the chains until the gangway was level with the trailer's floor.

'Seventy-five again,' called Hugh. 'Let them run, Johnnie.'

With the trailer tightly packed, it was the lorry's turn to be filled. The trailer must be drawn on to the road, backed, uncoupled; then the disencumbered lorry churned the mud again as it reversed to the fanks to receive the rest of the lambs.

'Now,' said the driver, 'that's the sheep a' settled. Wha' aboot the rest of yous?'

'It's the first time in twenty years,' Hugh explained, 'that there's been only the one lorry come with two men. It's aye been two lorries and two men that's come before, and there was aye plenty of room for the herds to go wi' their sheep.'

'Aye, shepherd,' the driver replied, 'an' if ye were goin' back fifty years there'd be no lorries in it at all. Indeed, it's a queer thing if they were here ten years ago. Your memory's awa', ye auld goat.'

'I'm putting up wi' no more o' your in*sults*,' warned Hugh.

'Here!' cried the driver. 'Stop gabbling, man; it's time we were awa'. Shove the boy and the dogs in at the back wi' the sheep. The boy can watch that nane o' them get tramped. You can come in aside us, Abraham, and your son can sit on your knees.'

'He's no' my son.'

'An' is that my doin', ye auld fule? Here, are ye wanting tae be late?'

Duncan scrambled in somehow with five dogs and their chains, seventy-five lambs, three coats and three sticks, and a parcel of clothes and food. If he sat down he couldn't stretch his neck, and if he lay flat the dogs licked him all over his face. When

the lorry jerked into motion it seemed as though everything fell on top of him.

' Are ye a' right there, Duncan ? ' Johnnie yelled.

' *No!* ' he replied, but nobody heard him.

It was a foul journey. No chance to see the country or the sheep it carried, to watch the people in the thronged towns, or the private cars go flashing by. To Duncan it was a rough passage of jolts and knocks, stiff discomfort, suffocating heat, and the ammoniacal stink of dogs and sheep. If he had been younger he would have cried, but he just had to clench his teeth and contain his misery until the lorry lumbered to rest in Cranok sale-yard. The dogs tumbled over his legs when the doors were thrown open, but the lambs huddled away from the noise and light. Duncan crawled down, feeling tired and sick, and handed sticks and coats to Johnnie and Hugh.

' Your clothes are in a mess, boy,' Johnnie casually remarked, but they were all too busy getting the lambs safely penned to bother about a boy.

There were lambs everywhere, in pens, in alleyways, in lorries, and on the road, flock after flock coming by train, on wheel, or on foot to the clamouring auction of Cranok sale. The lambs were all of the hardy black-faced breed, sheep of the heather, the rocks, and the hills. There were no park-fed sheep, no white-faced Cheviot or half-bred lambs, no crosses by superior Border Leicester or Down rams out of England. The farms they came off were the high places, the black hills where no green grass grows, outlying grazings where snow lies thick, the glens and the corries, the unfertile straths.

When Duncan wandered with Johnnie to see

other men's sheep it was like a voyage of exploration through a concentrated Scotland. From the Gaelic pens and herds they went to those with the challenging Border names and the Borderers' singing tones, then to the West Country twang, and the mild soft speech of the Perthshire men. The sheep, like the men, were products of history and local soil. The herds were all shouting at one another, for Cranok sale is a place where shepherds meet. They come there with their sheep, year after year, growing from boys into men, becoming bent with weather and the passage of seasons, until they cease their herding to drool before the cottage fire, or lie in churchyards of the lonely glens. Then men will ask after Hamish or Ian, and say how ill he looked at the Cranok sales last year.

Duncan moved from pen to pen in his dung-soiled suit, listening to the burring north England speech of big buyers from the South, who talked and argued with the auctioneer. He met Alicky Mag, come in with the small-boned lambs from Glendruid.

'Man, Duncan,' Alicky screeched, 'and have they been rolling ye in the midden of Glendarroch?'

Duncan grinned self-consciously, and turned to the Strathord pens, where Mackenzie, in dyspeptic depression, leant over the rails in contemplation of his flock. 'Aye, Duncan,' he said, 'and this'll be your first Cranok sale. May ye live to see many of them, boy. Now, if ye were buying wether-lambs the day, would ye no' fancy the Strathord tops?'

Duncan was ready with stockman's repartee. 'I might look at them if I was needing some seconds for late wintering!' he grinned.

Mackenzie made a clumsy, jovial cut with his stick, and Duncan ducked. He wandered up the endless alleys between the pens, liking the hardy set of some Lammermoor lambs, the clean open faces of the Lanark and Ayrshire border. He disliked a pen of muzzy-faced Perthshire lambs, and wondered how any man in his senses could buy the sickly, dry-coated lambs from the island of Aegus. He lost himself for a time among the thousands of sheep new-gathered from the bee-loud hillsides of the South and West, then found himself suddenly back at the Glendarroch pen.

He thought there was much to be learnt by the viewing of other men's goods, just as his father had said. The Glendarroch lambs were too lean for tops ; they were too close in the faces and too high off the ground. Still, they had fine bloom on their coats, and were bright in the eye. It was said they did well on the Italian ryegrass and second-crop clover of the mild Ayrshire coast. They had character, were known to live well, and the same farmer had bought them for fourteen years. It was different with the Glendruid lambs, which died like flies when they saw good meat, and were bought by gentlemen-farmers who were new to the game, and thought them cheap.

From all sides came the chatter of commercial anticipation. 'Lambs will be half-a-crown up. Thon daft butcher body from London is up the day.' 'Aye, he'll gar things gang.' 'Lambs were nae mair than yin an' saxpence up at Hawick.' 'An' nae muckle better at Boswells.'

Duncan joined Hugh and Johnnie. Hugh was in high excitement. This was to him the day of

days, when he met friends unseen since the previous year's sale, when talk was free and drams were plentiful.

' To hell wi' Hawick and Boswells,' he spat with traditional contempt for the Border herds. ' A West Country black-face lamb will aye find a buyer.'

' Awa' wi' ye ! ' shouted a Peebles man. ' Argyllshire scab and Argyllshire fluke.'

Hugh glared and gripped his stick.

Then a masterful figure came striding down to the pen, a great big burly bareheaded man with black close-curling hair, in brown tweed knickers and carrying a monstrous crook. ' My God ! ' he bellowed like a jovial bull, ' if it's no' Hugh Maclean, the best herd in the West.'

' Man,' cried Hugh, ' are ye still alive ? '

' Alive ! ' roared the giant. ' It takes a devil of a lot to kill a MacBride, as King Hakon of Norraway said when he split open one's head and it laughed in his face. Do you know a cure for wool-ball, Hugh ? '

' Aye, Dan—plenty of milk in the ewes.'

' You're wrong, Hugh. The best cure is chloral and whisky.'

' Cut out the whatever ye call it, Dan, and I'm with ye in that.'

' And who's the young laird ? ' asked Dan, looking Duncan over with a humorous smile.

' Duncan Gillies, my grandson, and son of little Johnnie Gillies that's married on my lassie.'

' Well, Hugh Maclean,' roared Dan, ' ye may be a grand active old tup, but they don't take after ye, man. Where's Johnnie Gillies ? I haven't seen him for years. Aye—there ye are, Johnnie. Your

lambs are no' as good as they were last year. You're breeding better bairns than lambs in Glendarroch.'

Johnnie laid his hand on Duncan's shoulder, who was flaming red. 'I'll tell ye this, Dan,' laughed little Johnnie Gillies, 'the lambs are like your stories, boy, too many of them and no' what they were.'

Dan showed his great strong teeth in a boisterous laugh. 'Do ye aye read them, Johnnie?'

'Whiles, when there's nothing else doing, Dan. I liked them fine when ye were clipping sheep, but I've no manner o' use for your murdered brides.'

Then Alicky Mag came up, wrinkling his nut-brown face in a welcoming grin. 'Dan?—is it Dan?—big Dan MacBride himsel'?'

'*Alicky!*'

They shook hands, the little man smirking up with his toothless smile, the big man bending his bull-dog head in joyous mirth.

'Ye drunken wee rascal,' growled Dan MacBride, 'd'ye mind of our night in Westown together?'

'*Mind*, Dan?' cackled Alicky Mag. 'Will I ever forget?'

A man came banging a bell from the sale-ring with its conical roof like a Chinese temple. 'Now, gentlemen, *please*,' called the keen-faced auctioneer, 'we *must* make a start.'

He had an anxious day before him, the pleasing of a thousand critical customers, the simultaneous satisfaction of those who bought and of those who sold. He moved towards the ring, followed by the crowd of dealers, drovers, farmers, and herds. The

first lot of lambs were already circling the sawdust-covered ring when he mounted his rostrum, perched his bowler hat behind him, hitched up his trousers, and turned to the business of the day. Duncan craned and peered to see something of the sheep.

'The first lot are from Corryheim, gentlemen—good sheep off a high sound place, and they've been sold here for a lot of years now.' The auctioneer tapped the rostrum with his short cane stick. 'Say away for these Corryheim top wether-lambs. How much am I bid? Twenty-five shillings? Twenty? Fifteen? I'm bid twelve, only twelve shillings bid for these character lambs.'

Duncan heard the price rise first by shillings, then sixpences, finally threepence a head. He couldn't see who was bidding, nor how the auctioneer spied the bidders. The Corryheim shepherd, an elderly man with a quiet, sad face, prodded the procession of lambs into circular motion. Then he followed them out of the ring, sold to a Carlisle dealer at sixteen and threepence a head. It was whispered around how the Corryheim lambs had made sixpence more at the last year's sale.

The monotonous auction dragged on all day. There seemed no end to the energy of the red-faced auctioneer. Duncan, running backwards and forwards from pens to ring, heard the low rumble of 'One and thrup I'm bid, one and thrup, *twenty*-one and thrup. Gentlemen, these lambs are cheap at the money. One and thrup. Are they to go at that?'—then the bang of the stick when the sheep were sold, the rattle of gates opening to let them out, and their scampering feet on the mud and stones.

Duncan helped drive in the Glendarroch lambs, and listened to the bidding with fluttering heart. How he hated and loathed the dumb, hesitant buyers! Would they never start? The auctioneer was down to twelve shillings when somebody bid, and the price went creeping up by shillings, six-pences, and threepenny-bits. Then came the dreadful suspense while the auctioneer paused with his threatening stick. 'Are they to go?' he cried. 'At sixteen shillings—sixteen shillings!'—Bang! The stick was down and the lambs streamed out.

Duncan followed them back to the Glendarroch pens. Johnnie and Hugh were laughing together as they stumbled after the flock, their legs slipping and splaying grotesquely on the liquid mud.

'Are ye pleased wi' the price?' Duncan asked.

'Fine that, boy,' grinned Johnnie. 'A shilling up from the year afore is not what many folks are getting the day.'

'An' we'll no' need to hang aboot wi' the sheep,' Hugh exulted. 'They're to be lifted by float, and there'll be no herding and hanging aboot Cranok station till the stationmaster wakens.'

Big Dan MacBride came rolling along, shouting cheery encouragement to the waiting herds.

'Are ye through, Hugh Maclean?' he shouted.

'Aye, Dan.'

'Then come on for a quick one before they close.'

Johnnie Gillies frowned.

'Who's thon?' asked Duncan, when MacBride went swaggering away with Hugh.

'A daft body wi' brains,' Johnnie answered. 'He was coming out for a minister, but got stickit

in college.   He's mad on the sheep and the ways
of the beasts, and makes his living writing stories
about them, but this last whiley he's got his sheep
a' mixed up wi' brides and baths, an' murders an'
suicides, an' thon sort o' trash.'

'He's a lively one, isn't he?' said Duncan.

'Aye, boy,' Johnnie replied, 'but ye've no' seen
him right started yet.   Wait till ye hear him singing
his songs to the herds in the bar the night!'

Duncan was tired by night, tired of the pushing
and bustle of men, of the constant movement and
smell of sheep, of the endless patter of the auctioneer.   He had a pain in his stomach from eating half-
cold meat-pies and overstrong tea in the dreary little
restaurant attached to the mart.   One day of the
fair had been more than enough, but he must stay
with Johnnie and Hugh in a cheap hotel, and see
the ewe-lambs sold on the following day.

The hotel was doing so well in its bar trade that
there was little attention to food and beds.   The
small bedroom smelt of damp and a nauseant mix-
ture of fading scents.   The bed was narrow and
hard, and Johnnie and Duncan were to sleep
together.   Duncan fed with Johnnie in the dismal
coffee-room, which still smelt of breakfast, though
supper was on.   The cloth was spattered with a
week's misdirection of eggs.   There was a picture
of a bull, and a stuffed salmon over the fireplace,
filled with pink paper.

Duncan jibbed at the fat slabby slices of ham and
the petrified scones.   'Are ye seek, boy?' asked
Johnnie, seeing the paleness of his face.

'No, I'm fine.'   Duncan made a brave attempt
to force the foul stuff down.

From the bar came the rumble of voices, and the roar of rude laughter, stamping of heavy boots and the banging of sticks, the tinkle of glasses and the rattle of cash.

The maid, a pimple-faced slattern, smirked into Johnnie's brown face. ' I'll need to ask you to shift, gentlemen,' she said. ' There's that many coming in to-day we're rushed off our feet.'

' But there's nobody here ! ' Johnnie protested, sweeping a puzzled glance round the deserted room.

' The commercials will soon be in, gentlemen,' sniffed the maid. ' There's plenty of room in the bar-parlour downstairs.'

' I'll no' shift,' said Johnnie stoutly. ' I'm no' wantin' a drink.'

The maid grew angry. ' A fine cheek ye have,' she sneered, ' sayin' what you'll do and no' do ! Coming in here wi' your boots and clothes wi' a mess and a stink like yon. The commercials would never put up wi' you if they came in.'

' *Stink !* ' Johnnie screamed in righteous wrath. ' I've smelt more stinks in this damn dirty bothy of a place than I've smelt in a year.'

' I'll call the manager if ye give me a word more impudence,' said the maid.

But the manager was there, standing unob- trusively in the background, prepared for any trouble on the night of a Cranok sale. A tall, lean, sallow-faced man he was, with a secretive silent walk. He stepped forwards from the shadow of the door. ' Come away now, shepherd,' he said in forced geniality and a Westown accent. ' Go down to the parlour with your pals, and I'll send you in a drink.'

' An' start me drinking for the rest o' the night,' cried Johnnie. ' A fine game thon ! '

' There's no need to do that,' said the manager.

' We're goin' out on the street,' replied Johnnie, ' an' there's nobody can stop us from doing that.'

' You're welcome,' the manager laughed, nodding to the window. The sky was blackened and the rain was hissing down. ' Take my advice,' he added, ' and make yourself comfortable downstairs. There's a fire there, and you can order lemonade if you like.'

' Come on, then, Duncan,' Johnnie grunted ; ' we'll go down and sit for a whiley, but we'll no' be long out of our beds.'

The bar-parlour was a blaze of geniality. Shepherds from the Western Isles sat on the narrow benches round the wall, talking together in the soft Gaelic tongue. Borderers and Ayrshire men, less shy and silent in their ways, laughed and drank round the beer-swilled counter. In place of honour before the fire stood big Dan MacBride and Hugh Maclean. Duncan slipped round to the horseless stables to comfort the dogs in their chained security, then crept quietly to where Johnnie was sitting in solitary gloom.

' My God ! ' laughed Dan MacBride, looking round, ' there's little Johnnie Gillies squatting in a corner like a calving quey. What's wrong wi' you, man ? Ye werena aye a lump o' peat.'

' It's the boy,' whispered Hugh, grinning over his beard. ' Johnnie watches him like he was a young tup coming out for the Highland Show.'

' An' he's right ! ' roared Dan. ' I've never met a Gillies yet that wasna proud o' his bairns.'

'Dan,' said Hugh quickly, 'your glass is empty, boy. Here, you,' he called to the aproned barman. 'Two more o' the same.'

'Hugh!' said Dan, gradually expanding with society and warmth, 'I can tell you the name of every clansman in this room. They're as different as ewes when you get to know them.'

'An' would you be knowing that I was a Maclean?'

'You couldn't be anything else.'

'An' can you tell me the name o' that big long black-headed man in the corner, Dan?'

'He's a Macdonald by the spit o' him, Hugh. The Macdonalds are all tall, dark, sour-looking devils.'

The man heard the talk and looked up with a scowl. 'My name's John Grant, if that's any use to you,' he said.

'Is it, now?' grinned Dan MacBride. 'Then your mother was a Macdonald.'

'What the hell's it to you what my mother was?'

'A good woman, I hope,' laughed Dan MacBride. 'Now, d'ye see thon little wee wiry dark-haired man, Hugh? He's a Macleod.'

The little man raised his sad grey eyes, and their long dark lashes fluttered like the wings of a perching bird. 'Mackerlich's my name,' he said.

'Well,' said Dan, 'and that's a clan I never heard tell of. Have a drink with me, Mackerlich, and tell me the story and home of your clan.'

'Thank you,' said the little man, stepping to the fire. 'I've read your stories, Mr MacBride, and there's not many faces I know here. I'm new over from Skye to a Dumbarton herding.' He spoke

slowly, as though English was strange to his tongue.

'So, you've never heard of the Mackerlichs before, Mr MacBride? There's not many of us. When Prince Charlie was in the West, there was a Spanish girl with him that had come over in one of the French ships. She was left behind when the Prince sailed off, and the boy that was born was called by the people Mackerlich, son of Charles. So the children he left and their children's children are the Mackerlich clan.'

'Half Spaniard, half Royal Stuart!' yelled Dan MacBride. 'Man, it's great blood ye have running in your veins. A drink all round, and I'll give ye a health, men. We've a Jacobite song in the making here. Your health, sir,' he cried, turning to the little dark man. 'Your health, and the health of your clan, the smallest clan in Scotland, and best breeding of them all.'

'Wait, Dan!' shouted Johnnie, 'that's a health worth drinking, and Duncan and me will take a dram with ye there.'

'Here!' Dan called to the barman. 'Two drams of your oldest, mildest, and best, for little Johnnie Gillies and the fine laddie he's brought from Glendarroch this day.'

The herds rose to their feet, holding glasses aloft, some of them moved and tearful, with dim memories of sorrow for a broken race, some not understanding, some willing to drink to the Devil if a neighbour paid. The little man stood silent in the middle of them all.

'The Mackerlichs!' said Dan.

'The Mackerlichs!'

The little man raised his head. 'Thank you, gentlemen,' he said simply, 'for drinking so kindly to myself and my people.' He picked up his stick and his ragged cap and drifted out, sad and lonely, to the wet darkness of the night.

'Prince Charlie!' sighed Dan MacBride. 'Man, Hugh, I've met an old man who talked to an old, old woman who had seen him.'

'An' what did she say of him, man?'

'That he'd have been better to have died at the head of his men than to have come home beaten.'

Johnnie poked Duncan in the ribs. 'Mind ye on that, boy,' he urged; 'that's right. It's the truth.' But Duncan was nodding, the bar was a dancing blur before his tired eyes, his lids would no longer keep open. 'Come away to your bed, boy,' whispered Johnnie. 'It's time ye were stretched.'

Duncan lay beside Johnnie on the hard bed, listening to the crashes of laughter, the nasal Gaelic singing, the lewd choruses of a Cranok sale night. He heard Dan MacBride roaring songs of Burns that are seldom heard, then Westown student ballads that none could print.

He thought of wee Johnnie alone in the double-bed at home, wished he were there too, and fell asleep.

XII

The rain had cleared by morning, and sunlight glinted on the wet pavement of Cranok town. Duncan and Johnnie were out before the sun was well up. They felt they must escape from the close dampness of the bedroom and the musty odours of whisky and beer that reeked in the downstairs

passages. Duncan was glad to get the clean air into
his lungs, and to feel the cool dawn-wind whispering round his head. He was keen enough now to
face a second day of circling sheep and bargaining
clamour.

' Where's grandfather ? ' he asked.

' Sleepin' likely,' Johnnie growled.

There was no more said of Hugh. They unchained the frantic dogs and let them gallop along
the streets beneath the close-shut windows of still,
sleeping houses. There was nobody about and the
town was quiet, save for the cheery rattle of an
early milk-cart. The black rain-clouds were drifting to the east, and a dark greyness in the distance
showed where the rain still fell.

' We'll away to the unction mart and see how the
ewe-lambs are doing,' said Johnnie. ' We'll get
them shifted to the sale-pens before the floats start
coming in.'

Cranok sale-yard seemed a dead place after the
clamour of the previous day. A couple of sleepy
drovers were leaning against the outer gate, talking
lazily together, without animation. The alleyways
were a sea of churned mud, beaten up by hooves
and hobnailed boots, and then washed smooth by
the lashing rain. The blue slates of the covered
ring flashed and glittered in the sun. Two white
pigeons scratched and cooed on the rones. Most
of the pens were empty of sheep ; the lorries had
rumbled away through the night with the wether-
lambs. Duncan helped Johnnie to drive the be-
draggled and empty ewe-lambs round from the
back of the mart to the Glendarroch pens.

' The rain's spoilt them, boy,' Johnnie grumbled,

' taken the bloom off them. They'll no' sell well wi'
their bellies all drapply like thon.'

' Will they be going down to Ayrshire too,
father ? '

' No, boy ; it's likely they'll go away up to
Nortown ; it's there most of the Cranok ewe-lambs
go. They gimmer them up there to make up the
crossing stocks.'

' What's a crossing stock ? ' Duncan asked, for
his knowledge of sheep was that of the Western
hills.

' Crossing stocks ? ' said Johnnie. ' They're
black-faced ewes tupped wi' the Leicester tup to
give cross lambs, an' they need to buy in black-
faced gimmers to make up their stocks, breeding
none of their own.'

' An' does it pay ? '

' Aye, boy, if it's a good sound hill, not too bare
in winter, and not too high.' Johnnie paused.
' Are ye needing your breakfast, boy ? '

' I could be doing with it,' Duncan answered.

' Then we'll away back to thon thing that's
calling itself a hotel, an' see if thon pock-faced
lassie is out o' her bed yet.'

She was. When Duncan and Johnnie came down
the street she was waiting for them, capless and
unwashed. ' Was it you that unlocked the door ? '
she demanded.

' Aye,' sneered Johnnie. ' Were ye thinkin' we
climbed through the keyhole ? '

' I'm wanting no more of your impudence,' she
stormed. ' What right had you to open the door
when there was nobody up ? '

' Well, ye should have been up yersel'.'

' At five o'clock ? '

' Aye ! Ye don't know you're alive yet.   When's breakfast ? '

' Seven o'clock, and it's just past six now.   And will you keep your dirty dogs off my clean mat.'

' Come away up to the mart again, Duncan,' Johnnie sighed.   ' It's more homely like there.'

' Aye, I believe that,' the slut called after them. ' Shepherds and sharn agree fine together.'

They wandered about, up and down the slowly awakening streets and around the more lively mart. Floats and flocks were already streaming in, and the bleating of lambs, barking of dogs, and shouting of droving herds made Duncan feel that the hills were not so far away.   It was a quarter to seven when they returned to the hotel.   Hugh and Dan were down at the bar, sour-faced and grey, drinking a hair of the dog that had bitten them.   Other herds were round about the door, discussing the prospects of prices and weather.

Duncan ate his breakfast of hard yellow paste that had once been egg, and the leathery lean and frizzled fat that passed for bacon.   The maid threw down the plate before him as though he were a dog. She was different with big Dan MacBride.

' Here, Jeannie, or whatever your name is,' he chuckled heartily.   ' Away through to the kitchen and ask Maggie to cook me something fit for a man to eat.   Tell her it's Dan MacBride that's asking.'

' Right, Mr MacBride,' she smirked, ' I'll do that. What are you for ? '

' Bacon and eggs and tea, Jeannie, my lass.   But see that it's not been cooked yesterday.   Well, boys,' he added, turning to Johnnie and Duncan,

' and ye missed a fine splore last night. Man, but we made a night o' it.'

' I heard thon,' Johnnie grinned. ' You were in grand form last night, Dan, but I doubt you're no' feeling as fine the day.'

' Am I no', Johnnie Gillies ? Am I no' ? Let me tell you, my bonnie man, that I'm fit to sell every sweet ewe-lamb off the island of Aegus. I'm near fit to sell thon giraffe-like bitches you've brought down off Glendarroch.'

' They'll maybe sell wi'out your clacking, Dan MacBride. A living giraffe is better than a dead Aegus lamb, and that's what the Nortown dealers will be thinking the day.'

The maid spread Dan's breakfast before him. It made Duncan envious to see what the invisible Maggie had been willing and able to do for Mr MacBride. ' Thank Maggie from me,' grinned Dan to the maid, waggling his massive haunches and lowering his tousled head to the plate like a ravenous mastiff.

Hugh Maclean shoved his head round the door. ' Are ye there, Johnnie ? '

' Aye.'

' It's time we werena here.'

Duncan hardly recognised his grandfather, so changed by a night's debauch. His eyes were staring, glazed, and red-lidded, his face and neck red and swollen, so that the band of his shirt seemed overtight. His brindled beard was matted and wet with spilt drink, and his voice was curiously hoarse and dead.

' Have you had your breakfast, Hugh ? ' asked Dan.

' To hell wi' meat !   Come on to the sale.'

The mart hummed with activity.   The voices of
the sellers were the same, but those of the buyers had
changed.   They were comfortable, strong-featured
men, these Nortown dealers, quietly jovial, and
broad in their dialect.   No point of a man or a
sheep escaped the shrewd judgment of their calculat-
ing eyes.   They gave nothing away, least of all what
they thought, and dressed well below their means.
The auctioneer was as energetic and active as though
there had been no sale on the previous day.   His
profession made money and died young.

Duncan was less confused by the bustle and stir,
and in consequence saw more of the sale.   He was
bold enough to creep down close to the cold iron
railings, and to shove his head between them to
judge the sheep.   He had got over his fear of the
auctioneer taking his slightest movement for a bid,
and had the courage to give a knowing tilt to his
bonnet, or to pass the back of his hand over the
point of an aristocratic nose.

The Aegus lambs were sold, each flock followed
by its rightful shepherd and by Dan MacBride, who
appeared to have assumed some sort of suzerainty
over the island's sheep.   He stumped round the
ring, with his gigantic crook, smiling his broad
grin, wagging his bared dark head, and urging
Jimmy, or Ian, or Angus, or Bob, to bid on the
lambs or they'd miss the best chance of their
lives.   He seemed to know everybody, and coined
appropriate names for the few outside his acquaintance.

' That man must own a lot of sheep,' exclaimed
a tall young farmer, new to the sale, when Dan

stumped in after the fifth consignment of Aegus lambs.

' He owns nothing but a pen and a damned cool impudence,' grunted the young farmer's friend.

A little old shepherd had been listening to what was said, as shepherds will. He intervened in a conversation which had nothing to do with him. ' Thon's Dan MacBride,' he shouted, ' and he's mair nor impudence an' a scraping pen to his name. He's a warm heart, a ready lauch an' a free han', and thon's mair than ony man frae Nortown has. There was yin o' them boucht ma lambs the day. He stole them, an' then cam' greetin' roun' aifter me fer a luck-penny.'

' Hear, hear ! ' roared Dan, who had heard his name mentioned and caught the conversation's drift. ' Stand up for Aegus and Dan MacBride, Cherlie, and I'll stand you a drink when this robbery's by.'

The Nortown dealers watched Dan's antics, as though they were those of a trained baboon. It took more than genial raillery or shepherds' chaff to make them open their purses or bid against one another.

' Sixteen and six, sixteen and nine. Are you all done, gentlemen, at sixteen and nine ? ' The auctioneer boomed away.

Johnnie slipped down to Duncan and handed him the printed catalogue of sale. He had his thumb placed on the Glendarroch entry. ' Mark down the prices, Duncan boy,' he whispered. ' Here's a pencil to you. Mark you down what you think they're worth when the lambs come in, an' see how near ye can come to the price. It's fine practice for

you. An' come out and give us a hand when they're at the Strathord lambs; they're three pens before us.'

Duncan nodded sagely and turned to his job. He formed his judgments and marked down the final price, until the Strathord lambs came tumbling into the ring. He needed no catalogue to tell him whose they were; they were old acquaintances, friends from home, and he knew more than half of their faces. Duncan, serious and self-important, forced a passage through well-filled trousers to the outer air and the Glendarroch pens.

He wasn't taken with the look of his own sheep. Their belly wool was tucked up and matted with the mud and rain. They looked too high off the ground, higher than they would have seemed after a fine dry night. He scowled at them, and little Johnnie Gillies laughed. 'They're no' just looking their best the day, Duncan,' he admitted, ' but they'll sell, boy, they'll sell. The man that bought them last year's down again looking for them. He never lost a beast o' them through the winter, an' they did well with him at the gimmering.' Johnnie winked. 'An' Dan MacBride's to give us a hand.'

'Can I follow them in?' Duncan pleaded.

'Surely, boy, surely—you've had plenty to do with them. There'll be as many men as sheep in the ring, wi' yoursel', mysel', Dan, and Hugh. If we canna sell them between the lot o' us, there's something far wrong wi' the lambs.'

'Glendarroch!' yelled the yardsman.

Gates were flung open, dogs barked, Hugh and Dan came striding along, sticks rattled on rails, and the Glendarroch ewe-lambs, bleating and baa-

ing, leapt to sale and their breeding future. Duncan felt all eyes on him as he entered the ring.

'Glendarroch ewe - lambs!' the auctioneer shouted. 'Now, gentlemen, you know these lambs; they're off a namely, well-doing stock.'

A thick-set dealer spat over the rails as he stared at the sheep. 'Bloody camels,' he grunted.

The auctioneer heard the remark and leant down from his box. 'This gentleman here objects that these character lambs are bloody camels,' he said, without a smile on his expressionless face. 'If he's come to buy the Loch Ness monster, we'll bring it into the ring within a minute. We sell all kinds of live-stock here. Now, gentlemen,' he continued, straightening himself again, 'these lambs are high-standing, I'll admit, but you'll be glad of that if it comes a hard winter, as the herds expect. How much for these lambs?'

The bidding started at twelve shillings, and the faces of the four amateur salesmen were disappointed and sore. The bidding stuck at fourteen and six. Even the auctioneer looked surprised. 'Come now, gentlemen,' he insisted, 'I can't take that price. I sold the wether side here yesterday at sixteen shillings.'

Then Dan MacBride intervened. He put one massive hand on Duncan's shoulder, and dragged him to the ring's centre. He waved his gigantic crook at the sea of caps and faces. 'D'ye see this loon?' he roared. 'He's Glendarroch breeding, and you'll no' find a finer boy in Cranok the day. But when he was weaned he was such a long-legged ugly brat o' a bairn that his mother near broke her heart. The boy's done well, and so will the lambs.

Damn ye all for a pack o' Nortown robbers, I'll buy them mysel'! *Fifteen shillings* I bid for the Glendarroch ewe-lambs.'

Duncan was glad when Dan's speech and his own shy agony ended together. His face and neck were both flaming red.

The auctioneer smiled. 'Fifteen shillings I'm bid by Mr MacBride. The judges are on them now, gentlemen. Fifteen shillings—*thank you*, sir, fifteen and six.'

Thankful and proud, Duncan followed the ewe-lambs out, well and fairly sold at seventeen and threepence a head.

'Fine, Duncan boy,' Johnnie grinned. 'We'll have a cup o' tea and a pie, an' then for home. The lambs are to be trucked by the mart. They're going to Nortown on a special train.'

'Then Dan didn't get them?' said Duncan.

'No, boy, he'd have been in a fine mess if he had.'

They ate their half-cold pies and drank their well-stewed tea in the busy restaurant attached to the mart. All about them shepherds and farmers leant elbows on the table and blew on their tea, for it, at least, was hot. Dogs lay beneath the tables, thumping their tails on the bare floor, or poking inquiring noses on their masters' knees. Now and again one would yelp as a hobnailed boot trod on its outstretched paws.

'Are ye through, boy?' asked Johnnie, pulling out his heavy watch. 'It's time we was moving to the station if we're wanting to be home the night.'

Johnnie paid for them both, as he had done at the hotel, then calling to the dogs, forced a passage through packed humanity to the outer door. They

tramped together, with a clatter of boots and sticks, past the mart, and through the busy streets, to wait for the Westown train at Cranok station.

There were but few people standing on the passenger platform, but the goods-sidings were loud with the rattle and bumps of shunting trucks, the short-lived puffing of shunting engines, and the babel of droving dogs and men. Duncan had never been on a train before; his experience of transport was confined to buses and cars, lorries, steamers, and white-sailed yachts. He liked the flat line of the engine's smoke and the trembling of the rails when the train came along, tearing round a clump of firs to whistle its way into Cranok station.

'Wait you, boy!' cried Johnnie. 'I've clean forgotten to buy tickets. Keep an eye open an' see if your grandfather's coming.'

Duncan was sure that the train would go without them, but was comforted to see Mackenzie of Strathord, a bent and lanky figure, come over the iron bridge with his plain-looking dogs. 'Aye, Duncan!' he shouted breathlessly. 'Dinna let the train away wi'out me!'

Then Johnnie came hurrying from the ticket-office, laboriously counting his change. 'Have ye seen Hugh?' he shouted to Mackenzie.

'Aye, boy, he's a good dram in already. God knows when he'll be home. He's wi' Alicky Mag, and they're going in to Westown by the last train to make another night o' it there.'

'The old goat!' Johnnie muttered.

They climbed into a third-class smoking carriage, although none of them smoked. But Mackenzie had been used to do so before his stomach grew

ill, and he led the way partly from habit, and partly to avoid the bother of women and bairns. The dogs were coaxed and kicked by turns until they were safely stowed beneath the seats.

'Are we right?' called Johnnie to the passing guard.

'Where are ye ga-in'?'

'Westown.'

'Aye, ye're richt.'

The train bumped and hesitated into motion. The dogs moved uneasily beneath the seats—one of them whined. The sun beat warmly on the window-panes from the cloudless sky of an August day.

They passed endless lines of stationary sheep-trucks, which yet seemed to be moving the opposite way. There was the drowsy hum of binders from a half-cut field of corn, a scent of smoke from burning grass by the railway track. Duncan lay back in his corner seat. A pool was gathering at his feet where Mackenzie spat. He was drowsy, contented, happy. He was going home, and he was glad. Cranok sales were by for another year. He wasn't sorry. He listened to the drone of Mackenzie and Johnnie speaking together. His dirty cap pitched over his face—his legs stretched luxuriously—he slept.

He was shaken awake by Johnnie as they steamed into Westown station. Dazed, he wondered, for a moment, where he was.

'Come on, boy,' laughed Mackenzie. 'You're lucky to be able to sleep like thon. We change here. Get your chain on your bitch.'

They clattered out on to the platform to search

for the Dalloch train that would take them to the Lochend boat. All the hurrying, neat-dressed people stared at the herds and their dogs, stumbling and slipping and taking ridiculous strides on the asphalt pavement.

'Put your bonnet straight, boy,' Johnnie whispered. 'We'll need to look kind o' respectable here.'

'Aye,' muttered Mackenzie. 'They stare at country folks here as though they were something out o' the ark.'

They were soon well lost in the echoing station, which seemed to them like a good-sized town. In an arguing pastoral group they gathered beneath an enormous clock. Duncan was fascinated by the way its hands leapt forward at regular intervals; for a moment it occupied his whole attention. He just stared at it.

'Well, I'm going to ask the way to the train,' said Johnnie, concluding an ever-warming argument with Mackenzie. He strode across purposefully to the railway bookstall. 'Here, lassie,' he inquired, 'can ye tell me the way to the Dalloch train?'

The girl stretched for a time-table with an air which regretted that fools were born. 'Want one? Threepence,' she murmured.

'No! I'm wanting to know my way to the Dalloch train.'

'How should I know? They'll tell you over there,' and she pointed to the ticket-office.

'Thank you,' said Johnnie, and hurried away. He popped his head into one window—it was the wrong one. He stopped at the second and was

sent back to the first. He went to the fourth before he got his information. ' Just over there,' he pointed. ' Number ten platform, boys, an' we're needing our time.'

Duncan was stirred to activity by the prospect of missing the train, and of having to spend a night in this vast unfriendly town. He disentangled his legs from Meg's chain, and chased after Mackenzie and Johnnie. They scrambled and jingled together into a third-class smoking compartment of the Dalloch train. Duncan lay back with a sigh of relief.

' Are we right ? ' asked Johnnie of a passing inspector.

' Where are ye ga-in' ? '

' Dalloch.'

' Ye're right.'

' Fine,' said Johnnie, pulling up the window. ' We're right, boys, and there's no' another change till the boat.'

Mackenzie spat.

Duncan was glad when the dreary tenement houses, the lines of faded washing, the children swarming like rats, were left behind. It had turned a hot afternoon, and the slum windows were wide open, as though gasping for air. Then the stifling town was clean out of sight, and there was the river, the ships, and the crops to look at and admire.

It was but a short run to Dalloch, and soon they were out again, slipping over the smooth worn cobbles to the Lochend boat. Duncan drank in the smell of the tar, and the cool salt breeze off the sea. He heard the familiar sound, the clock-clock of the boat's gentle beat against the wooden piles.

The ship was packed with Westown trippers, laughing and singing and playing accordions, but there were plenty of country-folk too, and the blue-jerseyed sailors were old friends. Duncan walked through the crowd, between the varnished seats where the old people sat, and leant over the rails. Small waves lapped against the ship's sides, and a black-headed gull floated like a bobbing cork on the smooth water. The siren hooted, the trippers cheered, and the boat swung round its nose to Lochend and home. Duncan raised his eyes, and watched the sun dipping down over the shadowed bulk of the hills.

It was growing dusk by the time Lochend was reached, and the waiting buses had their side-lamps lit. Duncan, Johnnie and Mackenzie, with their dogs and sticks and small parcel of clothes, climbed into the vibrating bus that would take them to the mouths of Glendarroch and Strathord. The trippers were left behind, coupling up, arm linked in arm, the girls and their boys, to seek the expensive shelter of lodgings in Lochend. The bus clattered into motion and sped along the road round the sweeping margins of the loch.

It was no time before the girl conductress in her jaunty hat pulled the cord and rang the bell for the bus to stop. ' Glendarroch,' she called, and Duncan and Johnnie stepped down to the road.

' Have you the parcel, Duncan ? '

' Aye.'

' Good-night, Mac.'

' Good-night, Johnnie. Dinna fall asleep, Duncan.'

The bus was away, its lights fading into the

distance. Duncan turned to the long tramp up the glen to supper and bed.

It was dark before the cottage was reached, and the twinkling light of the lamp set in the wee window was their welcome home. They put the dogs in the stable, and walked wearily across the yard, through the stone lobby to the warm and lighted kitchen. The kettle was singing on the fire, the table was laid for three, and Mary was opening the hot oven door with a cloth to bring out the stew. She turned to smile at them as they blinked like dazed bats after their long walk in the dark.

' Where's father ? ' she asked.

' Dinna ask me that, Mary.   Dear knows ! '

' Is he—is he—— ? '

' Aye, Mary, the usual.'

' I shouldna have let him go, Johnnie.'

' He's no' a bairn.'

' But he's no' well.   Sit down ! Duncan boy, you'll be tired.   Take off your boots and sit in to your tea.   Did ye like Cranok ? '

' It's fine—once in a year.'

' Then you're glad to be home, Duncan ? '

' Aye, I dinna like towns.'

' Wee Johnnie's been wearying for ye to be home. He was for sitting up, but it was too late. He was sore that he didna get.'

' He's too young yet,' said Johnnie.

' He'd be no use,' grinned Duncan. ' He'd have done nothing but laugh at thon unctioneer.'

XIII

Three days passed. Then, in the early morning, Hugh Maclean arrived. He strode up the glen road with his two cowed dogs at heel, and when he was home went straight to his work without speaking a word. Mary urged him to sit down and eat first, or to go to his bed, but he snarled at her like a savage beast. She was afraid to persist.

Duncan saw him setting off for the East-end heft, slashing at the bracken as though foul fiends lurked there. Whenever one of his dogs ran past him he lashed out with his stick. He lurched a little from side to side as he walked, and his left leg seemed to drag. Duncan and wee Johnnie were at school that day, and when they returned Hugh was a changed man.

He sat by the fire, a helpless hulk of flesh, one arm hanging limp, his face smooth and his lips sagged and dribbling on the left side. His eyes had a vacant stare, and he was trying to speak through saliva which filled his mouth. He mumbled to himself, as though he spoke with a stone between his teeth. Mary, white and scared, was trying to pull the boots from his helpless legs.

'Dinna worry your grandfather, boys,' she whispered; 'he's no' well. Your father's away for the doctor. He'll no' be long before he's back.'

Duncan felt Hugh's eyes upon him, and that made him uncomfortable and shy. There was something uncanny in the way the mad gaze followed him round the room. Wee Johnnie had slipped away, to cry for a minute and then throw stones in the burn.

Duncan didn't like to leave his mother alone. She had Hugh's boots off now. Then Hugh tried to laugh, but all that came was a flapping snuffle.

'Come here, you wee bastard,' he said in his toneless and lisping voice. Duncan turned to him, afraid. 'You're no' a Gillies. Did ye know that, boy?'

'Wheesht, father, wheesht!' Mary implored.

'Little Johnnie Gillies is no' your father, boy.'

'For God's sake, wheesht, father!'

Hugh laughed again, the horrible lifeless sound. Duncan felt sick, as he had done after the fight. 'Your father was a gentleman——' the voice droned on.

'*Father!*'

'Jack Knight he was called, you young bastard ye are.'

Duncan stiffened as though struck. He remembered the supper following the laird's shoot, the silence as of something dreadfully wrong that had followed his mention of that name. Jack Knight—was his father. That explained it all. Little Johnnie Gillies had nothing to do with him, for all the kindness and knowledge he gave. Some unknown man—some gentleman—was his father. Then who—who might his mother be? He stared at Mary. Her face was white and still as though dead. He saw how her worn hands were clenched so that the knuckles shone. He saw the panting movements of her breasts, and the swallowing motions she made in her throat. Was she, then—his mother?

Hugh's half-paralysed mind seemed to sense the question. 'Aye, boy, she's your mother. But she was never married on your father, Jack Knight.

Ye're a bastard, see? And she—Mary Gillies—
she's nothing better than a whüre!'

Furious anger blazed in the eyes of Duncan
Gillies, anger that this droning hulk of a diseased
thing should so miscall his mother. He didn't know
what the word meant, but he knew it for something
foul. He rushed forwards as though to strike Hugh
dead, his fists clenched and his chin lowered. Then
he stopped. For Hugh had seen what he meant to
do, and had begun to sob like a frightened bairn.
There was abject terror in the blue eyes which had
never shown fear before, anguished helplessness to
be in the power of an angry boy.

'Dinna, Duncan!' Mary cried.

Then she burst into tears, and Duncan had never
heard such a terrible, tearing sound before. At first
he thought that his mother was laughing, but the
ghastly look on her face held nothing of mirth.
She went on and on, standing there before her
father, the sobs racking and wrenching the whole
of her body. Then she fled from the room, and
Duncan heard her fling herself on the bed, crying,
'Johnnie! Johnnie!'

He turned to Hugh, and the sick man was pointing with horror-stricken face towards the outer
door. 'Maggie! Maggie!' he was muttering.
'What's the do wi' you, lassie? You're all bleeding, lassie—all bleeding—bleeding—bleeding—
bleeding—bleeding——'

It seemed as though Hugh's mind had stuck on
the one note, and could not get off it. He went on
muttering the one word over and over again. His
right hand gradually slipped to his side, and his
muttering grew inaudible. His mouth drooped

open and he began to snore—spasmodic, grunting snores, that frightened Duncan. Mary's sobbing grew fainter and died down.

Duncan didn't know what he should do ; whether to go to comfort his mother, or to stand beside the sick, snoring man in case he should die. He thought that Hugh would strangle by the way his head was lying, but he could not force his hands to lift it up, or even to touch the horrible thing. He wondered whether he should light the lamp to chase the shadows from the darkening room, but he was afraid the noise he would make might waken Hugh, and start the lisping voice and flapping laughter all over again. It was an intense relief to hear the drone of the doctor's big car come up the glen, and to know that help, at last, was at hand.

They came in single file—Dr Brown, with his quick sidelong look at the unconscious man, that rapid professional glance which took in everything and gave nothing away ; Johnnie Gillies, with the visible relief of one who has fetched the doctor and can do nothing more ; Bob Macintyre, ready and able to shift the most heavy and helpless man to his bed.

' Well,' said the doctor, ' he can't stay there. Will you take him to bed ? Just lay him on it ; don't take off his clothes until I've had a look at him. Don't shake him up more than you can help.'

Bob Macintyre hitched up Hugh Maclean by his sagging arms, and Johnnie took a grip of his feet. When they lifted Hugh, his snores turned to something like a groan, and the doctor looked quickly round. Then Bob Macintyre, wishing to show his strength and to justify the invitation of his help,

ran backwards so quickly that Johnnie lost his grip
on Hugh's feet, which bumped and slithered on the
floor.

'For God's sake be careful!' the doctor snapped.
He turned to Duncan. 'Where's your mother?'
Duncan pointed dumbly towards the door. 'Upset,
is she?' asked the doctor, shooting up his grey
eyebrows. 'I'll go and see her.'

Duncan was left alone. He found courage to
put a match to the lamp, and so drive the snuffling
shadows from the room. Wee Johnnie crept in and
sat quietly by the fire. Through the open door came
the rumble of hushed voices and the snores of the
paralysed man.

'Man,' whispered wee Johnnie, 'grandfather
must have an awful dram in the day.'

'It's no' that,' said Duncan. 'He's dying.'

'Man,' whispered wee Johnnie again, 'is deith
like yon?'

They heard the doctor taking leave of Johnnie
in the lobby. 'I'm afraid not, Gillies. He's changed
even since I came in. He's not suffering at all—of
course.'

'Thank you, doctor. Can you see your way?'

'Yes. And, Gillies—don't let your wife lift him.'

'No, doctor.'

Duncan listened to the restrained, purposeful
tramp of the doctor going down the brae, then to
the drone of the car speeding back to Lochend.

Johnnie wandered rather aimlessly into the room.
He seemed shy before the boys, not knowing quite
what to say. He ruffled his black curls and fidgeted
with the fire and the lamp. 'Have you boys had
your tea yet?' he asked.

' We're no' for any,' Duncan muttered.

' You'll need to have some.' Johnnie stared helplessly about him, wondering where everything was. He opened and shut cupboards and drawers in a lost, male fashion. ' I'll see if your mother's fit to come through to you yet,' he finally said.

It was a little time before Mary came. She never looked at them as she prepared their meal, until Duncan shyly touched her as she passed. Then she showed him her white, drawn face and tried to smile. Duncan and wee Johnnie ate in silence, with Mary putting the food before them and filling their empty cups. Through the half-open door came the rumble of Johnnie and Bob talking together in low sick-room tones, and the sound of the sick man's breathing, which had changed to a stifled whistle.

' You'd better go to your beds now, boys, and try to sleep,' said their mother.

They were frightened to go to the big double-bed —to be left alone in the intimidating darkness—to listen to that uncanny sound. ' Can we leave the candle burning the night ? ' wee Johnnie asked.

' Aye, but keep it well away from the bed.'

Duncan lay awake for a long time—listening. Wee Johnnie was asleep and the candle burning low. It flickered and guttered, one moment lighting up the room, then dying down to a match-like point of flame. From time to time Duncan heard the shuffle of hurrying feet, the creaking of doors, and the whistling sound, which like the candle would grow momentarily strong and then die down to nothing at all. The flame shot up in a burst of light and went out quite suddenly, leaving the room

pitch-dark. Duncan listened and listened. The snoring began again. Then it stopped, and something told Duncan it had stopped for good. The shuffling feet were no longer hushed; the voices were talking above whispers. Doors slammed.

A dog howled from the stable, and Duncan felt the hair rise stiffly on his neck, and shivers of trickling cold run down his back. The dog howled again with all the wild sorrow of its animal soul. There was the sound of heavy footsteps on the brae—Bob Macintyre going down the glen to tell the news.

Duncan knew that Hugh Maclean was dead.

XIV

Before a fortnight was passed, Duncan knew he was glad that his grandfather had gone. Everything was easier, both in the house and among the sheep. Johnnie whistled more as he went about his work, and Mary was more gentle and kindly than of late. It seemed as though a thunder-cloud had rested for years over the house, and then had been taken away to let the sunlight through. There was more talk and laughter around the kitchen-table when they gathered in for meals; but in the stable Hugh's old bitch, Sheila, sickened and died.

Yet something bothered Duncan. The clouds of worry gathered for the first time to tire his brain. He kept thinking of what Hugh had said, of the gentleman—Jack Knight—who was his father. His mother had never spoken of it, though the way she sometimes looked at him showed what was on her mind. Duncan had taken everything for

granted since ever he could remember: Johnnie was just the father who taught him what he wished to know—Mary was his mother who fed him and mended his clothes when they were torn—Hugh had been a grandfather who was sometimes better avoided. Duncan had thought all fathers were like Johnnie, all mothers like Mary, all grandfathers like Hugh. So Hugh's death and revelation had upset the whole series of relationships on which life was based.

One evening, after vainly searching in the tall bracken for a maggoted lamb, Duncan and Johnnie walked back towards the house through the rustling sounds of an autumn evening. The young things —rabbits and hares—made more noise than grown beasts as they bolted clumsily away.

'Father,' said Duncan suddenly, 'who *is* my father?'

Johnnie strode silently on, his brown face puckered with thought of what to say and what was better left unsaid. 'That's a queer-like question to ask, boy!' he exclaimed. 'What makes you ask that?'

'Grandfather said before he died that Jack Knight was my father, me a bastard, and my mother no better than a whüre.' The words came tumbling out in an angry stream. Duncan heard the shaking of his own voice, and strove to control the trembling of his lips.

Johnnie laid a comforting hand on his shoulder. 'Did your mother hear Hugh say thon to ye?'

'Aye, she was there.'

'Then that's what upset her that night.'

'Aye, it was that.'

'Well, Duncan boy,' Johnnie sighed, 'you'd have needed to know sooner or later, so ye may as well know now.' Johnnie stopped to whistle in his young dog, which had gone bounding through the bracken in the rustling wake of a young rabbit. He turned again to Duncan. 'Dinna you be ashamed of your mother, boy. You'll never find a woman like her, though ye live to be a hundred.'

'I'm no' ashamed of her,' said Duncan stoutly.

'And ye've no need to be, boy.'

Then Johnnie told how he had gone away one cold November's day to a winter's herding in the South, how the young gentleman, Jack Knight, had come in his place. He told of the hard weather of that winter, how the snow had come to the hills before tupping was well started; how Mary, who was but a young lassie, had been left alone with Jack Knight, who was only a boy; how Hugh had had his mind on the sheep and forgotten his daughter; how they had come to love one another, and how Duncan was the result of that love. He told how he had come home to find Jack Knight away and Mary lonely and in trouble, of how he had married her, and sworn to be a father to Jack Knight's boy. 'And Mary's been a good mother to ye all, boy, and a good wife to me.'

Duncan plodded along, taking it all in, turning it over and over in his boy's mind. 'Why did Jack Knight no' marry her?' he asked.

'Because he's a gentleman!' Johnnie's mouth was set, for once, in an ugly sneer.

'And I'm no' your son, father?'

Johnnie Gillies walked on and on without speaking. There was a queer sort of shaking in his voice,

too, when he spoke. 'I've been a father to ye, Duncan boy, and I'd like ye to think of yoursel' as my son. But I'm no' caring much about that if ye'll be good to your mother. Ye'll promise me that, boy?'

'Aye, father.'

Mary wondered what they had been talking of when they came in. They were so serious-looking and so gentle with each other. That night, Johnnie told her all that had been said.

XV

Money was scarce in Glendarroch cottage during the winter that followed Hugh's death. There was only the one man's wages coming into the house; there were three bairns to feed; and it was clear, even to Duncan, that there would be a fourth before the winter months were by. Johnnie had been to see the laird, and came home smiling because he had been made head shepherd, his wages raised, and a place kept open for Duncan when he was done with the school.

'The laird's to see if he can get Duncan off the school for the lambing,' he grinned, 'and he's to let him have five pounds in the year for the work he puts in at week-ends, and mornings and evenings. That'll help us, Mary.'

'Och, Johnnie,' she exclaimed, 'the boy'll no' be much of a scholar with all the herding he'll have to do.'

'He'll be none the worse herd for that, Mary.'

Duncan was glad that rules and regulations could still be stretched a point by the laird's waning

influence. He only wished they could be broken
altogether, and he be free of what he called ' thon
silly besom,' his teacher, and ' thon pack o' bairns,'
his companions in learning.

There was now less money to buy from the
butcher's, and baker's, and grocer's vans which
brought tentacles of trade to the farthest recesses
of the hills. Duncan and wee Johnnie found what
time they could to set wire snares for the hares,
and steel-fanged traps that bit the soft legs of the
scuttling rabbits. They would lie awake in the
night, listening for the frantic squeals that pro-
claimed a catch, and would poke each other glee-
fully in the ribs as the screaming subsided to
whimpering or death. Next morning they were
out at daybreak to pull the tight nooses from the
necks of strangled hares, and break the shrinking
backs of the trapped rabbits. They gutted the
beasts with their sharp new knives, and brought
the steaming bodies to the kitchen for their mother
to skin and cook.

Johnnie went out a lot with the rusty double-
barrelled gun, and Duncan sometimes accompanied
him. Johnnie was sparing with the cartridges. He
never let blaze at anything that moved, whether
beast of the earth or fowl of the air. He waited
until it sat down within fifty yards, dwelt on his
aim, and never missed. ' This is no' sport, Duncan,
we're at,' he would say. ' It's our dinners we're
after—no' fun.'

Duncan learned to catch the light-brown trout in
the burn, so different in colour from the black fish
over in Glendruid. They were better-tasting too,
with pinker flesh and a flavour of sea-trout or

salmon. At first, when he tried to fish, his line and hook were always getting caught among the alder, birch, and hazel trees, but he soon learned to make his cast clear of the branches, and send hook and wriggling worm swinging right out over the rippling stretch of the burn. Johnnie showed him the places to fish, not in the clear pools or quiet parts, but where the water was troubled and broken into leaping whiteness by shallow-lying stones.

Duncan never forgot the excitement of his first catch, when his line, drifting swiftly downstream, became suddenly taut, and the point of his rod dipped downwards, when the weight and pull of the fish bent down his arms, and the reel whirred away as the line spun out. Then drawing in again with the reel singing away, tautening and slackening until the trout tired, and a jerk of the rod brought the slippery, lashing fish on to the short green grass of the bank. It was a game that Duncan and wee Johnnie never tired of, and one that took them wandering up the burn's side on any Saturday afternoon, when the sky was clouded and they were not too busy with the sheep.

It was fine open weather in the back end of the year. On the first day of October a lorry came up the glen to take the ewe-lambs to their wintering on a green Dumbarton dairy-farm. It was the same driver who had driven the sheep to Cranok sale, but with a smaller lorry and without his mate. He had not forgotten his earlier visit to Glendarroch. 'An' where's auld Abraham the day?' he shouted, as the lorry screeched to rest before the buchts.

'He's dead,' said Johnnie shortly.

'Aye, aye,' said the driver. 'I just thocht the

auld man wad wag himsel' tae deith ane o' thae days.'

'Aye, it was a shock he had.'

'An' nae muckle wunner! Tak things easy, Jack. Thon's my motto for an easy life an' a lang ane. Man, yer sheep hae growed.'

'Aye,' Johnnie agreed. 'They've done weel wi' the open weather and things aye growing. Duncan boy, give me a hand to get them out.'

The Glendarroch ewes were cast at six years old, so that there were only a hundred and fifty odd ewe-hoggs to send to wintering. There had been a time when the stock was younger and cast at five, but since then the bracken had come creeping down the braes to cover the best bits of grazing in the hollows, the drains had fallen in and become choked, turning pasture back to swamp, and there was a death-rate and strange diseases among the ewes that had never been heard tell of in earlier times. Above all else, Jock MacCulloch wouldn't allow enough of the tall, rank heather to be burned. But the hoggs that year were good—level, well-grown, and fleshy, with fine keen eyes and a bloom on their coats. The only danger was the braxy, when they were thriving so well, but the dairy-farm where they were going was notably free from that trouble. Johnnie and Duncan packed in the sheep, and then watched the lorry go lurching and swaying on its long journey to Dumbartonshire.

Johnnie was full of great plans as he turned for home. 'It's no' for me to be saying things against Hugh Maclean that's gone, poor man,' he said. 'He was as good a hill herd in trouble and rough weather as ever I've seen, and a fine lamber and clipper on

top of that. But there was the one thing against him, Duncan boy, though it's maybe no' me that should be saying it. He wasna using the right kind o' tup for the place. I mind o' him having a fine beast, a fine low-set, square-backed tup, the year I was away. He got it out of Cranok, and a fine price he paid for it too. It wandered away over to Strathord, and left Mackenzie some of the bonniest lambs you ever saw in your born days, Duncan boy. But it left nothing on Glendarroch worth a docken. Them Cranok tups are too fast-growing a strain for a place like this, Duncan; the lambs take far too much out of the ewes. Then he went in for these long-legged, bare-coated, brockit-faced South-country gowks o' things that we have on the place the day. Have ye handled them this back-end, Duncan boy?'

'No,' admitted Duncan, who was drinking in every word.

'Well then, ye should, boy. They're as lean and hard-backit ewe-necked giraffes o' beasts when ye get down on them as ever I've seen, and I've seen some queer-like beasts calling themselves tups in my time. When I was down about Cranok, herding thon winter, the boss was for buying his own tups. He said he liked them low-set and sym-et-ri-cal. Was thon no' a daft-like word to use for a sheep, Duncan? And all they were when he'd bought them was just bad beasts made bonnie wi' shears. My, boy, we'll need to be hurrying There's old Macfarlane coming up for you. Where's thon wee black deil o' a Johnnie? If he jinks the school again the day, I'll skelp his backside to him.'

Duncan was preoccupied during his drive to

school, and refused to join wee Johnnie in any of his ploys. His mind was far distant while Miss Gray was trying to explain the simplest of simple fractions. He was thinking all the time of a problem deeper than arithmetic. He was forming mental pictures of suitable rams to mate with the ewes of Glendarroch.

When he got home with wee Johnnie in the evening's dusk, who should be gibbering at the cottage door but Alicky Mag from Glendruid, with a fiddle tucked under his arm, and a wide grin cracking his nut-brown face. 'Aye, Duncan,' he screeched, 'ye're getting too big a boy for the school.'

'Fine do I know that,' grinned Duncan. He was pleased to see the little man again.

'An' thon wee black tinker o' a brother o' yours, can he dance yet?'

Wee Johnnie laughed and cut a wild caper. 'Can ye drink water yet, Alicky? Are the puddocks deid yet?'

'It was *you*, was it?' screamed Alicky, and flung his cap to the ground. 'Wait till I get a hold of you, boy.'

Wee Johnnie bounded away through the yard and byres, laughing all the time, and Alicky, cackling like a bald old hen, hirpled in the rear, his fiddle tucked under his arm.

'Ye'll never catch him, Alicky,' cried Duncan. 'Ye'll need to learn to run first.'

'My,' gasped Alicky, panting back to the door, 'it's my idea they teach you nothing but impudence in the school. It's time ye learnt the fiddle, boy. I met your father the day looking for ewes out over the Glendruid march, and he asked me to come round here to learn you. He's no' wanting you stravaiging

over the hills in the dark nights, he says. I doubt he's thinking you've an eye on a lassie somewhere, boy.'

' An' what about yoursel', Alicky? Ye'll go down a peat-hole one o' these nights.'

' Dinna fear for me, Duncan ! Dinna fear for me ! Give Alicky Mag an October moon to see by, his fiddle to make the daft white hares dance on the top of the hills, and the deer coming creeping round him to hear him play.'

Duncan shivered to hear the queer old bodachan talk like yon.

' The stags'll soon be fighting, Alicky.'

' And what's better music than thon, Duncan ? Man, it's me that likes to hear them banging their feet and horns thegither wi' a crack ye can hear a mile away, and the bellowing o' them grumbling and rumbling on the Glendruid hills. But I didna come here to clack, Duncan ; it's fiddling we're to be at the night. Mistress Gillies, your mother, has asked me in to my tea, like the bonnie woman she is, and we're to go out to the byre to play so as not to waken your sister, wee Jean.'

It was a merry meal, with Alicky squeaking away of the terrible things he would do to wee Johnnie for putting ten puddocks in his drinking-well. ' It's the queerest thing in the world, Mistress Gillies,' he grinned, ' that one o' your boys should be a real gentleman, and the other just a damned wee tinker like Johnnie.'

A painful silence fell like a pall over the merriment of the meal.

' I'll put a lamp in the byre for you,' said little Johnnie Gillies. Duncan sat on an upturned box, with the fiddle and bow in his slender hands, and

the quiet eyes of the cows turned on him from their
stalls. He made screeching and ugly noises for the
best part of an hour, while Alicky Mag lectured
and showed him what should be done.

' Ye'll be a fiddler in no time, Duncan,' Alicky
exulted. ' Now I'll play ye a wee tune mysel', and
then it's over the hills to Glendruid for me. No,
I'll no' play for ye the night, Duncan boy. I'll
play a wee tune for poor Hugh Maclean, may peace
be wi' his soul. It's a tune that was learnt me by a
fine young herd from the island of Skye. He told
me the seals would follow the boat when he played
it, wi' the salt tears running down their faces to fall
in the salt o' the sea. Listen, Duncan boy ! '

It was a sad old tune like the sea-gulls crying,
timed to the ring of the rowlocks and plashing of
oars. Alicky paused when the playing was done.
' Did ye hear anything, Duncan ? ' he whispered.

' What d'ye mean, Alicky ? '

' Did ye no' hear the steps o' a man come clump-
ing across the yard when I was playing thon bonnie
tune ? '

' I heard nothing.'

' Ach, man, what was I thinkin' on ! An' would
big Hugh Maclean be coming to the playing of a
tune he didna know ? It's a reel—that's what he'd
be asking for—and it's a reel I'll play.'

Duncan sat shivering on the upturned box, while
Alicky Mag was scraping away with tapping foot
and flashing bow. The reel stopped suddenly in
the middle of a bar. The old man leant forwards—
listening—listening, his mouth half-open, showing
the toothless gums. ' Wheesht, Duncan, wheesht ! '
he whispered. ' D'ye no' hear the stamping o' feet

on the yard outside, an' the noise o' a big man birling aboot?'

'Ach! there's nothing,' sneered Duncan.

Then the dogs howled together from the stable, and the cows rose uneasily, rattling their chains.

'What did I tell ye, boy?'

'For God's sake, stop your daft capers!' cried Duncan, and ran for the house as though hounds of hell were racing at his heels.

Behind him, from the byre, came the screeching voice of Alicky Mag. 'Man, Hugh, and it's pleased I am to see you again.'

Duncan dashed into the kitchen like a panic-struck hare, and stood shaking before the fire, his eyes seeing a dribbling twisted face in the shapes of the glowing coals.

'What's wrong, Duncan?' Mary asked.

'Aye, boy,' said Johnnie, rousing himself from his evening doze. 'What's the do wi' you, boy, and where's old Alicky Mag?'

'He's aye in the byre.'

'An' why did ye leave him there by himsel'?'

'Och, he's daft, father—no' canny. He's talking away there to himsel' or something else. Did ye no' hear the dogs howling?'

Then Alicky Mag came in, grinning and smirking and nodding his old bald head. 'An' did I give ye a fright, Duncan?' he screeched. 'Man, Hugh was asking after ye, boy.'

Little Johnnie Gillies was angry. 'Here, ye auld goat,' he shouted, 'it was to teach Duncan to play the fiddle that I asked you over here, and no' to put the fear o' death in the boy. What d'ye mean wi' your daft-like, indecent capers?'

'Little Johnnie Gillies,' the old man whimpered, 'an' is thon a way to talk to a neighbour herd?'

'I'll just tell ye this, Alicky,' Mary interrupted, 'that if there's to be any more of this kind of nonsense, ye needna show your face in Glendarroch again. And if you go on drinking the way you've been doing, it's the asylum you'll end in.'

The little man was terribly angry. He spoke in the mincing, well-bred voice that he put on only when excessively wrathful or hopelessly drunk. 'Mistress Gillies, I am gravely insulted!' he said. 'If it was not for the great love I bear your son Duncan, I would not trouble to cross your doorstep ever again. But the boy has great art, great talent, in his playing. I would walk many a long mile for the pleasure of seeing his fine fingers at work. He is also a very apt and attentive pupil, Mistress Gillies——'

'Aye, Alicky boy,' said Johnnie, who knew from experience that the speech might last all night, 'we're much obliged to ye for your interest in Duncan, and we'll be glad to see ye back any time, and I'll come to the byre wi' the two of yous and see that ye stick to the job that brought ye over, the next time ye're here.'

'Fine!' squeaked Alicky Mag. 'An' I'll be leaving the fiddle wi' Duncan to try a tune on it himsel'. An' it'll no' be long before I'm back to learn him more. An' I'll be saying good-night to ye, Mistress Gillies—I'll need—to—be—saying—good-night.' The old man's twinkling eyes had strayed towards the cupboard where he knew the bottle was kept. 'I'll need to be saying good-night, Mistress Gillies, for it's a long way over the hills to Glendruid.'

'You'll be taking a dram before ye go, Alicky?' grinned Johnnie.

'Well, just a wee one to drink Duncan's health, fine boy that he is. An' may ye soon have another like him, Mistress Gillies.'

Mary blushed and fidgeted before the fire.

'Ye couldna give me just a wee drop to put in my bottle, Johnnie?' Alicky pleaded. 'The cold whiles grips me now when I'm out at night. I've got a bottle here, Johnnie.'

Johnnie poured out enough to send the old man happy to Glendruid. 'Fine!' Alicky piped. 'It's a good friend and neighbour ye are, Johnnie Gillies. Now I must away. An' Duncan, dinna let thon wee tinker brother o' yours lay a hand on thon fiddle; he's got hands like a puddock's feet.'

Alicky strode into the October night. The new moon laughed, a crescent-shaped bride on the bed of the sky, and the old, her shadowy travel-worn lover, lay quiet in her glistening arms. The grumbling roar of rutting stags sounded deep thunder from the distant Corrie, and a flight of duck like a speeding arrow shadowed the moonlit clouds.

Duncan held the lamp while Alicky Mag unchained his snarling dogs, then stood beside the open door of the cottage watching the wraiths of dogs and man fade into the lonely darkness of the moor.

Mary was speaking when he returned to the kitchen. 'I dinna know what Lady Waterton's factor is thinkin' on, keeping the daft old man as herd in Glendruid. I doubt the bottle gets more attention nor the sheep.'

'Alicky's no' a bad herd,' said Johnnie. 'Better

nor you'd be thinkin', Mary. An' they wouldna get another soul to bide in a peat-hole o' a glen like yon. A married man wouldna get his wife to bide there a month, and a young chap would be wanting away to Lochend every day of the week. And then, poor Alicky's no' well paid.'

'He's getting worse on the drink, Johnnie.'

'Aye, poor old soul, he'll go daft in the end, I'm feared.'

Duncan carefully stowed away the fiddle, and kicked off his boots at the end of another day. 'I'm thinkin',' he said, half to himself, 'that Alicky's daft because he's wiser than other folks are.'

XVI

October days drifted away and October nights grew dark. Bracken bent and turned brown, and white frost glistened on it in the early mornings. The sun had a soft caressing warmth in the afternoons, but sank early in a painter's paradise of coloured sky. The hills rumbled and echoed to the bellowing of sex-mad stags, and the birds, their breeding done, drifted away with mournful calling to the warmth of southern lands or the restless beat of the sea.

Duncan felt a tug at his heart and a pain at winter's coming. He quivered in answer to the stag's roar, and would steal out in the still evenings to listen to them, while the heavy dew moistened his hair and shadows swept over the moors. Then he would return to the warm kitchen and kick his boots against the polished fender in a vague and restless seeking for he knew not what.

As the end of his schooling drew near, so much greater became his resistance to its tiresome immobility. He wanted so much to be up and doing, to be amongst men and sheep, fighting the annual and year-long battle which began with the buying of tups and ended with the selling of lambs. He wanted to feel the force of the wind's challenge and to test the strength of his limbs against the blizzard and snow. He dreamt of the days of his coming release when he would be free each morning to stumble out across the yard to darkness or bright sunshine, rain, hail, or sleet, unchain his dogs, and meet the sheep as they came straggling down the hillside to another day. He had never been so impatient with the school, with Miss Gray, or old Macfarlane—even with wee Johnnie.

He spent much time in the byre making weird noises on his ill-tuned fiddle. Now and then he would pick out something on it that had the semblance of a tune. That pleased him and made him smile, in the warm byre with the silent cows and the sweet-smelling hay. Once a week Alicky Mag would come over from Glendruid to cackle and flatter and teach. A whisky dram at the lesson's end was all that the old man asked.

Sometimes Johnnie came out to the byre to sit crouched on a stool, his head nodding downwards after his hard day's work. He had left the glen but once since Hugh's death, and that was to buy two new shearling tups, square, long-coated, black-faced rams, at sensible prices. He had gone to Crimmond for them, as he had longed to do every season while Hugh lived.

It was a great occasion on the twenty-third of

November when the tups were let out, and the two new Crimmond rams were driven to mate with the East-end ewes, the best in the stock. Duncan watched them go in the early morning, and when he returned home in the evening was glad to hear from Johnnie that they were working well. But the very next day the better of the two was lost, and Johnnie was out on all the hefts searching for the strayed beast. He was tired and worried by evening, thinking of all the possible ways in which a tup might come to grief on a strange hill—the peat-holes—the squelching bogs—the slippery rocks —the burns in autumn spate. 'Duncan boy,' he said, ' I'd like ye to give us a hand to find thon tup the morn.'

At once Duncan was eager attention, throwing down his scribbler and pencil, his unfinished sum, on the brightly-lit linoleum beneath the paraffin lamp. He looked up with adventure in his grey eyes, hearkening to the lashing rain on the window-panes. ' What hefts will I be taking ? ' he asked.

Johnnie stretched himself in an effort to drive numbing sleep from his exhausted brain and to gather his straying thoughts. ' I'll need to be looking the holes and burns on the East-end mysel',' he explained, ' an' that'll take me the best part of the day, boy. It's likely somewhere there that the beast'll be. I'll need to take a turn down to the Macintyres too an' see if they've come across him. If you could look the Pot and Corrie, Duncan boy, an' see Mackenzie over in Strathord, that would be taking some work off me. It's no' likely the beast will have come down and crossed the road over towards Glendruid. It'll either be on the East-end,

Craigdarroch, Corrie, or Pot. Will ye manage that, boy—the Corrie and Pot, I'm meaning ? '

' Aye, father ; fine that.'

' That'll mean another day from the school,' Mary said.

' An' what o' that ? ' yawned Johnnie. ' A Crimmond tup's surely o' more importance than sums about how long a tap will be taking to fill a tub. Water's no' that scarce in the hills that a few buckets running over is going to make much difference.'

Mary laid down her knitting, and her clear blue eyes grew troubled. ' Maybe Duncan will no' aye be in the hills,' she said.

' Are you for making Duncan a scholar ? ' Johnnie laughed. ' Ye'll be trying yer hand on wee Johnnie next.'

Duncan smiled, showing his fine teeth. ' I'll away to my bed,' he announced. ' Wee Johnnie can get the answers to my sums at the school the morn. I'll be out in the Corrie first thing and see if Mac's aboot.'

Duncan wakened to wild rain next day. It blew in solid sheets over the western hills and swept hissing down the inundated glen. Duncan struggled out in the dusk to release Meg, and was soaking wet before he had crossed the yard. Water poured down from the choked and overflowing rones of the sheds, falling in muddied cascades to the slippery cobbles. Pools, lying in sunk hollows beneath the walls, were whipped by the wind to fluttering waves. The cracked glass-panes of the stable windows were streaming wet. Overhead the heavy grey clouds drifted to falling rain on the hill's face. The burns

roared down in yellow spate, carrying branches torn from the trees, stones swept from the stream's bed, earth and gravel snatched from overhanging banks, down the steep ravines to the surging waters of the river below. Everywhere was the lash and swish, the ripple and roar, the echoing boom of the hills in flood.

Duncan pulled his cap down over his ears, gripped his rain-wet stick, and strode out for the Corrie. Meg shrank in size as the rain soaked through her coat, slicking black hair against her sides. She was draggled and miserable before she had run a yard.

It was a long weary climb over the greasy heather and quaking bogs to the high hills. The rain, sweeping horizontally before the wind, buffeted Duncan until his head rang, until the left side of his face lost all feeling and became a lump of paralysed ice. His jacket and the long trousers he wore wrapped themselves in sopping tightness round his limbs ; his hill boots squelched and spouted water from the seams ; his cap was a cold imprisonment to his soaking hair. Rain ran in spasmodic trickles under his upturned collar and down his shrinking neck, and fell in great splashes when he shook his head. He half closed his eyes to keep out the whirling rain-drops, which made him blind, and his lashes held the water for a second, then, overflowing, sent it streaming down his cheeks.

Duncan plodded on, his head bent downwards to shield his face, and felt the blood spring up in him, rushing to his skin to battle with the cold, and surging through his limbs to bring strength for the climb. Exercise brought exhilaration, and the sense of struggle banished all fear. Duncan was glad to be

matching his breeding and his strength against the
anger and tumult of the hills in storm. This was a
fight, a man's job ! He would win through to the
Corrie, to the screeching winds on the flat top of the
watershed, to the broken wire and rusted posts
which showed the line of march between Glendarroch and Strathord.

He skirted the rich hollow of the Pot, keeping to
the high peat-hags on its left. Duncan knew that
after such a night of rain the Pot would be a sodden,
sucking, treacherous swamp, where even a sheep
might be drawn down, down, until only its
agonised head showed above the bubbling mud—
then a pair of horns twisting desperately from side
to side—then nothing but the slowly settling peat.
He feared to feel the grip of that sticky stuff upon
his sinking heels.

The shoulder of the Craig loomed through the
flying mist. It was scarred by white waters of the
tumbling burns, racing down to join the bigger
stream with its source in the Corriemore. A group
of sheep stood with their heads down and their
arched backs turned to the wind and rain. They
were perfectly still, conserving their animal heat
by passive immobility. Two hoodie-crows drifted
helplessly like autumn leaves before the baffling
storm.

Duncan gave up hope of searching the Corrie for
the missing tup. He would try to do so on his way
home, when the Atlantic rains might have beaten
themselves to death on the towering peaks of the
western hills. Meanwhile he would scale the Craig
to the watershed and to Mackenzie in Strathord.

The Corrie's precipice sheltered him as he

clambered up the slopes of the Craig. But at the top the wind met him again like a demon released, like an artillery's salvo, like the contemptuous blow of a mountain giant. Duncan staggered and slipped, while his wet clothes flapped against his limbs and cut against the smoothness of his skin. He bent forwards so that the line of his body was that of the wind, and struggled blindly to the rusted wreckage of the old march fence.

The whirling mists below him were all he could see of Strathord. He heard the thunder of flood water falling over rocks, and the roar of the river Ord racing down its valley to the loch. There was a tang of the sea in the wind up there, and Duncan licked his lips to savour the salt, blown landwards with the rain.

Then he followed the downward slope of the hill, keeping clear of the leaping streams, which might lure him to precipice and death. He knew the shape and lie of the Strathord grazing—the cup-like gash in the hills with the buchts and shepherd's house on the flat ground above the river—the easy way down to the left—the difficult, steep rock climb to the right. Even in the confusion of mist he could find his way.

He slithered down over the rocks and moss. The wind swept breath away so that he must momentarily turn his back to the storm, shelter his head under his patched tweed jacket, and stand with panting sobs until strength returned. Then round again to face the slash of the rain on his stinging cheeks, to slide and run, tumble and fall, to the relative peace of the valley below.

Down there in the wet blanket of mist he could

hear the lowing of a cow and the rattle of an outhouse door. The sounds led him across the rain-
soaked heather and grass to the dim shadow of
Mackenzie's house. His boots rang on the cobbled
yard and a dog howled from the stable. He knocked
on the green door that led to the stone-flagged lobby
and the cottage kitchen. He heard the shuffling
sound that told him the housewife had left the range
and was coming uneasily to the door, wondering
what disaster or alarm was foreboded by the shadow
of a man in the frightening mist.

Duncan saw Mackenzie's young wife before him.
Her blue eyes were heavy, as though with sleep, two
flaxen plaits falling over strong, broad shoulders,
her forearms bared and soft and white, soft and
white. She smiled, and the red lips curled over even
teeth in a lazy way, and dimples showed on her red-
brown cheeks.

' You'll be Duncan Gillies ? '

' Aye.'

' Come away in, Duncan boy. You're fair
soaked, laddie.'

' Where's himsel' the day ? ' Duncan asked.

' He's away over to Glendarroch to ask for some
tup that's lost. He's no' long away, no more than
an hour.'

' He must have passed me in the mist on the
Glendarroch side of the march,' said Duncan. ' I
was coming over to ask for a tup that we've lost oursel's—a fine tup that was bought in Crimmond the
year.'

' You'd best come in, boy. You can be dryin'
yoursel' before the fire. I'll no' look till ye've got
your clothes on, Duncan.' She laughed in a strange,

intimate way, and Duncan felt shy and ashamed. He bent his head to hide his eyes, and the rain splashed from his cap's peak, to patter on the stone floor. 'Away now, boy,' she said, giving him a little friendly push, 'away and put that drowned-looking dog of yours in the shed over there, and come in for some meat and a warm to yoursel'. You're no' shy of a married woman, are ye, Duncan?' She laughed again, and there was wildness in her laughter.

'I'll need to be getting back,' he muttered.

'Indeed an' ye'll no' do that before you're dry, Duncan.'

She slipped one of her bare arms round his slim shoulders, to which his sopping clothes were closely moulded, and pulled him into the kitchen. He felt the warmth of her arm against his neck, the full round arm, so soft and white, so soft and white. He wanted to lean his wet head against its comfort, but was too shy to do anything but stumble by her guidance to the glowing fire. She drew a chair forwards for him, then, hearing Meg scratch and whine beyond the door, went out to put her away in the shed's warm shelter.

Duncan gazed at the red coals. He began to understand how tired he was, how the shattering force of the rain and wind had drained his strength. He felt sleep steal over him, and stretched his bruised legs in relaxation's ease. His head nodded, and a picture of flaxen plaits, ruddy cheeks, and white bared arms swam and danced before his fluttering eyes.

Then she was back again, brushing the rain from her blue print dress, and the full curves of her body

showed beneath it when she bent. ' You're not to sleep with your damp clothes on, Duncan,' she laughed. ' What would your mother say, if I didna look after her bonnie boy ? I'll bring you a clout to dry yoursel', and a jacket and breeks to put on. Come on wi' you, now, and I'll no' look. I'll make a cup o' tea to ye when you're changed.'

She brought some old darned clothes of Mackenzie's. Duncan slipped off his own wet suit in the slowly growing pool at his feet. He heard Mackenzie's wife getting out plates and cups to make ready his tea. He hurried over his changing, showing as little as possible of his nakedness because of his shame. Dressed in Mackenzie's outsize garments, he turned anxiously to the table, to make quite sure that she had not looked.

There was a warm light in her eyes, and she was laughing at him. There was the dreamy softness of the pigeon's song in her voice when she spoke to him. ' Duncan,' she said, ' if my skin was as bonnie, as soft and white, as yours, I'd no' be ashamed to show it.'

He blushed and shivered, and the warm blood ran like wine through his trembling limbs.

' Sit in to your tea, boy,' she smiled, ' and I'll get your clothes dried. I was only teasing you, Duncan.'

He ate hurriedly, with bowed head, and was sensitively conscious of every swish of her dress, every movement that she made. The picture of the restless warmth and blueness of her eyes swam before him as he drank his tea.

Rain lashed against the house, streamed down the windows, and the wet mist shut in the house like a shroud. Steam rose in clouds from the clothes hung

across the kitchen on the pulley-ropes, and water dripped from them, to form spreading pools on the floor—the stone-flagged floor, covered with scrolls and curious devices of coloured chalks.

Duncan felt a warm arm brush his cheek as his cup was filled. ' How old are you, Duncan ? '

' Thirteen, past.'

' My, you're a well-grown lad for your age, boy. I thought you would be older.'

She moved away again, and Duncan felt that some of the warm interest was gone from her voice. He could not bear that it should go so soon. He turned his head and followed her with his grey, adventurous eyes. She surprised his glance, and laughed at him again, raising her head to show the smooth white column of her throat. ' Aye, you're a well-grown lad,' she said.

Duncan, overcome with wild confusion, buried his face in his white tea-mug. ' It's time I was going,' he muttered. The thought of his uncompleted task returned to him, the worry of the unfound tup, of his having missed Mackenzie, of the long road home.

' Your clothes are no' dry yet,' she said, stroking their wetness with her toil-worn hands, ' but they're maybe no' as damp as they was. You'll need to keep moving, Duncan boy, and no' catch cold.'

He changed into the steaming warmth of his half-dried suit, forced his feet into the squelching boots, and rose stiffly to go home. ' Many thanks to ye,' he mumbled in shy awkwardness.

She came to him with the lazy strength of her graceful limbs, with the sleepy look in her half-closed eyes, and the full lips smiling, showing her

even teeth. 'An' is that all the thanks you'll be giving me, Duncan, my bonnie boy? Is that all?'

Then she stooped down and held his lips with her own, until the life seemed drained from his body, to leave him trembling and weak. She pushed him through the door, laughing all the time. 'You'll come back to see me again, Duncan?' she asked.

He took one step towards her, the blood hammering and beating in his head. He wanted to bury his face in the warm white arms. Then, frightened at the strange desires which swept across his brain, he turned away. 'Aye! I'll come back,' he whispered, and ran through the rain for Meg.

The wind was behind him going home, and he had to lean backwards to keep his balance. It seemed as though the storm would thresh him downwards to the ground, and beat his face against the jagged rocks. Meg was bowled round and round, her coat swept up in tufts of rain-soaked hair. She whined and whimpered when the wind's force drove her sideways against hard stones. The air held coldness and a threat of snow. Deer sprang out of the mist like silhouetted monsters, then the flying rain hid them from view. Wreaths took form and shape of clinging lips and smooth white arms. Duncan struggled onwards, driven by duty towards his home, but with sick yearning at his heart to linger in Strathord. The wind, rushing through cracks and tunnels in the rocks, seemed voices crying out his name in smothered laughter, then dying to whispers like the pigeon's cooing, bidding him return. He stumbled against Mackenzie on the Craig's slopes.

'My, Duncan boy, I thought ye were a bogle.'

The shepherd was panting, his shoulders hunched

and his face pinched and blue. There was the restless, agonised look in his eyes, as of a man who fears death. He leant on his stick, his red hair straggling out from under a cap with the peak turned backwards on his scraggy neck. He rested a moment, while a more healthy colour spread over his face. 'The devil's surely in the tups the year,' he muttered.

His plain dog wagged its tangled tail and sniffed at Meg. Duncan was dazed and speechless, thinking of flaxen plaits and a honey-tasting mouth. He forced his tongue to movement, and his frozen face to a sickly smile. 'Have ye been down at Glendarroch, Mac ? ' he asked.

' Aye, I've been there, Duncan boy. There's no sign of my tup, but your father's found yours.'

' Where ? '

' On its back. In a bog-hole on the East-end heft, with only its legs showing above the water. He shouldna have gone to Crimmond for his tups. Old Hugh knew what he was doing with his hardy Cranok sheep.'

' Aye,' Duncan replied, ' there was one did you a fine turn the year it left a lamb or two worth the buying in Strathord.'

Mackenzie made a half-hearted lunge with his stick, and Duncan ducked in a lifeless way. The wind whistled around them, drowning the words they said, making mockery of the farce and misery of their fooling.

' Were ye down at the house, Duncan ? Did ye see the mistress ? '

' Aye, Mac ; she made me take a cup of tea.' Duncan's face was so red with the whipping rain that his blush could pass unseen.

'Aye, Duncan boy,' said Mackenzie, 'it's lonely for her there when I'm out on the hill, a young lassie like thon and no' used to the glens.'

Duncan thought of the half-closed eyes of mocking blue. He hated Mackenzie, who was going back to his wife in Strathord. The bent, sick, cheat-the-wind beast of a red-headed pining stot! What right had he to cool his ugly face on the bare, soft arms? Why should he be kissed by the honey-tasting lips? Duncan was afraid of the angry, searing thoughts, the bitter, jealous hatred that drove like the winter's storm across his mind. Why should he want to strike old Mac, the friend and companion of many a great sheep-gathering?

Mackenzie's scared eyes grasped the change in Duncan's face. 'My, Duncan,' he exclaimed in surprise, 'you're growing a big lad. Have ye got a lassie yet?'

Duncan gave a startled gasp of fear. Did Mackenzie guess? 'We'll be needing our time if we're to be home before dark,' he grunted out, and sped down the winding sheep-track of the Craig. He squelched recklessly across bog and moss to the Pot, never heeding the sucking mud and rising bubbles of gas. Meg crept at his heels, a chilled, exhausted, trailing ghost of a dog, and the rain lashed them mercilessly with its ceaseless bombardment of flying drops.

Mackenzie watched the boy race down the hill like a thing gone mad, and wondered what wild fears were in the laddie's heart. He shook his head, and turned to the climb before him. His pain caught him an agonising stab, and his eyes grew panic-stricken. He wondered whether his strength

would prevail against the hurricane, that foe of weakly men, and bring him safely home to fireside and to wife.

Duncan was soaked again to the skin when he had left the Pot behind and was on the firm heathery ground that led down to the house. The cottage loomed out of the mist. Peat-reek and wood-smoke scented the air. The lamp, already lit, glimmered out through the wee window. He was home! He chained Meg in the stable beside the other three dogs, and rubbed the shivering beast with wisps of hay. Then he went to seek hot milk to bring back warmth to her chilled bones.

Pools of water gathered at his feet as he stood swaying drunkenly on the kitchen floor. Wee Jean toddled away from him, he looked so strange. Johnnie wrestled to an upright position in the old green arm-chair. 'You're fair done, boy,' he exclaimed. 'You've had a long day for nothing at all. The beast's in a hole.'

'Aye,' muttered Duncan. 'I met Mac on the Craig.'

'Get your wet things off this minute, Duncan,' Mary ordered. 'You must be soaked to the skin.'

But Duncan seemed suddenly to have outgrown his mother's commands. He stood, swaying but determined. 'I'm needing milk,' he gasped—'hot milk for the dog.'

Mary stared—then quivered as though a ghost had spoken. She filled a pan and moved it on to the leaping flames.

Johnnie staggered to his feet and fumbled for his boots beneath the chair. 'I'll see to Meg for you,

Duncan boy,' he said. ' Get you some dry clothes on and a warm bite inside you.'

When he had changed, Duncan fell fast asleep in the chair. He never heard Jean prattling at his knees, nor wee Johnnie come bounding in from school. Mary wakened him to come to his tea, and he ate and drank as one dazed. Then he stumbled off to bed and fell asleep as soon as his tired legs were stretched. It seemed that his head nestled down on warm bare arms that were soft and white.

XVII

Duncan was to think of Mackenzie's bonnie young wife for the waking and dreaming hours of a week of late November rain. Then, like unseasonable weather, interest faltered and died, and he was at play with wee Johnnie and at work with his father on the sodden hills. Sometimes, too, the story of his birth would bring worry to him, to be swiftly forgotten in the interests of sheep and school which were nearest to his heart and age.

As December slipped away in twilit days of rain, plans were laid in Glendarroch for fitting celebration of Hogmanay. It had always been Hugh's custom to make much of Old Year's night, to have one or two neighbouring herds in for an evening's drinking and fun. Alicky Mag and red-headed Mackenzie had been the boon companions of those nights which, begun in the house, had often ended in the byre. But now Hugh was dead, and fast becoming a sentimentally whitewashed memory, Mackenzie's mind was fixed on his stomach and his wife, and only little Alicky Mag, the life of them all,

was left of the three herds who had once forgathered with song, mirth, and a bottle apiece at clippings, markets, and Hogmanay.

It showed how the years brought change when Mrs Macintyre sent a letter by the postman asking Johnnie, Mary, and Duncan to spend a quiet Old Year's night with them all down the glen. It had never happened when Hugh was alive, for the Macintyre boys were not drinking men, when their mother could keep them from it. Mary, of course, must send a letter by return, saying how she could not leave wee Jean alone with wee Johnnie in the house at night, and would the Macintyres all come up to Glendarroch instead.

The note was away, and evening come, before Johnnie asked, 'And what about Alicky Mag the year?'

'We canna ask him, Johnnie,' Mary answered with worried look. 'Him and Mistress Macintyre's no' speaking since the day his dogs broke out on her hens.'

'The old man will take the strunts at that,' Johnnie warned.

'Well, he'll just have to,' she answered with decision. 'It's been real good of Mistress Macintyre asking us all down, and the most we can do is to ask her back and no' bring people in that she's no' speaking to.'

Duncan, pretending to be busy at his home lessons, listened to all that had been said. 'Have Alicky,' he pleaded. 'He's more fun nor all the Macintyres put thegither.'

'Aye, you're about right, Duncan,' Johnnie agreed. 'It's likely thon squint-eyed Jenny'll be coming an' all, Mary?'

'Aye, Johnnie ; why not ? '

'Because I just canna stand the sight o' her.'

'That's no way to talk about your neighbours,' Mary complained. 'It's right good of Mistress Macintyre to be inviting us. It's no' that often that farmer folk take notice of herds.'

'Aye, we're fair getting into society,' Duncan laughed.

Johnnie quelled the twinkle in his own dark eyes. 'Ye're no' to make fun o' your mother, boy,' he said.

So Alicky Mag was unbidden to the feast, and at seven o'clock of a starlit Hogmanay the Macintyre family tramped up the glen. Mrs Macintyre and Jenny led the van, with the Macintyre men plodding behind them like a Westown police patrol. Duncan squinted through the wee window when he heard their steps, and felt the flat depression which the approach of funless people brings. 'They're coming,' he groaned.

Mary gave the last housewifely touches to the spread table. 'Put wee Johnnie's boots away,' she whispered to Duncan. 'He's left them there for anyone to trip over.'

Duncan did what he could to help and went through to the firelit parlour, where the two Johnnies sat in the starched discomfort of prepared hospitality. 'You left your boots lying about,' said Duncan, and wee Johnnie's slicked curls wobbled as he laughed.

Then they heard Mary at the outer door receiving the Macintyres with the age-old ritual of an anxious hostess. Johnnie whispered across to Duncan, ' See and behave yoursel' the night, boy. It's no'

oursel's we must be thinking on the night—it's your mother. She's had no kind o' a party that I can mind of. It's aye been a kind o' bar-parlour here before.'

Duncan nodded, and rose beside his father to receive the guests. There was the customary chatter of meaningless greeting. 'Aye, Jim—aye, Bob—sit ye in, Mistress Macintyre—how's yoursel', Jenny?'

They squashed somehow into the red-plush chairs, the faded sofa, the rickety cosy-corner. The yellow glass eyes of the mangy fox eyed them all with a malevolent stare, and generations of photographed Macleans blinked over their collars and through their hair from the pinewood mantelshelf above the leaping flames.

'Aye, Duncan,' said Mrs Macintyre, folding capable hands on an ample lap, 'it only seems yesterday since you were born. I said to your mother whenever I saw you that there'd never be a curl in your hair.'

Duncan blushed, feeling foolish, and Mary excused herself to dish the pie.

'Jenny, go and give Mistress Gillies a hand. It's no' little she has to do with all the bairns about the place.' Mrs Macintyre confirmed the order with a little shove at her daughter's drooping back, and a professional glance to judge the secret progress of the fourth young Gillies. 'Aye,' she continued with a sigh when the other two women had been set to work, 'it's no' the same here without Mr Maclean. Such a quiet decent man he aye was too, and a kind, joky word for everyone he met.'

'Aye,' Johnnie grunted. 'And what sort o' a tupping have ye had, Jim?'

'No bad, Johnnie.'

'Have ye many ewes eild?'

'I dinna think it.'

'Oh, you men and your sheep!' exclaimed Mrs Macintyre, resuming her interrupted grip on the evening's conversation. 'D'ye ever talk of anything else when you get together?'

'No before the ladies,' Johnnie grinned, and the Macintyre men awkwardly shuffled their feet.

Jenny squinted in at the door. No man could tell where or at whom she was looking. Her nose shone after work before the fire, her fair hair straggled wearily after stooping, and her face showed the pinched thinness of an unloved life no longer young. 'Mistress Gillies says will ye all come through to the kitchen to your tea, and will Duncan and wee Johnnie bring in a couple of chairs apiece.'

Mrs Macintyre heaved her lean yet massive frame from the sofa's uneven comfort, and showed her excellent teeth in a hungry smile. It seemed that she had already accepted the position of unquestioned authority which was hers by personality abroad and by right at home. 'Come along now, Duncan,' she urged. 'Do as your mother asks, like the fine boy you are.'

Duncan scowled as he struggled with the red-plush chairs, and wee Johnnie made a rude face at Mrs Macintyre's portly back. Johnnie screwed down the lamp, to leave the parlour in emptiness and dusk, to the representation of things once alive, to the mangy fox and the photographed Macleans.

The kitchen sparkled in the light of fire, lamp, and massed reserves of flickering candles. In the soft illumination everyone seemed more young,

more kindly, and less shy. They arranged the chairs, the hard-backed plain everyday chairs that were the kitchen's customary denizens, and those of faded plush reserved for christenings, funerals, and special occasions. The crockery had all the variety of shapes, sizes, and colours necessitated by the service of a company of eight. The linoleum was scrubbed to snowy whiteness for the satisfactory dazzlement of a widow neighbour's critical eye.

'Well, Mistress Gillies,' said Mrs Macintyre, settling herself cosily down in the small space at her disposal, 'I must say you manage wonderfully considering the work you have with all your bairns.'

'Aye, you stopped at a lucky number, Mistress Macintyre,' Johnnie grinned, and Mary looked uncomfortable, wondering what her husband might yet be roused to say.

The pastry was broken on the steak-and-kidney pie, and thick steam and appetising odours rose in clouds to the low, smoke-grimed roof. Cups and saucers rattled as the tea was passed round, and hard-skinned hands stretched out for scones and oatcakes, butter and jam.

'And how are the hens laying, Mistress Gillies?' Mrs Macintyre asked when all were served.

'Not well at all, Mistress Macintyre. There's a lot o' them not done moulting yet, and those that are will be laying no more than an egg a week.'

'You should go in for White Leghorns and colony houses, Mistress Gillies—them with slatted floors, I'm meaning. What breed gives *you* the best results?'

'Indeed, an' I canna tell you that, Mistress Macintyre. Our hens are just hens. I'm feared

we're getting a wee bit behind the times up here in Glendarroch.'

' You should try to get in to the poultry classes in Lochend, Mistress Gillies. But what am I talking of ? It's a whiley yet before *you'll* be free o' bairns on a winter's night. I've kept Jenny at it regular these last three months, and I must say she's not wasted her time.'

Johnnie's mouth had been quivering and twisting for several minutes. He had something good to say, and at last it must be said. ' Do you women ever clack of anything but hens when ye get thegither ? ' he laughed.

Mary glared in outraged disapproval ; Duncan and wee Johnnie nodded and grinned, and spluttered out crumbs. Mrs Macintyre shook herself angrily like a ewe newly out from the dipper. There was a long pause, broken only by the crackle of slightly overdone pastry against rows of unusually perfect teeth, the rattle of cups on saucers neither so even nor so white, by the long low whistle Bob Macintyre blew on his over-hot tea.

' An' what sort o' tupping have ye had, Johnnie ? ' asked Jim Macintyre.

' No bad, but we lost a new tup.'

' The one ye were looking for ? '

' Aye, the Crimmond tup.'

' An' what came o' it ? '

' Drowned in a peat-hole. We searched the whole place for it. I kept Duncan back from the school to give me a hand. He was out over the Craig to Strathord on a day o' rain no' fit for a dog to be out in.'

The Macintyre men stared at Duncan in frank

admiration of his hardy precocity. But Mrs Macintyre scented an opportunity of adding to her encyclopaedic knowledge of local gossip. ' An' did ye see Mistress Mackenzie ? ' she asked. ' Jamie Dunlop—that's him that comes with the Cop. van, Mistress Gillies ; he doesna come up your length—well, he was telling me that she's never right dressed unless she's going into Lochend, which is every second day of the week, if we're to believe what's said.'

Duncan tried at first to restrain his blush. He had never related the full story of his Strathord adventures. He dared not have told of the warm bare arms and the honey-tasting lips. Now it all came back to him again—the flaxen plaits and the half-closed eyes of blue, the clinging skirts and the lazy limbs, the cooing voice and the arms so soft and white, so soft and white. He felt the blood rush, a resistless surging flood, to his face and neck, and lowered his eyes in a wild confusion.

Mrs Macintyre nodded her grey head sagely and pursed up experienced lips. ' Aye, you'll have seen bonnie Mistress Mackenzie,' she said.

Duncan felt seven pairs of eyes on his crimson cheeks. He heard wee Johnnie bubble rudely in his tea, and Mary move uneasily in her chair.

' Aye,' said Johnnie fiercely, ' I doubt Mistress Mackenzie's a bad woman, an' I'm sorry for her man.'

Duncan pictured a red head buried in warm, soft arms, and thought misfortune not by any means all on Mackenzie's side. But tongues were busy tearing all shreds of reputation from a bonnie young wife, as a licking cat will scrape meat from a

butcher's bone. With tongues so busy they ceased to stare, and Duncan could safely raise his face without meeting the merciless scrutiny of sex-starved Macintyre eyes. Wee Johnnie winked wickedly over the rapidly melting pile of fresh-baked scones.

'Aye,' concluded Mrs Macintyre with matronly decision, 'what Mistress Mackenzie needs is a bairn to keep her in about the house and give her something to think of when her man's away.'

Johnnie Gillies laughed and winked all round the table : 'Can Jim or Bob no' do anything about it ? ' he asked.

'Some more tea, Mistress Macintyre. Will you just pass over your cup,' said Mary, in a desperate effort to avoid a scene. It seemed to her that Johnnie was out to spoil the success of her social evening, and she had no sympathy with Mrs Mackenzie's striving for unwifely freedom. 'If there's nobody for another cup, I think we might go ben to the other room.'

'Jenny,' Mrs Macintyre snapped, 'you'll give Mistress Gillies a hand to clear away and wash up.'

The others clattered through to the parlour, where Johnnie stoked the fire to a crackling blaze, and turned up the lamp to a yellow glow. Mrs Macintyre sighed down in replete contentment on the uneven sofa, and the Macintyre men made themselves politely uncomfortable on the edge of chairs. Duncan and wee Johnnie sat side by side, their eyes full of the dreamy vacuity which follows good food and fresh air. From the kitchen came the rattle and scrape of dishes and knives, and the high-pitched cracked voice of Jenny Macintyre humming a sentimental tune.

The unmusical noise forced an idea on Bob Macintyre's pie-dulled brain. ' You'll need to give us a song the night, Johnnie. You used to be a grand hand at the singing,' he said.

' Aye,' Mrs Macintyre agreed, casting purse-proud eyes round the over-furnished room, ' it's just a pity there was no piano here for Jenny to accompany you, Johnnie. She's been having lessons in Lochend this winter, and I must say she's no' wasted her time.'

' Ach ! ' grinned Johnnie, ' I'm no' needing a piano. I'll just keep time wi' my fut.'

Mary and Jenny came in, buttoning the sleeves of their blouses. ' We'll just leave the rest till morning,' Mary said. ' Sit you down in the sofa, Jenny, and many thanks for your help. She was real useful, Mistress Macintyre.'

' Johnnie's going to give us a song,' Bob Macintyre announced.

Mary looked a little alarmed, wondering what kind of song Johnnie would sing. Something to annoy Mistress Macintyre, as like as not.

' Come on, Johnnie,' Jim Macintyre urged.

Little Johnnie Gillies planted himself firmly with his sturdy back to the leaping fire. He ran his hand bashfully through his black curls, which were slightly flecked with thin streaks of grey. His brown eyes danced with mischief, and his humorous mouth twisted up to one side. ' I'll sing ye a song I havena sung since I was married,' he grinned. ' It's kind o' in keeping wi' the talk we was having ben the kitchen. It's called " The Bonnie Wife o' Mettick," and I learnt it from a herd on the other side o' Cranok.'

Johnnie threw up his head and broke into a jig-like tune, keeping time on the carpet with the heel of his Sunday boot. The first verse was in a quiet strain, but with the hint of broader humour to come :

> The bonnie wife o' Mettick,
> She was full o' fun and capers,
> She would kiss the daftie postman
> When her gudeman was awa'—
> She would skirl and toss her heid up
> When the minister was preaching,
> She would dab her nose wi' pouder
> When the factor came to ca'——

The Macintyre men had caught the rhythm and were keeping time with their feet. Mrs Macintyre was all smiles and nodding grey head.

Johnnie paused, torn between the evident approval of his guests and Mary's no less obvious uneasiness. He risked a second verse, which more than fulfilled the promise of the first.

'That's enough o' thon, Johnnie,' said Mary with decision.

'It gets better as it goes on, Mary.'

'Then there's the more need to stop, singing a thing like thon wi' your two boys listening to you.'

'Huts !' cried Mrs Macintyre, 'it's Hogmanay, Mistress Gillies.'

'That's no excuse for being indecent, Mistress Macintyre.—Duncan, will you give us a tune on your fiddle ? '

'Ach ! I canna play it right yet, mother,' he pleaded.

'Nonsense, Duncan boy, you're aye at it.'

'Come on, Duncan,' Johnnie laughed. 'You can play better nor I can sing.'

' All right,' Duncan sighed, ' I'll fetch it.'

' Will I need to bide while he's making thon scraiking ? ' wee Johnnie giggled.

Duncan made a playful lunge at his brother as he went out. He took down the fiddle and bow from the kitchen shelf, and feeling desperately foolish and shy, returned to the parlour. Taking up position before the fire, he made several tentative squeaks, while wee Johnnie simulated pain. Then he plunged into his attempt at the slow, sad, rowing tune that Alicky played—the tune that brought tears to the eyes of the West Coast seals. He played on, making more discords than he did in the byre, until the plaintive melody was done. Then he stood with the fiddle and bow hanging at his knees, and a sound in his ears of the slow gathering of summer waves and their lazy breaking.

' That's a sad tune for a boy to play,' Mrs Macintyre said. ' Can you no' play us a tune that's a bit more lively, Duncan ? '

So Duncan essayed the old dance tune, ' Jenny, catch your skirts up,' but he could get no life or time in the thing for thinking of the divergent eyes and silly humorless smile of drab Jenny Macintyre. He thought that if she ever lifted her skirts it would be to keep clear of the mud and not to dance. His fiddling was a failure. He could tell it by the expressionless faces and still feet of the Macintyre men, by Mary's concerned look, and by the kindly, encouraging smile that Johnnie gave him. He hurried away to hide his fiddle and his bow.

When he came back to the parlour the hands of the black marble clock were at five minutes to eleven, and the talk was all of the sheep and hens.

Wee Johnnie's black head was nodding with boredom and approaching sleep.

Then, from outside came the distant music of pipes, a march that was familiar to them all—the rousing tune with which Alicky Mag serenaded the mistress of a house where a day's clipping was over and done. Somewhere, out in the coldness of a starlit moor, the little man was parading the peat, sending a Hogmanay greeting to a house which Death had barred against him.

They were all silent while the playing lasted, and then when it was over, Mary said: 'Perhaps, Mistress Macintyre, you wouldn't mind us asking the wee daftie in for his Hogmanay dram. It's good of him to come all the way over from Glendruid to give us a tune.'

'It's no' us he's playing for,' Duncan murmured. 'It's for Hugh he's come.'

There was a strained uneasy silence at these words. Mary trembled, as though cold.

'Huts!' exclaimed Mrs Macintyre. 'That's a silly-like way for a young boy to talk.'

'I'll get out the bottle,' said Johnnie, in a brave effort to relieve the uncanny tension. 'It's getting on for twelve. Perhaps you'll be taking a wee dram yoursel', Mistress Macintyre, for the sake of old times.'

'Thank you, Johnnie.' She shivered. 'It's not often I take one, but I could be doing with one now.'

Duncan wanted so much to go out and call Alicky back to the company and warmth. He thought of the little man watching the light in the window, and waiting for the door to open and a hail to sound over the wintry moor. He longed to spring from his

chair before it was too late, when Alicky, pocketing his thirst and hoisting his pride, would stride off in bitter loneliness to the black gulf of Glendruid glen. He knew he had been foolish to guess the reason of Alicky's playing, for the mention of Hugh's name had made them all strange and taut, as though waiting for the door to open and something to come in that were better unseen.

Johnnie brought the glasses and bottle and poured out a small respectable portion for each of the guests. Then he turned his back and helped himself to a more manly dram. He beckoned Duncan outside the door. 'Duncan boy,' he said, pointing to a corner of the lobby, 'there's the gun there and a couple of cartridges in it. Go you outside, boy, and wait, and when it's twelve o'clock I'll come out and tell you, and you'll fire two shots in the air.'

Duncan was proud of his promotion to this important duty, which had always been his father's before, and he at once forgot Alicky Mag and all uncanny things. He slipped outside to the moonless night and the million stars. The world was still and hushed by the frost, as though waiting. Nothing stirred on the black moors, on the dim shadows of the hills, or in the valleys below. Everything was still.

Then at last Johnnie poked an excited face round the door, whispering 'Now!' and Duncan lifted the old gun to his shoulder and pressed the triggers. The reports roared out, breaking the silence of the world, and the gun's butt punched his shoulder like a kicking horse.

Was that a shot or an echo from Glendruid?

Was that a fainter echo from beyond the Corrie in Strathord? It must be Alicky and poor old Mac in their distant glens, shooting the Old Year out— bringing the New Year in.

Duncan rushed back to the parlour, leaving the gun in the lobby, and burst in upon a babel of voices and a blaze of light—Johnnie kissing Mary, Mrs Macintyre kissing her sons, everyone holding glasses, everyone wishing each other a Good New Year.

Johnnie laid a hand on Duncan's shoulder. ' May this be the best year ye've ever had, boy,' he said.

' Aye,' Duncan grinned, ' it'll be that all right. I'll be done with the school.'

They sang ' Auld Lang Syne ' together, and then the Macintyres prepared to leave, because they wished to first-foot the MacCullochs. Mrs Macintyre struggled into her black hat and coat and her purple feather boa, and Jenny into more fashionable green, with a piece of brown fur like a frayed rabbit skin around her stringy neck. They all shuffled through the darkness of the lobby to the keen frost of a New Year's Day.

Duncan and wee Johnnie rushed back to the kitchen to snatch a slice of gingerbread apiece before their mother came in. Duncan stole back to the lobby to see whether there was time for the secret eating of a second.

Johnnie and Mary were standing at the door, facing the starlit night. Johnnie had his arm around his wife's waist and was saying, ' It was a grand evening, Mary, and ye managed fine.'

' Aye, Johnnie,' she sighed. ' I'd like to see more people.'

XVIII

It was the postman who brought the story up the glen, on a mild February day when the hills were hidden in drifting smoke and dotted with twisted tongues of yellow flame, when the air was heavy with spring incense of burning heather and charring whins.

He told it all to Mary as she stood, bare-headed and heavy with child, the day's paper clasped in her reddened hands. He told of how Alicky Mag, the daft wee bodach that he was, had been taken away at last; how he had broken into the shop of Jimmy MacBain, the licensed grocer in Lochend, and had stolen a half-dozen bottles of whisky there.

'Aye,' said Mary, 'I thought it would come to that.'

'But that's no' the best o' it,' the postman sniggered. 'Jockie Ewan, that's him that drives old Macfarlane's summer bus, saw Alicky coming out, and went straight to East, the *po*lice sergeant, and him and a constable and Jockie went up to Glendruid thegither. They found the old man playing the pipes to himself in thon tinker's tent o' a house o' his, with the empty bottles about him and no' a stitch to his back. When they were for breaking in, that grey-beardie collie o' his near tore the throat out o' East. They had to go back to Mac-Culloch's and fetch a gun to shoot the dogs before they could lay hands on Alicky and put clothes on the man.'

'An' is he off to the jail?' Mary asked.

'No, no' the jail, Mistress Gillies. He's away to the asylum. He's clean daft, they're saying, and

winna talk unless it's in Latin.' The postman laughed again and wheeled round his bike. ' No letters the day, Mistress Gillies ? Well, I'll no' be keeping you.'

Mary told the story to Johnnie when he came in from the heather-burning with red-lidded eyes and blackened hands. Duncan heard about it when he came home from school. He was more sorry than he could tell. Alicky had always been kind and jolly with him, ready to teach him the fiddle, or Latin grammar. The sheep-gatherings would be poor dull things in future without the old man's cackling fun throughout the hot day, and his piping in the cool evening when the work was done.

On the following Saturday, Duncan wandered by himself across the Glendruid hills and came down on the silent shuttered cottage by the coal-black river. He walked through the weed-covered garden, hushing his footsteps as though in Death's presence, round to the well where wee Johnnie had wrestled with the heavy stone and dropped ten wriggling frogs in the dark pit. The glen was silent and deserted as it had never seemed before, and the little light-boned sheep were cropping the grass right down to the cottage gate. Duncan shivered at the misery and loneliness of it all. He thought of Alicky shut up in some sunless room, perhaps bound down, with nobody to laugh at his fun or to keep time to his fiddle or his pipes. There was no knowing what might be done to the little man put away like that and with nobody in the world to speak for him. It was likely he would never come out again to the sheep and the hills and the bottle he loved so well.

Duncan thought there was no use in his lingering in Glendruid, making himself feel unhappy and uncanny with thoughts of his old friend. He struck out across the hills to Glendarroch, and looked back only when he was safely out on the high watershed. Then he gazed down on the deep hollow of the glen, the river coiling through it like a black-scaled snake, and the cottage a little white match-box on a handkerchief of green. He stared so long that he imagined smoke curling up from the squat chimneys, and when he turned away his eyes were full of tears.

In the weeks that followed there was much talk of who would come as herd to Glendruid. Mrs Macintyre knew all about it when she came up the glen on a wild March day to see Mary safely through her fourth confinement. She had heard from Jock MacCulloch that Lady Waterton's factor was putting in a single man, a young fellow, until the May term, when the stock was to be sold to the Forestry Commission, which meant to clear the sheep from Glendruid and plant trees instead. ' And that'll be the first sheep delivery there's been hereabouts for many a long day,' she said.

Duncan asked his father what a sheep delivery was, when they were sitting together in the dim-lit byre awaiting the baby's birth. Dr Brown's big car was at the brae-foot, and wee Johnnie was curled up fast asleep on a pile of hay.

Johnnie seemed thankful to talk, and pulled a chewed strand of hay from his quivering mouth. ' A sheep delivery, Duncan boy, is a great day. It's something between a sheep-gathering and a grouse-drive. The folks come in from miles away,

and there's a fair army o' men driving in the sheep and the young lambs, and dogs and bairns, and unctioneers valuing, and white clouts waving until the sheep's fair scared to death. The man that's selling has his valuer and the man that's buying has another, and the two valuers fix on an oversman to keep them both right, and atween the lot of them they put a price on each age o' sheep, and put on a bit more for acclimatisation, and a shilling or two for hefting, and a bittie more on top o' that to give the man that's selling a fair thing to retire on.'

'What price will they put on the Glendruid ewes?' Duncan said.

'I wouldna like to say, boy. It a' depends on who's valuing. It'll likely be a good price wi' the Government buying, maybe fifty shillings a head for the young ages.'

'But they'd no' make the half o' that in Cranok,' Duncan exclaimed.

'They would not, boy. But a sheep's no' the same value in a sale ring as on the hill it's born to. The Glendruid stock's bound to the ground, and must be valued on the hill. If they was putting on a new stock there, the half o' the sheep would die.'

'But the Glendruid sheep's no' worth fifty shillings,' Duncan persisted. 'They're poor beasts.'

'If they were a better stock, Duncan boy, they'd no' make as much. There'd be less acclimatisation value on them.'

'I dinna see the sense in thon, father.'

'Ye would if ye were selling, boy.'

Silence fell on the byre again, except for wee Johnnie stirring in his sleep, and the quiet movement of the cows. Duncan's head was beginning

to nod when the tramp of footsteps on the cobbles outside heralded the coming of news. Mrs Macintyre opened the byre door, letting in the cold air and making the hay stir. There was a white shawl over her head, and the maternal look in her eyes which a birth evoked. 'It's another boy, Johnnie,' she said.

Duncan followed his father to the warm kitchen, bared of lamp and table, lit only by a guttering candle, and scented with a strange sweet sickening scent. There was a weak wailing in the house, as though a lost lamb, born out of season, had been brought to shelter from a world of storm.

Mrs Macintyre came bustling through to stir the fire and heat a kettle and a pan of rain-water. The doctor followed her, his spare figure bent with age and fatigue, but the twinkle still in his kind brown eyes. He nodded to Johnnie and smiled at Duncan. 'You've grown a big boy,' he said. 'You make me feel old. It seems but yesterday since I brought you into the world. I think your father was disappointed you weren't a girl.' Duncan grinned and shuffled his feet. 'Well, I must go,' said the doctor, buttoning his coat. 'I'll be up soon again to see that everything's right. Mrs Macintyre is a good nurse.'

Duncan hated the fortnight that followed, when Mrs Macintyre took his mother's place and firm charge of them all. He was thankful when he saw her black hat bobbing down the glen road, and Mary, pale and tired-looking, poured his porridge again and filled his cup.

The baby was called Hugh after its grandfather, for nothing but good was now remembered of big Hugh Maclean.

Duncan's schooldays drifted away through a stormy March and blustering April weather. The laird was unable to obtain his release for lambing work, and Johnnie became a thin ghost of his usual self by the time the wind shifted out of the east and trembling ceased among the Glendarroch ewes. It was a hard lambing that year, with the draw-moss late and the gimmers without a drop of milk, the old ewes lean and 'sookit doon,' and too many twins because of a week of mild weather and a late flush of grass at the beginning of tupping. The kitchen was filled with lambs weak and dying, and the byres loud with the bleating of those hand-milked.

When the wind changed round to the south in the later days of May, and warm weather came, then everything burst into glorious growth on the sleeping hills. It was like the sudden bursting of a pent-up dam of life. The dead-brown winter colour left the heather. Patches of grass among the brittle fronds of bracken lost their greyness to the summer sun and turned in a night to shimmering sheets of emerald green. Days grew warm and the wind caressing, late-lambing gimmers could suckle their lambs, and morning dawned with a promise of sun on the day of sheep delivery at Glendruid farm.

Duncan and his father set out with the dogs to meet Mackenzie and the Macintyre men, to advance like a skirmishing army over the Glendarroch side of Glendruid grazing, driving the ewes and young lambs before them to the buchts' security, and shrewd appraisement of the valuators' eyes.

It was a fine walk across the flat moor to the Glendruid hills, with the peewits, larks, and curlews

making summer melody in clouds of rising mist.
It was to be a grand day by the very feel of the air,
and by the way the sun gained swift victory over the
dampness of night. Duncan was whistling, and
Johnnie joined in with the clear purity of note and
rhythmical gaiety which gave a lilting lightness to
a simple tune. The dogs knew that something
special was afoot, running on ahead in twisting
courses, following their noses and the scent of a
dancing hare, then standing with cocked ears and
eyes of inquiry, waiting for the whistling men to
lead the way. Far over to the right a dog was
yelping, and Duncan knew that would be Mackenzie, still hidden by mist, come down the Corrie
from Strathord. Johnnie put the little fingers of
his two hands in his mouth, forcing his lips outwards to a line, and blew a far-carrying whistle,
first to the right, and then to the left. Answers,
like faint echoes, came through the mist, and the
liquid summer song of nesting whaups. Soon came
tramping of feet and the bark of dogs, and shadows
loomed big in the silvery light of the morning mist.
The Gillieses, Mackenzie, and the Macintyre men
had met to gather the sheep off the northern slopes
of Glendruid glen.

They were all agreed that it would be fine weather
for the delivery, and likely to be a warm night for
the young lambs finding their way back to the hill.
They all agreed that Glendruid would be a queer-
like place without Alicky Mag. Then they set out
together, five men and seven dogs, to gain the high
watershed before the sun was up. The mist had
lifted from Glendarroch by the time the top was
reached, but it lay late in Glendruid, a white blanket

held in the black grip of the rocks, and the Druid, like a silver snake, coiling through the hidden depths of the sunless glen.

' Man,' said Mackenzie, ' it'll be a queer uncanny place wi'out sheep on it, and the whole of it covered in a forest o' trees ! '

' Aye,' Johnnie agreed, ' an' a fine nest for vermin to come out on the Glendarroch lambs, I'm thinkin'. Wi' all this planting the hills will soon be like what my grandfather used to tell of, wi' foxes and wild-cats and sea-eagles making a bigger loss among the sheep than braxy and trembling put thegither.'

' Ach ! ' Mackenzie grunted, ' I'd sooner have foxes and cats than bracken and maggots. My father would aye say that his father had no manner o' use for sheep at all. He would be saying, if he was alive the day, that the old folks were right and that a West Highland grazing was made wi' black-cattle and spoilt wi' sheep. I'm telling ye mysel', boys, that Strathord will no' carry half the sheep stock in another twenty years.'

' Aye, Mac,' said Johnnie, ' you're maybe right. There would have been a time when all these hills were covered wi' wood. I've burnt many a good tree that was dug from the peat, and after the trees there would have been nothing but the black-cattle, and then the sheep. It's likely enough we're going round the other way now, and the sheep will go and the cattle and trees come back.'

' An' what o' the men, Johnnie Gillies ? ' asked Mackenzie. ' What o' the men ? '

Johnnie spat on a stone. ' They'll come back when London's burnt, and no' till then,' he said.

The mist was lifting, and rock after black rock

rose above the thinning cloud to sparkle a welcome to the risen sun. The men spread out in a straggling line to beat the lambs from birch-sheltered ravines and bracken brakes. Duncan was between Johnnie, away on his left, and Mackenzie on his right, and strode down the steep brae with Meg darting hither and thither, and ewes and lambs leaping before them both. There was one little sickly lamb, blinded with the rotting yellowsis disease, and Duncan picked it up to carry it under his arms. He could see the dot-like moving figures on the opposite side of the glen, and the fine May morning was full of shouting of men and barking of dogs. Furtive wisps of mist hid in shadowed places like delayed night-revellers surprised by day, and the river glittered and flashed as some winding column of a steel-clad host.

Men were already gathered round the shepherd's house and the buchts, and down the hill from all the boundaries of the glen sheep were streaming for inspection, valuation, and final sale.

Duncan closed in on Johnnie, and they bunched the sheep together. It was a poor-looking flock they drove, with a thin crop of lambs for the number of ewes, and of the lambs many were evidently motherless by the dryness of their ragged wool, their pinched chests, and out-blown bellies, too early filled with a diet of grass. Two ewes were trembling despite the lateness of the season, and fell over at intervals among the rough heather, to lie there with spasmodic kicking until once more lifted to their feet.

' They're looking bad the year,' Duncan said.

' Aye,' Johnnie agreed, ' worse nor usual.

There's no saying what death there's been here
the last couple o' months, with the wind in the
east and a new herd in the place. Alicky used to
keep the ewes off the worst trembling bits until the
grass was well up, but the new man wouldn't be
knowing about thon. Aye, Duncan boy, they're
looking real bad.'

The Macintyres and Mackenzie joined them at the
foot of the hill with the sheep they had gathered. As
the flock increased in size, so much greater the confusion grew. Ewes left the van to come baaing in
search of their lambs, and lambs with frantic bleating
broke past the dogs in a frenzied effort to regain
their dams. Progress was pitifully slow across the
moss-grown bridge. The sheep could not be
hurried for fear of jostling a weakly lamb into the
black and swollen waters of the Druid river, and the
ewes, when safely across, would double in their
tracks and try to regain the bridge. At last the
bleating throng were safely over and streaming
across the short grass to the buchts. There were all
too many willing hands to help in their penning.
The shouting, the barking, and the clamour of unknown voices reminded Duncan of Cranok sale.
But there was an air of jovial holiday-making at the
sheep delivery which was absent from the auction
mart.

Only the factor and the Commission's repre-
sentative were directly interested in the sale, the
twoscore neighbours and onlookers were there for
friendly talk, a quiet dram together at the joint
expense of seller and buyer, some frank comments
on the valuator's judgment and the Glendruid sheep.
The herds from adjacent grazings, however, were

present for the special purpose of rescuing strayed members of their flocks from the wholesale delivery. They would have opportunity of examining the sheep as they ran through the narrow wooden race, of claiming and identifying them by the special ear-marks and horn brandings legally registered for each grazing. It was their last opportunity, for after the sheep were delivered and painted with a red band on the horn they became the buyer's property.

The Glendarroch contingent penned their gather-ing of the Glendruid sheep with sober expedition, but there was all the fun of the fair among the crowd who followed the sheep from the Lochend side of Glendruid glen. Half a score of men were shouting together, and some twenty dogs chasing a single ewe like hounds in a stag's pursuit. Two men held a wide white sheet between them to restrain the leap-ing lambs that ventured an escape. It seemed that they were already half-drunk, for they kept tripping over the cloth they carried, shouting with wild laughter. An old red-bearded man hurled his knotted stick into the flying pack of ill-disciplined dogs, and the beast that was struck turned snarling on its neighbour. Other dogs joined in. Soon the glen was hideous with the worrying clamour of fighting curs. From all directions herds' dogs bounded to join in the fray, and the savage brutes were at each other with bared fangs and gaping red throats, their neck hair rising in bristling collars of unconscious defence. From the wrestling mass a black head rose, splashed with spurting blood. Somewhere in the midst a dog yelped as though burnt with fire.

Duncan and Johnnie and Mackenzie were hold-

ing in their dogs and bitches with anxious faces and
aching arms, but the Macintyres had chains in their
pockets and lashed theirs to the bucht rails.   Then
they advanced together to the fight, faces expressionless, jaws jutting, proud in their strength.   They
strode fearlessly among the squirming mass of
canine ferocity, and Duncan, breathlessly admiring,
witnessed a gallant scene.   The Macintyre men
caught dogs by the scruff of the neck, or the end of
the tail, and flung them clear of the struggling mass
with effortless ease.   The beasts came tumbling
through the air like thistledown, and ran whining to
their masters' feet, blood running from their ears or
throats.   In a minute the fight was over, the glen
quiet, and the Macintyres walking in solid silence
back to the buchts.

' They're hardy, Duncan boy ! ' Johnnie exclaimed.

'Aye, they are that ! ' said Duncan.   He was to
walk just a little like the Macintyre men until the end
of a bustling day.

When the sheep were all gathered, the inspection
began.   Johnnie and Duncan, the Macintyres and
three other herds from neighbouring grazings to the
south of Glendruid leant over the slatted race to
watch the sheep stream through.

' Now, Duncan boy,' Johnnie warned, ' you keep
a look-out for the Glendarroch marks—eill stob
on near ear, two notches below on the far ear, a C
on the near horn.   Give a cry if you see a sheep
of ours.'

Duncan's eyes were sore and his head swimming
before the last of the twenty and odd score Glendruid ewes were through the race.   He had hoped to

spot a sheep that his father missed, but Johnnie's
eyes were keen and trained through long years to
quick recognition of lug-marks and brands on horns.
None of the four Glendarroch stragglers escaped
his eye. Between the Macintyres and Glendarroch
there were seven ewes recovered and left unpainted
on the horn.

Duncan met the new herd, a young green lad at
his first herding, Gillespie by name, and asked what
sort of a lambing there had been in Glendruid.
Gillespie stretched his long limbs and yawned, and a
sullen cloud passed over his cheeky face. ' Lambing ! ' he exclaimed, in a queer nasal intonation.
' There's no lambing here at all, boy. It's just death
and nothing but death in this damn coal-pit o' a
place. I wouldna bide here another term though I
was paid for it, and I'm telling you, boy, there's no
pay in a herd's job worth a damn. I'm through wi'
the sheep now my time's up here.'

' An' what will you be doing then, boy ? ' asked
Duncan, staring round-eyed at the strange, foul-
mouthed, cigarette-smoking youth who wished to
be through with the sheep.

' The army for me, boy,' Gillespie boasted.
' Wear the kilt and have the lassies running after it.'

Duncan turned away. He had little use for a
shepherd without interest in sheep, and there was a
vulgarity about Gillespie which was strange to the
hills.

There was meat and drink for everyone in the
shepherd's cottage at Glendruid that day, and the
fun would have been high had Alicky been there to
lead it on. But all those who had known the little
man were sad at his absence. As Johnnie said on the

way home, it had been more like a funeral than a sheep delivery.

Duncan tramped back to Glendarroch with his companions of the morning, and they all turned again to take a last look at Glendruid. The Forestry Commission were to run a sheep-proof fence right along the skyline to protect the young trees, so that not even the pursuit of a strayed tup would lead a herd down to the empty glen.

'They're to put a keeper on to kill down the rabbits and white hares,' Johnnie said. ' I'm thinking he'll find a few sheep's horns among the brackens.'

'Aye,' sighed Mackenzie, ' there must have been an awful death there the year. Thon boy Gillespie knows his job all right, if he'd have put his mind to it. But they were saying he's been that taken up wi' a lassie in Lochend that he's seen more of her nor of the sheep. Did ye ever see such a lot o' pining beasts, Johnnie Gillies, to have made seventy-eight shillings for a ewe and her lamb ? '

Bob Macintyre had been making mental calculations. ' They canna make less than a thousand pounds loss when they come to sell in the back-end,' he said.

Duncan let them all talk away. He wasn't really listening to what they said. Their words fell on his ears like a meaningless drone. His were queer thoughts for a young boy. He was thinking what an easy job the keeper would have when it came to the killing of winter white hares. If what little Alicky Mag had said was true, then they would come dancing from the peat-hags whenever the cottage door was opened, and clean their faces in the sunlight

—waiting for a fiddle to play. But perhaps they knew Alicky was gone and would dance across to Strathord on a moonlit night, to the strange woman there, who would love the warm white softness of their fur.

XIX

The letter came to Glendarroch on a Monday morning in July. Mary was out, waiting for the postman, with Johnnie's old raincoat over her head because of a heavy thunder-shower. The postman gave it her with questioning glance, because the address was in strange handwriting, and the envelope of a fine texture rarely seen in the glen. Mary took it with anxious haste, thinking it must be some further official warning of the truancy and misdeeds of her boys. She was thankful that the address was in fine upright handwriting, and not the impersonal typescript of authority. She took a glance through the birches by the burn to make sure Jean was still safely at play and had not fallen into the pool, then hurried to the cottage, where wee Hugh wailed from the dilapidated pram. After stoking the fire she rocked the pram until Hugh was quiet, ere sitting down wearily on the green arm-chair to read the strange letter which the post had brought.

Her ragged nails were black against the envelope as she tore it open, to unfold the firm sheet with the embossed address in its right-hand corner. She read slowly, spelling out the more difficult words. The letter was from 43 Drumortin Gardens, Auldtown, and it brought death to the hidden hope which had kept Mary's heart alive.

'My dear Mrs Gillies,' she read, 'I am writing to ask a great thing of you. My only child, Jack, was killed three months ago in an aeroplane accident. He was unmarried, so that his death has left me a lonely old woman. My niece, Anne Winterton, has been living with me lately, but she is soon to be married. It is she who has told me of Jack's son and yours, for I knew nothing of it before. She has told me what a splendid boy your Duncan is. I want you to allow Duncan to come and live with me. I know how you will hate to lose him, but my niece tells me you have other children. I think it would be a splendid thing for Duncan. I can easily afford to give him the best possible education, which will allow him to take his true place as his father's son. I shall be very good to him, for my niece tells me he is so like Jack, and I feel that I love him already. Of course he would often come to see you; he could stay with you on many of his holidays if you wished it. I am sure that this is a great opportunity for your boy, and I am sure you would not wish him to waste himself.

Please think it over well, and then let me know. Yours very sincerely,

ELIZABETH KNIGHT.'

He was dead! He was dead!

That was all Mary could think of as she stared blindly before her, the white sheet and envelope fallen to the floor. Nothing else mattered now that hope had gone from her life and the world was grey.

She had always thought that in some magical, mystical way, her love must win through, that somehow, somewhere, if only in dreams, Jack would come smiling and lift her into his arms. If ever he had come again, she knew she could not have gone to him because of Johnnie and the bairns. Yet

to have loved a man for fourteen years—to have seen him but once—and then that he should die !

Mary closed her eyes in weary sorrow. A painting as of happiness grew amid the sadness of her mind—a picture of something splendidly alive come newly in from a world of death, of a smile with the warm brilliance of a summer sun, of a voice with the age-old music of the rivers and hills.

It seemed that the July day grew suddenly cold, that the hushed expectancy of thunder turned to whipping winds of winter storm. She opened her eyes, and the room was lamplit and in shadow. The door swung open and the wind screamed in ; flakes of snow drifted to the kitchen's ceiling. He came to her, white powder on brown and tangled hair, melting snow on long lashes over bold grey eyes, skin smooth as the down on a pigeon's breast, throat and limbs with the graceful strength of sapling trees. His eyes rested on her, a caress, a kiss, in their soundless song.

The wind sighed through trees beside the burn. Rain pattered on the frozen surface of the drifts. Snow crashed in thunder from the laden roof. A quick thaw—and was that someone stealing through the darkness of her room ? Would her heart beat quietly that she might listen ! Was it he—the dear brave lad—blood swiftly throbbing to his milk-white throat ? Was it he with cheek smoother than the softest silk, and lips that drew all life from her body to his own ? Was it he, or just the dead ash settling in the fire ? Oh God ! What was she thinking of ? He was dead, dead—the bold grey eyes had seen their last adventure.

Mary staggered to her feet, wiping her face in

child-like movement with her hand. She blinked because of the bright sunshine which followed the summer storm and streamed in dancing sunbeams through the open cottage door.

Johnnie Gillies stood by the wee window, the letter in his hand. He turned quickly when he heard her move, and his face was twisted in anxiety. 'Aye, Mary,' he said, 'I doubt you cried yoursel' to sleep.'

She rubbed her eyes in a dazed way. 'Johnnie,' she said, 'he's dead.'

Little Johnnie Gillies lost his temper with her. It was the first time since their marriage. 'Aye,' he cried bitterly, 'he's dead, and so it's no matter to you that wee Jean's been near drowned in the burn and near frightened to death wi' the thunder. I've put the lassie to her bed. No! your man and your bairns'll no' be counting much now that *he's* dead. God knows what good he ever did ye when he lived! I'm thinkin' ye've been half-dead yersel' from the day he left ye. An' on top o' that, his mother's wantin' to take Duncan from us and turn him into some kind o' a gentleman that'll no' look us in the face. What did he or she ever do for Duncan that I've not done for him? Can ye tell me that, Mary? Can ye tell me that?'

She shielded her face with her hands. 'Och! Johnnie,' she sobbed, 'dinna be that hard on me. I didna cheat ye when I married ye. Ye'll mind on that, Johnnie?'

Tender sorrow chased the anger from his face, the bitter reproaches from his lips. He came to her and laid his hands on her bowed shoulders, brushing her uncombed hair with his rugged cheek. 'I

shouldna have said thon to ye, Mary,' he whispered.
' You've been a good wife to me and a good mother
to the bairns all these years. If there was other
things in your mind, Mary lassie, that was no fault
of yours. There's none of us can just manage our
hearts to suit our heids. Away ben to wee Jean,
Mary—I've made a fair boorach of her clothes.'

She kissed him in a way she had not done for
years. ' Johnnie,' she said, ' you mind what I said
to ye that night you were asking me to marry you ?
It was true, Johnnie, what I said to you then.'

She hurried away to wee Jean, and he whistled a
tune to himself as he gazed out on a rain-soaked
world, which flashed a million diamond points to a
summer sun.

That night, when all the children were in bed
and the brief northern night had fallen, Mary and
Johnnie sat before the kitchen range, reading and
re-reading the letter. They were very tender to
each other, allowing their hands to linger when they
touched, caressing with the kindness of their eyes.
There was no passion in their voices, neither of
anger nor of love—just the quiet sympathy of old
companions.

' I canna think of Duncan leaving,' Johnnie said.
' He's aye been the life of the place since ever he
started to toddle about it. He's a fine boy, Mary,
and the pride of us all. He wouldna like to start
his schooling all over again, now that he's near done
wi' it. His mind's set on the sheep, Mary, and I
wouldna like to think o' him boxed up in one o'
thae great schools, wi' a top hat or some such
rubbish on his head, and the hills and the herding
in his heart. I'm no' eddicated mysel', but I'm

thinkin' it would be making a kind o' fool o' the laddie to take him away from the man's job he's set on and treat him like a bairn all over again. I wouldna like to think o' Duncan all dressed up like one o' thae dummies in Macgillivray's shop-window in Lochend.'

Mary listened patiently to everything he said, nodding her head when she agreed. But there was much of Johnnie's talk with which she could not agree. 'It's no' me that's wanting Duncan away from us,' she said. 'I needna tell ye that, Johnnie.' He nodded. 'But Duncan's just a laddie yet,' she went on. 'He canna just know right what he's wanting to do wi' his life. He's seen that little o' the world, Johnnie. It's all the sheep wi' him because there's nothing else he's seen. But he might be thinking different when he's a grown man. I wouldna like him to think we'd stood in his way, Johnnie. He'd never blame us. Duncan's no' that kind. But he might give us a look one night, Johnnie, when we were old folks sitting by the fire. I wouldna like to see blame in his eyes, though he'd never speak against us wi' his tongue.'

'Well, Mary, we might just ask him what he's for himself.'

'I doubt we know his answer wi'out asking, Johnnie.'

Johnnie stared into the fire for a long time, as though trying to read the riddles of life in the changing shapes of the glowing coals. Then he raised his head and spoke again. 'You're thinking that Duncan should go, Mary?'

'Aye,' she answered, 'and I'll be telling you why, Johnnie. There's a lot in breeding, Johnnie.

Ye canna deny that after all ye've said about the Glendarroch tups my father used. I'm thinking that, though Duncan seems to be one of oursel's, he's just no' that at all. I'm thinking that when he's a grown man he'll be wanting more than a hill herding for his job and a herd's lassie for his wife. I'm thinking too, Johnnie, and you'll no' be angered at me saying it—I'm thinking that him—him that's dead wouldna just like his boy to grow up wi'out manners nor learning.'

' Then he should have done something about it when he was alive,' Johnnie growled.

' He offered, Johnnie,' she said. ' It was on a day after a shoot here, when Duncan would be eight years old. He came up the glen in his car that day. He told me then that he'd no notion a bairn had been born. He was for doing something for Duncan after all those years, and I wouldna let him.'

' Why did ye no' tell me o' that before, Mary ? An' what was it he came for, Mary Gillies ? ' There was jealous anger in Johnnie's eyes.

' No ! no ! Johnnie,' she cried. ' It wasna for that he came at all. We did no more than speak for a minute or two. Indeed, there would have been nothing more he was wanting after the long years. I didna tell ye, Johnnie, and I wouldna let him see Duncan then. It's kind o' easier for me now—now that he's dead.'

' And now ye'd like to turn Duncan into something like his father, Mary ? '

' Dinna say that, Johnnie ; dinna say that ! '

' I'm no' sneering at him that's dead, Mary. But I'm askin' ye what kind o' a man was this

Mr Knight? I never clapt eyes on him mysel', but from what I've heard he'd have been like the other gentlemen. And what do the gentlemen do? When they've a minute to themselves they're out on the hills wi' a gun and a dog, or wi' a rod beside the burns. The worse the weather and the harder the going the better pleased they are. If a gentleman can fish and shoot an' keep the belly off him, there's no' much more he's wanting to do except maybe to ride a horse. I'm telling ye, Mary, that if there's gentry's blood in Duncan it'll no' be turned by a herd's life. There's no' that much difference between a gentleman and a herd. There's more between either of the two of them and a shopkeeper in Lochend.'

'Aye, Johnnie,' Mary smiled, 'that's maybe true enough what you're saying. But there's an awful difference between doing a thing because you're wanting to do it an' the doing of the same thing for your daily bread. If Duncan was to be going to Auldtown, there'd be nothing to hinder him shooting and fishing on the hills. It's likely he'd have that much money he'd no' need to work at all.'

'Folks are no' like thon,' Johnnie argued. 'The more money they've got the more they're needing, and the gentlemen are no' idle bodies like they once was. There's none of them but does something for a living, if it's no more than to go and get theirselves killed.'

Mary sighed and stirred restlessly in her chair. 'I'd like fine for Duncan to be a gentleman,' she said.

'Aye, now we're getting at it,' Johnnie grunted. 'I see your mind's set on the boy going, Mary.

You're like all the women. You'll break your heart at Duncan's going, and likely break his, and all just to see the boy dressed up in London clothes, and speaking in a voice would make you think his neighbours were deaf. I dinna see the sense o' it mysel'.'

Mary was stubborn in her conviction. 'It'll maybe break my heart to see him go,' she confessed, 'but it wouldna be right to hold him back. Duncan's no' bred like the rest of us, Johnnie. Och! I'm no' thinking he's better nor the other bairns, nor better nor you, Johnnie. He's just no' the same, for he couldna be that.'

Johnnie rose slowly from his chair. His eyes were full of patient resignation and dumb sorrow. 'I'll say no more, Mary,' he sighed. 'I see your mind's made up. It's no' for me to stand against you. The boy's no' mine, though I've been a father to him.'

'Then ye'll make him go, Johnnie?'

'Me?'

'Aye! you, Johnnie. He doesna heed what I'm saying to him. If you ask him to go—he'll go.'

For a minute it seemed that Johnnie would grow angry again. His eyes flashed, and his mouth twisted as though holding back hot words. He clenched his fists until the knuckles showed white beneath their skin.

'You're asking a lot of me, Mary,' he said, 'but I'll do it the once for your sake, Mary. I'll do it the once—and no more.'

PART THREE

DUNCAN ALONE

I

IT was the late afternoon of a September day. The train steamed between the dreary tenement houses into the echoing vault of Auldtown station. Dirty smoke and a haze lay over everything.

Duncan wished he could grow invisible and be hidden from all the strange faces that would so soon surround him. He hated everyone, even his father, for prevailing on him to go. He didn't want to be a gentleman if it meant living among houses and noisy people. The thought of years of school and study was hell to him. He would never know what the Glendarroch lambs had made at Cranok until a letter told him. He wouldn't see the hoggs go away to their wintering ground. He was home-sick before he had well left home.

The carriage slid slowly to rest past the line of porters, relatives, and friends. Duncan pulled his suit-case from the rack—a neat new suit-case bought with his grandmother's money. He rubbed the dust from the grey overcoat and ready-made blue serge suit purchased on his grandmother's credit at Macgillivray's shop in Lochend. He pulled his grey cloth cap to an independent angle and stared out through the open window in search of Miss Anne Winterton, who was to meet him there.

It was like looking for a Glendarroch ewe at the Glendruid delivery. There was such a sea of faces, such a bustle of porters and slamming of doors. In

the end it was Miss Winterton who found Duncan Gillies, standing, a forlorn and lonely figure, with his suit-case by his side.   He saw her coming towards him, tall, confident, in brown tailor-made tweeds, swinging long legs with athletic grace.   He noticed how white her teeth looked in her brown face when she smiled.

' Hallo! Duncan,' she cried.   ' You've got safely here ? '

' Aye,' he grumbled, and made a fumbling gesture towards his cap.

' Where is your trunk, Duncan ? '

He pointed dumbly to his suit-case.

Miss Winterton engaged a passing porter to carry the scanty luggage.   She led the way to the platform barriers and waiting taxis beyond.   Duncan gave up his ticket, glad to see it safely delivered after the recurring terror of its loss.   He stood beside a taxi, a little behind Miss Winterton, while the porter heaved the suit-case up beside the driver.   After a swift passage of orders and silver coin, Miss Winterton climbed into the vibrating car, with Duncan, like an obedient dog, close behind her swinging skirt.

The smoke and the station vanished together. Auldtown offered the princely welcome of a spacious street and castle-crowned precipice amid the sunlit glamour of a cloudless sky.   Duncan watched the hurrying throng of gaily dressed women and sombre men, the speeding cars, the lumbering buses and trams, the athletic hatless men and humanity's twisted wrecks.   Beside him Miss Winterton seemed unaware of the marvellous stir and incongruity of a city's streets.   She shot out remarks in a clear loud

voice, and gazed straight into his eyes in a most dis-
concerting way. Her hair was so perfectly arranged
beneath the small brown hat. Waves of it rested as
though sculptured above her beautifully curved ears,
and the colour of it was black with a purple sheen
like a raven's wing. Her eyebrows were so strangely
perfect in their outline, drawn high above peat-
brown laughing eyes, and her smiling mouth red as
the haws on an autumn briar. Her skin was so
satiny and yet so brown, except when she raised her
head to laugh, showing it soft and white in the
hidden curves of her throat. Duncan scarcely
noticed the words she said to break shy silence ; he
watched the way her lips moved over ivory teeth.
He was fascinated to the verge of adoration.

The car left the broad street between ancient
castle and modern shops to turn uphill past houses
of massive dreariness and unwashed statues of
absurd celebrities. It swung left-handed into a
solemn circle of brooding masonry. A railed-in
patch of soiled vegetation was at its centre—a mock
oasis in an urban desert.

'This,' said Miss Winterton, 'is Drumortin
Gardens.'

The taxi screeched to rest before a flight of broad
stone steps. Duncan stepped to the greasy pavement beside his guide. A gentleman passed, tall,
straight, slim, and correctly dressed in funereal black,
wearing a bowler hat, carrying a furled umbrella.
His reserved and elderly face made a half-hearted effort
to break its reserve. The lips above a grey moustache
moved in simulation of a smile. 'That is Dr Mansfield, the specialist,' said Miss Winterton to Duncan,
who knew neither Mansfield nor his speciality.

'Shall we go in?' smiled Miss Winterton. 'The man will see to your box.'

Duncan accompanied her up the stone steps. He would have followed those peat-brown eyes to heaven or to hell. The door opened in answer to the clanging bell—a capped and aproned maid with honest country face bowed a permission to enter—smiled a respectful welcome. Her reddened hands and work-moulded body reminded Duncan of his mother, or of what his mother might have been when pretty and still young.

Hushed stillness and peaceful dignity filled the dusky interior of a linoleum-covered hall. Pegs for coats and hats lined its right-hand side; it faded in the background to the massive doors shielding the kitchen premises and servants' quarters, as though both servants and cooking were a little obscene. A broad staircase with low banister led to a grand-father clock ticking out the time, its pendulum swinging with the inevitability of fate. An old lady stepped from a hidden landing to the head of the stairs, and Duncan saw Mrs Knight for the first time.

He knew at once that there was something very beautiful in her setting and in her self, standing at the head of the stairs as though carved in living stone. His impression was of a picture—of some-body not quite real, of a tall fragile lady with snow-white hair and in a plain black dress, with one delicate hand resting light as gossamer on a polished banister of oak. He looked up, and by some strange instinct removed his cap, stood for a moment bare-headed and grave, then smiled in frank pleasure at a work of social art.

The old lady spoke in a voice that seemed too strong for the frail body which held it, and there was surprised gladness in her tone. ' Yes, Anne,' she said ; ' he is Jack all over again.'

Duncan went up to her and shook hands shyly, saying nothing.

' We are so glad that you have come to us, Duncan,' she said.

He didn't know how to answer. Should he call her ' Mum,' as though she were his school-mistress ? He thought not, for she was so very unlike Miss Gray. Deserted by words, he repeated his shy smile, glad when the taxi-man breathed heavily upstairs with the case on his shoulder, followed by the maid who would see to its safe bestowal.

' Perhaps Duncan might go up with Jean to see his room ? ' Miss Winterton suggested.

' Yes,' Mrs Knight agreed, ' I am sure he would like to wash after his journey.'

Duncan stared, and Miss Winterton smiled. ' This way, sir,' the maid said, leading him up a farther flight of stairs to the landing above. The taxi-man met them at the door of a blue distempered room, and gazed in some astonishment at Duncan. ' This will be your room, sir,' said the maid. ' And the bathroom is next door on your right.'

Duncan inspected the room where he would sleep. The blue carpet was the softest thing he had ever stepped on in a house ; it was like the short green grass by the buchts at home. There was something unfriendly in the narrow single bed with its white coverlet and smooth arrangement. Some-how it recalled Hugh's death and the hushed terror

of the room where his still body had lain.   But the electric light was a fascinating discovery.

Duncan noticed the little shining buttons on the wall, and when he examined them found how easily they moved.   When the room was flooded with soft light he thought some accident had occurred, that he had done something awkward and silly, as he had dreaded to do.   He wondered whether he should call over the banister to tell what he had done, but returned instead to the shining button. He found that he could turn off the light, then spent a delightful minute in the sheer pleasure of making it go off and on.

The tall wardrobe was another discovery.   The grain of its polished doors was twisted and whorled in fascinating pattern, and when they were opened displayed shining mirrors in which Duncan could see the whole blue-clad length of himself from top of a tousled head to tip of a polished shoe.

A picture was hung above the bed—a picture of flower-clad slopes leading to snow-clad mountains. It seemed to Duncan an unnatural medley, as though the artist had taken strange liberties with place and season, implanting a nurseryman's summer garden in the midst of a corrie gripped in winter's ice.   He thought the colours were bonnie, but the subject daft.

The view from the window was depressingly drab.   It looked on to twisted leaden pipes, climbing like diseased ivy over the faded backs of houses past their prime.   A strip of sooted ground lay between, ground which, planned as gardens, had become what cats and smoke had made of it. Distant rumble of traffic penetrated the seclusion

of the residential quarter; some maid sang jazz and rattled pails in a basement area. The rectangular patch of sky glowed in the evening's pale light, a white cloud drifting across it like a wild thing revelling in freedom.

Duncan left the window to investigate the bathroom, which lay next door. He had heard and read of such things—a man once murdered wives in a bath—but the actuality was new. The glittering metal and white enamel, the shining mirrors and labelled taps, surprised him into admiration. It was real pleasure to turn the taps. Hot water actually issued from the tap called 'Hot,' and cold from that called 'Cold.' It was all very thrilling, and full of social pitfalls into which he might absurdly fall.

Anne Winterton surprised him in his explorations. She was dressed in a kimono of brilliant colouring and strange device. 'Hallo, Duncan!' she exclaimed. 'You here?'

'Aye.'

'Have you washed yet?'

'No.'

'Then what are you doing with the taps?'

'Seeing how they work.'

She laughed, filling the room with rare music. 'Hurry up and finish, then, won't you? I want to wash, if you don't.'

Duncan hastened to withdraw.

'Come here, Duncan,' she smiled. 'You'll *have* to wash your face and hands. They really are dirty. Look! You put this gadget in the hole in the washbasin, then you turn the taps on. You use this thing called a nail-brush, and there's the soap. I'll

give you five minutes to get clean, and then I'll come back.'

Her departure left Duncan offended. Her eyes might have the brown depths of a salmon-pool, her hair the sheen of a raven's wing, her teeth the whiteness of fresh-fallen snow, but she had talked to him as though he were a naughty bairn, and she Miss Gray. She had lectured him as though he were wee Johnnie or Jean. He could not easily forgive a thing like that—but he washed his hands. Then he slunk like a whipped, dispirited dog to the imprisonment of his bedroom. He stayed there until the maid, smiling in a friendly way, told him that dinner was served. A queer time of day, he thought, for folks to be having their dinner.

He found the two ladies awaiting him at the dining-room door, both dressed in black dresses which covered their feet yet left their arms and shoulders bare. He was disappointed in Mrs Knight, thinking she had looked so very much nicer in her other dress. Her parchment skin looked dead, her arm bones stranded by their ageing flesh as ribs of a wrecked ship are stripped by battering waves. Her shoulders lacked the merciful concealment of her clothes. How different from Miss Winterton, whose dress revealed the slim lines of muscled youth, and skin magnetic in vitality and health.

'We've been waiting for you, Duncan,' said Mrs Knight, and when she moved he knew that only the shell of her had died. With such superb dignity did she sweep through the door to her place at the head of the glittering table, ignoring the presence of the maid as though souls who served were furniture,

holding herself erect in stern contempt of crippling age. 'Will you sit there, Duncan?' she said, pointing to a terrifying array of cutlery, napery, and glass.

Duncan sat down. He wondered what kind of a meal this was, which, begun with the ceremony of a sacrament, might well end in his sacrifice to shame. He was directly opposite Miss Winterton, and her laughing eyes gave comfort. 'I believe you were too frightened to come down, Duncan,' she teased.

He blushed, lowering his eyes to the snowy whiteness of the table-cloth.

'You mustn't be shy, Duncan,' said Mrs Knight. 'We are so delighted to have you here, and we don't expect you to know everything.'

Duncan thought there must be a great deal to know, and vaguely wondered why it was so important. There seemed to be such extraordinary fuss over serving a bowl of soup. His scrubbed fingers wandered hesitatingly above the spoons, knives, and forks, in wild terror of using some culinary implement inappropriate to the simple task before him. He decided to watch Miss Winterton's procedure, and, by doing so in every detail, attained the grateful triumph of the meal's conclusion.

They returned to the lounge, to spacious width and a lofty ceiling, shaded lights and dim glimmer of old silver. Blue curtains excluded the window's alcove and the mild night air; pine-wood crackled and blazed on a tiled and open hearth. The grey carpet had the silent softness of an animal's fur—the very stillness of the air held privacy of privilege and dignity of age. From the stairs came the heavy tick of the grandfather clock.

Duncan sank down in a chintz-covered chair between the two ladies and before the leaping fire. Miss Winterton smoked a cigarette, and Duncan found pleasure in watching the graceful movements of her drooping arm and the lazy drift of the rising smoke.

Mrs Knight asked a question which brought ghosts stealing to the room. ' Would you like to see photographs of your father, Duncan ? ' she inquired.

He nodded his fair head.

She rose, and he noticed the stifled twitch of pain on her powdered face when she forced herself erect. She sailed in majestic rustling of expensive cloth to her private cabinet beside the fire. From it she drew a sheaf of fading photographs, handing them to Duncan with sadness in her smile. He examined them slowly, one by one, while the ladies read their books.

Was that, then, really his father—that solemn-faced boy in a white suit and a cap like thon sailors wore ? Or this—the lad in nothing but shirt and pants, holding a cup in his hands ? Yes, he would have won that jumping or running or something, like the folks did in the daily paper.—This one, all in white, would have been him playing cricket, likely, when he was at school. Aye ! That was a bonnie horse he was riding, and a fine figure of a lad he looked in his breeches and with a white clout round his neck.—Aye ! he could hold a gun, and it must have been a high shot he was taking with his gun right back on his shoulder like thon !—Here was just the head and shoulders of him, his head half-turned and a smile about his face. His father had been a bonnie gentleman indeed.—This one would

be him in Highland dress, with the kilt and plaid, the cocked bonnet and a crook no manner of use in catching a sheep.—There he was beside his aeroplane, all padded in leather and fur, drawing on gloves with a kind of stern look on his face.

Duncan laid the photographs down on the arm of the chair, and for a long time gazed into the leaping flames of the pine-wood fire. It seemed to him that it was kind of queer that this gentleman—this Mr Knight—should have had anything to do with his mother, with Glendarroch, or with himself. He did not think he was anything like that gentleman, except maybe in the face. Would he care for a life like thon?

It would be a fine thing to ride over the fields on a horse's back, though he didn't much care for the shooting he had seen. He didn't like the noise and blood and the broken birds. It would be fine fun to be up in an aeroplane—to leave the smoke of the towns behind—to sail up into the sky above the white clouds and flash in the sun like the flying gulls. He would like to run and win silver cups and hit a ball about a green field on a summer day. But there was nothing in all that so good as a day on the hill with Meg—as the bleating of sheep new gathered to the fanks—as the roll of the wool-sack under treading feet—as the peewees and whaups crying about his head on a morning in May—as the slow, sad tune his fiddle played.

When he raised his head he saw that Mrs Knight had laid down her book and was smiling at him. 'Would you like to play games, Duncan?' she asked.

'Yes,' he answered, for he had found 'Aye' a word unused in Drumortin Gardens.

' And shoot, and ride, and swim ? '

' Yes.'

' What would you like to do best ? ' Miss Winterton inquired.

' Fly,' he answered.

The smile faded from Mrs Knight's old face. Ghosts played around the silver candlesticks and fluttered through the silence of the room. ' You must promise me never to do that, Duncan,' Mrs Knight implored.

Duncan knew the mistake he had made. It was only five months since that gentleman—Mr Knight —had come tumbling to earth like a shot bird, to leave this old lady in sorrow and alone. It was because of that accident that he, Duncan Gillies, was sitting before a fire in Drumortin Gardens. Mrs Knight must hate all that had to do with aeroplanes or flying. He should not have mentioned the word.

There came a knock at the door. The maid, Jean, opened to ask whether she could speak to Miss Winterton.

' Yes. Please go, Anne,' said Mrs Knight.

Miss Winterton returned some minutes later, suppressed amusement in her laughing peat-brown eyes. ' Where are your pyjamas, Duncan ? ' she asked.

Duncan was covered in confusion. He had seen the striped fantastic things in Macgillivray's window in Lochend. They were something the gentry dressed up in when they went to bed. He was very angry with his mother for not having bought them for him before he left Glendarroch. Now he was faced with exposure and public shame, with the sneering surprise of gentlefolks who must

make an important ceremony of everything, even of going to bed.

'Where are they, Duncan?' Miss Winterton repeated. 'Jean can't find them anywhere.'

'I've none,' he stammered.

Miss Winterton frankly laughed. 'What on earth do you sleep in, Duncan?' she asked. 'Your birthday suit?'

'My shirt,' he blushed.

She laughed again, and advancing towards him, she ruffled his hair. 'Little savage,' she said. 'We must buy pyjamas for you to-morrow.'

Duncan hated to be laughed at. His face was crimson and his eyes flashed fire. Yet what a cool touch her white hand held! It was like the caressing wind of a summer evening playing soft music in his hair.

'I think you should go to bed now, Duncan,' said Mrs Knight. 'You must be tired after your long journey. You remember the way to your room?'

He nodded agreement, pleased that the long and difficult day had come to its end. Mrs Knight came to him and kissed him on the brow. He felt a strange tremor in her dry, cold lips. 'Good-night, Duncan,' she whispered. 'I am so glad that you have come.' Miss Winterton clasped his hand in a friendly grip, and gave him a friendly smile.

He climbed wearily and alone to the solitude of his bedroom. His feet made no sound on the thick stair-carpet. The room was in darkness, and he fumbled awkwardly until the switch was found. Then soft light flooded blue walls and polished furniture of brown. The white coverlet had been

removed, and the smooth sheets turned backwards on the bed.

Duncan undressed quickly, turned off the light, and slid beneath the blankets. He found the big room eerie, missing the drowsy movements of wee Johnnie by his side. He lay awake for a long time, listening to the muffled sounds of distant traffic, the rumble of maids gossiping, the shrill serenade of cats. He was miserable, more so than he had ever been in the fourteen years of his life. Hot tears welled into his eyes. He forced himself to keep from crying by remembrance of the hardy things he had done in his time—how he had struck the butcher with his bag—how he had run out to fight with a poker in his hand the night sheep-stealers came to Glendarroch. He recalled the struggle across the Corrie to Strathord on a day of lashing rain. But memories brought more sadness and no comfort. On this, his first night away from those he knew, he cried himself to sleep, burying his face in the pillow so that none should hear.

In his dreams, the screech of cats was the screaming of young hares caught in strangling snares, the rumble of traffic the music of the whispering burn trickling through shallow pools on an August night, the muffled voices those of Johnnie and Mary talking late together in the kitchen at home. As he dreamt of old familiar things, a smile spread over his sleeping face.

II

Daylight and early morning found Duncan awake, but the house still sleeping. Raindrops were on

the window-panes, and the light waxed and waned as clouds drifted over the rising sun.

When he opened his eyes Duncan wondered for a moment where he was, the bed and room and furniture were all so strange. Then he remembered, surprised at his misery of the night before. Nothing seemed quite so difficult or disheartening when the sun was up, and Miss Winterton was indeed a bonnie lady.

Duncan sprang from bed, his bare feet sinking deep in the soft blue carpet. He crossed to the window and threw open the lower sash to drink in the summer air and to hear the first faint stir of an awakening town. Sparrows twittered on the rones above his head, and the pleasant company of birds brought melody to his lips. He whistled the fine old dance tune, ' Jenny, catch your skirts up,' and a maid newly come from the country, cleaning boots in the basement below, looked up and laughed when she heard the familiar air.

Confused to find himself observed, Duncan drew in his head and closed the window, which slid upwards and downwards with such astounding ease. He dressed himself carelessly, licking his hands before the glass, then smoothing his rumpled hair, listening all the time to a buzzing on the landing outside, a rhythmical drone as though a bike of bumble-bees was loosed. Opening the door very carefully, he saw yet another maid, a sallow, dark-haired girl, running a thing like a blacksmith's bellows backwards and forwards across the carpet. She looked up surprised when she saw Duncan peering out. The humming grew faint and the tick of the grandfather clock became audible again.

' What time will it be ? ' Duncan asked.

The maid squinted over the banisters.   ' Six minutes past seven, sir.'

' And when will breakfast be ? '

' Nine o'clock, sir.'

' Eh ? '

' Nine o'clock, sir.'

' I'm hungry.'

' I can get you something cold, sir. What would you like ? I think I could get some ham and tongue and bread and butter.'

' Thanks,' said Duncan.

He paced the room like a prisoner, unable to sleep, afraid to go downstairs, waiting in impatient hunger to see what the maid would bring. It seemed an unconscionable time before she reappeared with well-filled dishes on a silver tray. He took them from her at the door, unwilling to let a stranger disturb the private sanctuary of his room. She smiled in a friendly way when she left him, so that he thought her a nice lassie, though not very bonnie at all. Pacing the room and munching sandwiches prepared to his order, Duncan passed a pleasant five minutes, leaving him one hour and fifty minutes of unwanted leisure to digest his food.

He was thankful to hear the deep boom of a gong sound through the house. Having heard a similar signal in Cranok hotel, he knew that it heralded food, permitting descent to the dining-room, and making him feel terribly shy.

There was no one in the dining-room. Steaming dishes and bubbling pans were on the wide sideboard, with little spirit-lamps underneath to keep them warm. Pleasant odours of bacon, eggs, and

coffee scented the room. Two places were set on the snowy table-cloth.

Duncan wandered about the room, examining the etchings hung on the stone-grey wall. He liked one depicting a flight of duck rising through winter mist from a reed-grown swamp. There was more life there than in the pictures of drab slum houses and flapping lines of sooted clothes. He paused at the wide windows with their view of pavement still shining wet from rain, and of the dead green of late summer foliage in the central and circular garden. He was turning away, when the urgent sound of swiftly trotting horses brought him hurrying back.

They stopped before the door—Miss Winterton, a graceful willow-tree in breeches and man's tweed jacket, on a light-boned bay—a little and twisted man, raising his bowler-hat, on a restive brown. The little man gathered up the reins of the led horse and trotted out of sight round the garden; Miss Winterton bounded up the steps, a splendid colour on her glowing cheeks.

Duncan gasped when she came into the dining-room. She looked so beautiful in her close-fitting masculine clothes, with the warm flush on her skin that an evening sun lends to snow-covered hills, the brown of sunburn hidden for the moment by the bounding pulse of the blood beneath. When she smiled the shadows of the room were gone.

' Good-morning, Duncan,' she said. ' Sleep well? You shouldn't have waited for me. What would you like?' She served bacon and eggs and poured out coffee for them both. ' Aunt Elizabeth always has her breakfast in bed,' she explained. ' I'm going to get my car out, and we'll storm this fair

city in search of clothes for you. We must do justice to your looks, Duncan. We made a list last night after you had gone to bed. The very first item is—pyjamas.' She laughed, bringing music about the breakfast table of the dull town house. ' It seems a dreadful shame to imprison you in the outward and visible signs of respectability,' she said.

When breakfast was over, Duncan waited beside the new-lit fire in the chilly lounge until Miss Winterton had changed and fetched her car. Duncan found that the view from the lounge was that of the dining-room window seen from a slightly different angle. He saw the car come swinging round the garden, a little spitting wasp of a thing, all wheels, inquisitive bonnet, and barking exhaust, with scanty body-work of flashing grey.

Duncan ran downstairs, retrieved his cap from the high peg, and stumbled shyly down the stone steps to the smiling welcome of Miss Winterton. He jumped in beside her and sank nearer to the ground than in any vehicle he had ever known. He faced a glittering confusion of clocks, meters, gauges, and ash-trays. The wind-screen sloped backwards at an angle.

' Suits first,' Miss Winterton laughed. ' We shall leave the pyjamas until you have gained confidence, Duncan.'

They sped away at alarming speed. For a moment Duncan felt separated from his substantial breakfast. Then he got used to it all, revelling in the sheer joy of rapid motion and narrow escapes.

The car shot out of Drumortin Gardens and up a steep hill, past dreary houses and representations of prominent men, then downhill again to the broad

sunlit street and a view of the castle-crowned rock. The brightly dressed women and sombre men, the cars and buses and clanging trams, the beggars and cripples at the pavements' corners were just the same as on the day before. It seemed as though night, a dark curtain, had fallen and risen before a theatre scene which had gone on all the time.

The car roared and dodged through the traffic like a doubling hare. It drew up by the broad pavement, opposite a shining stretch of glass, behind which distinguished figures of wax looked scornfully indifferent in model suitings and magnificent clothes. An elderly, splendid man in uniform of silver and pale sky-blue stood, a commercial sentinel, before the swinging doors. Rainbow ribbons and polished medals blazed on his stalwart chest. He saluted the car and Miss Winterton's well-cut clothes. He stared through what shrank in Macgillivray's suit as though it were mud.

Miss Winterton sailed through the shop with confident air, her manner suggesting that everything worth having already belonged to her, and that only the vulgar and worthless were beyond her means. It was soon clear to Duncan that shop-walkers and assistants were merely dirt, despite their smart appearance, and that none would dare to make fun of Macgillivray's clothes in Miss Winterton's presence.

'I want a complete outfit for this boy,' she said. 'Here is the list.'

Duncan was taken into a small private room, made silent with curtains and bright with glass. He discovered unsuspected aspects of himself in the ubiquitous mirrors, and saw his clear-cut profile from some flattering angles. He was stripped and

prodded and poked by stooping tailors with mouthfuls of pins. He was chalked and turned about and pinched and measured until he was tired. The tape slipping up and around his legs tickled him so that he wanted to scream. One tailor cried out numbers like a mistimed minute-gun, while another echoed him back, scrawling small figures in a mystical book.

Trying-on followed, with Duncan wriggling in and out of shirts, trousers, jackets, and vests. At intervals Miss Winterton was called in to approve, disapprove, or merely comment. A barely hidden smile twitched about her lips as she scanned the transformation which clothes can make.

' That will do in the meantime,' she said, nodding to a mounting pile of underwear and ready-mades. ' I should like those sent immediately to Mrs Knight, 43 Drumortin Gardens. When will you be ready for fitting ? '

' Yes, madam—certainly, madam,' the pink-faced tailor bowed. ' Let me see, now. To-day is Tuesday. We are very busy at the moment, but we shall do our best to have them ready for fitting by Friday morning.'

' You can't do it sooner ? '

' I'm *afraid* not, madam. Friday morning.'

' Come along, Duncan,' Miss Winterton called. ' You must be fed to the teeth with this rotten business. I *loathe* shops.'

Duncan thought that was a rude thing to say before the pink-faced tailor, who seemed an agreeable, harmless man. But, evidently used to such remarks, the tailor merely smiled, showing his false teeth.

Miss Winterton led the way through the crowded

shop, past the swinging doors, to the thronged and busy street. The animated splash of uniformed colour stooped to open the door of the wasp-like car. It sped away, the top of its wind-screen level with the mud-guards of a double-decked bus.

'Tired, Duncan?' Miss Winterton asked.

'Aye—yes.'

'Well, I think we've chosen some marvellous clothes. Don't misuse them, Duncan. Don't go to bed in your dinner-jacket and come to meals in pyjamas. Only very distinguished old men are allowed to do that sort of thing.'

They stopped before a florist's, a confectioner's, a fruiterer's, and a chemist's. Duncan sat in dazed wonderment while Miss Winterton made her purchases. Then she turned the inquiring nose of the car towards home.

The brilliantly painted van of the outfitter's establishment was just leaving Drumortin Gardens when Miss Winterton drove dangerously in.

'Good!' she cried. 'They've got here before us. You have just time to change before lunch and bring pride to Aunt Elizabeth's adoring face.' She left the little car tilted by the road's camber against the pavement's side. 'Come along, Duncan,' she urged. 'I'll tell Jean to take the boxes up to your room. Put on the grey suit with the grey socks and blue shirt and tie.—Heavens!' she gasped, 'I've forgotten all about shoes. We must get them in the afternoon. Do you think you could stand it?'

Duncan wearily grinned.

He could not help admiring himself in the long mirror of the polished wardrobe. He certainly looked bonnie in the new clothes, which fitted him

so well. He felt less shy as he walked hesitatingly downstairs, in answer to the clamour of the gong announcing lunch.

Mrs Knight awaited him, with her snow-white hair and in her plain black dress, a little smile playing about the corners of her quivering mouth. ' Duncan ! ' she exclaimed, ' you look quite distinguished.' Her cold lips kissed him on the brow. Then she sailed into the dining-room, to her place at the head of the glittering table.

Miss Winterton, a little late, ran downstairs to join them. She took in Duncan's obedience to her orders with one smiling quizzical glance.

' We've had a perfectly ghastly morning,' she said to Mrs Knight—' haven't we, Duncan ? ' Duncan grinned. ' He was really terribly good about it, Aunt Elizabeth,' she continued. ' Never gave a squeak when those evil-smelling tailors dug pins into him. Indeed, I think it would take a lot to make Duncan squeal. He's quite the most silent person I've ever met.'

' Duncan will talk when he becomes less shy of us,' smiled Mrs Knight.

A three-course lunch followed two substantial breakfasts into Duncan's unexercised interior. He began to feel a little crowded and more than a little sleepy. But he knew it was bad manners to reject food offered him, especially when it was much too good to refuse. He ate stolidly on. First the thin and watery soup, with small pieces of carrot, turnip, leek and parsley floating like coloured insects in a heated pool. Then lamb cutlets, crisp and brown, with butter-soaked mashed potatoes and the season's rearguard of home-grown peas. Fruit salad

followed—grape-fruit, orange, banana, and apple, with thick yellow cream from a pewter jug. Mrs Knight saw how much he was enjoying it all. She pressed him to a second helping, and rather than embark on a stammering refusal, he allowed the maid to replenish his plate.

Then queer things began to happen to him. His mouth watered and his head swam round. He knew he must act very quickly, were he not to disgrace himself. ' I'm going to be seek,' he muttered, and bolted for the door.

' Go and see that he's all right, *please*, Jean,' said Mrs Knight, with some irritation in her tone.

Duncan ran upstairs, and through waves of nausea he heard Miss Winterton's laugh and the words she said—' Don't be cross, Aunt Elizabeth. You can't expect our little kennel-dog to be house-trained yet.'

He was sick in the bathroom, with Jean, like an attentive nursemaid, at the open door. He felt physically better, but in mental agony. He dared not return to mocking laughter and disappointed wrath. He would hide himself like a whipped dog until the misery of his disgrace was forgotten and he could face the world with unblushing face.

' I'm for my bed,' he murmured to a sympathetic Jean, and regained the thankful privacy of his room. There he lay on the bed for what seemed an interminable time, until a knock came on the door, and Miss Winterton strolled in. She smiled at him and ruffled his hair with her cool hand.

' Better ? ' she asked.

' Yes,' he answered.

' Then I think you should go out, Duncan. A little fresh air would do you a world of good. I'm

going out to the hills in my car, and then I'm going to walk. Would you like to come with me and tell me all about the sheep ? '

He jumped up eagerly and ran down behind her to the wasp-like car.

They were off ! Out of dingy Drumortin Gardens, flashing through traffic and byways to the open road. There, away in the distance, were green hills, rising from golden stubbles to a cloudless sky. Wind whistled over their heads ; the shining road leapt up to meet them ; telegraph wires rose and fell at their approach. Cars, buses, lorries, charabancs were rounded like stationary objects and grew suddenly small behind. An express train thundered neck and neck with them, dots waving handkerchiefs from its carriage windows, until road and rail diverged, and the car swung on to a rutted track, twisting and winding like a slackened tape to the foot of the hills.

' Did you enjoy that ? ' smiled Miss Winterton.

' *Fine !* ' he answered.

They parked the car at the roadside, and strode together over the springy carpeting of smooth green turf. Duncan fell into the long hill-stride which made the way to the tops seem short. It took Miss Winterton all her time to force athletic legs to his pace. The slopes were of grass, with little heather and bracken, and scarcely a single rock showing through concealing soil, fine grazing for the black-faced sheep creeping slowly upwards as evening fell.

Miss Winterton asked all sorts of questions about the sheep and their shepherding, so that Duncan felt at home. He talked freely, face flushed with animation and pride in his detailed knowledge, until

a comradeship grew up between them on the crown of the hills. They sat down together on the sweet-smelling grass and looked back towards the spires of Auldtown rising above its industrial smoke, to the castle—a mediaeval monument towering above the turmoil of modern men—to the blue waters of a distant river. They talked of sheep and sheep men, of dogs and horses, of hills, and of the sea. Duncan's shy awkwardness had vanished by the time they turned again for home. He was calling Miss Winterton Anne.

He chattered all through the swift return drive, and his bonnet was cocked at the old independent angle when they alighted in Drumortin Gardens.

They had tea together in the spacious lounge, where dim firelight fell on the shining silver service and delicate china cups. Anne asked him whether he had enjoyed his afternoon, and he smiled his frank adoration and grateful thanks.

Then the door opened and the maid announced Captain Campbell. A tall fair man strode over to Miss Winterton, and he looked as though all the fine blood and food in the world had gone to his making. He was so splendidly tall and so massively broad under his rough brown tweeds, his face so ruddy and cheerfully smiling, his eyes so clearly blue. She rose to meet him with pleased alacrity—it seemed she had been waiting for him all that day.

Duncan found himself forgotten as they talked of drives that had been sliced and putts that would not go down. Captain Campbell, it appeared, had been golfing, and had played the worst game of his life.

' What have you been doing all day ? ' he asked Miss Winterton.

'Rode before breakfast,' she replied; 'then attempted to clip the wings of our little caged linnet. I gave it up this afternoon and returned him to his native sheep.' She smiled on Duncan, and Captain Campbell bent down to shake his hand.

'You are Duncan Gillies?' he asked, puckering his eyes in amused examination.

'Yes, this is Duncan,' Miss Winterton replied. 'You'll have tea, Jock?'

Duncan writhed in jealous shyness whilst they talked. He felt so desperately forgotten and forlorn, so unimportant, so completely out of things. They talked and laughed of people he did not know, and of things he could not do. They were so intimate in their common acquaintances, their interests, and their sports, that Duncan felt an unimportant stranger at a family feast. He was glad when Mrs Knight came in, because she was so obviously more interested in himself than in Captain Campbell. Everyone rose at her entrance, but she came straight across to Duncan. She handed him a brown leather pocket-book and a five-pound note to put inside it.

'My small present for you, Duncan,' she said.

He mumbled inaudible thanks, while Captain Campbell exclaimed 'Lucky fellow,' and threw back his head to laugh.

Duncan hated the easy condescension of that laugh. He saw how Anne Winterton watched every movement Jock Campbell made, how her eyes lit when he smiled, how her colour ebbed and flowed when he looked at her.

Duncan put the note in the leather case and slipped it in his jacket pocket.

'Why don't you go out before dinner?' asked Mrs Knight, smiling from Jock Campbell to Anne.

They seemed pleased at her suggestion, and Duncan was left with the old lady. She was silent until the tea-things were cleared away. Then she drew her chair forwards to the fire. 'Captain Campbell is Anne's fiancé,' she explained. Duncan looked blank. 'She is going to marry Captain Campbell quite shortly. Do you like him, Duncan?'

'No!' he answered. The truth sprang to his lips before he could remember his manners. He thought Jock Campbell nothing but a forced-out tup with a fine conceit of itself until hard weather came.

'Neither do I, Duncan,' laughed Mrs Knight.

The old lady talked of her dead son Jack—of how good and kind he had always been to her — of how he had hated confinement and discipline—of what a splendid sportsman he had been. Duncan scarcely listened to her droning on; he was thinking of cool hands in the unquestioned possession of an overfed, red-faced ram.

Captain Campbell stayed to dinner. There was a fourth place set at the glittering table. Duncan ate listlessly, while the conversation flitted from tennis to football, touched on badminton and golf, finally embraced bridge, when Mrs Knight broke into an eager torrent of enthusiastic talk. It seemed that these people were for ever outside, yet seldom in the country. Heather was merely purple stuff where grouse nested and were shot, turnips green shelter where startled hares scurried between drills and partridges rose in panic-stricken coveys. By their talk there might have been no stock on the hills or

crops in the valleys. Mountains were for climbing and grass for golf.

Captain Campbell recognised Duncan's presence when the sweets were cleared. 'Ever played Rugger, young man?' he inquired.

'Of course not, Jock,' Miss Winterton smiled. 'They don't play football in the glens.'

'Then is shinty his game?'

Duncan nodded agreement, although it was not. It seemed that ignorance of games was a disgraceful thing.

'He must take up Rugger,' Captain Campbell continued. 'He has a good build for a three-quarter. Don't think he'll ever have weight for a forward.'

'Captain Campbell has played for Scotland,' explained Mrs Knight, in tones that implied he had fought for God.

The misery of coffee in the lounge followed the long agony of the dining-room's meal. Duncan resented every glance that passed between Anne and her swaggering lover, the hateful proprietary air with which he lighted her cigarette. Then the interminable chatter recommenced—golf and tennis, which were nearing their season's close—hockey, badminton, and Rugger about to begin.

'You look tired, Duncan,' said Mrs Knight, seeing white boredom on his face.

'I'm for my bed,' he muttered in angry shyness.

'Good heavens!' Anne exclaimed, 'I forgot all about his shoes this afternoon.'

Captain Campbell laughed again—his intolerable, hateful laugh. Duncan stumbled towards the door.

'Aren't you going to say " Good-night " ?' the ladies asked.

Duncan walked back, the carpet between the chairs an endless highroad of humiliation. He felt Mrs Knight's cold lips on his brow, the casual hand-shake of Anne Winterton, Captain Campbell's crushing grip. Then he escaped.

He climbed in deadly misery up the stairs, his mind a wounded adolescent thing of silent suffering and damaged pride. Leaving the room unlit, he raised the blind to gaze out on the magic glitter of roofs beneath a crescent harvest-moon. He raised the lower window-sash to drink in the comfort of the early autumn night. Everything was strangely still. There was peace and worship in the very silence.

Then, away over the sleeping town, some curlews called, floating high above the shadowed houses and among the moonlit clouds. They cried with the magical low clear whistle they croon to the sands, when winter waves come tumbling in to the wet expanse of a lonely shore. They passed overhead, one bird calling to another, and then they were gone.

Duncan knelt beside the window, laying hands and head on the low sill. He wept far into the night, the soft wind, like cool hands, caressing his hair.

He waited until all was silent and the house asleep. Then he changed into Macgillivray's ready-made suit, placing his note-case in the pocket. He crept from his room, down the wide stairs, past the ticking grandfather clock. He struggled with the lock of the heavy door. It seemed to fight against him, threatening his defeat, but at last he succeeded.

Duncan slipped, a shadowy ghost, on to the deserted pavements of Drumortin Gardens. There he broke into a run, speeding over the first lap of his agonised journey home.

III

Duncan stepped off the bus at the end of Glendarroch road. He would never forget the hunted
feeling of his flight, a night and a day of confused
wandering and missed trains, a second night in the
cold loneliness of Dalloch pier.

But now he was home again. Happiness had
come with the first sight of Lochend, when the
rising sun made a passage of silver over smooth
waters, and white gulls dipped to the wake of the
speeding boat. The first gentle bump against the
pier, the singing of ropes through frosty air, the
sailors in blue jerseys and the piermaster official in
his shining hat—the rhythmical clop-clop of the
boat's side against seaweed-crusted piles—the birds
rising from the tangle on the Lochend shore—the
bus conductress in her jaunty cap—then Glendarroch road-end at last !

It was as it had always been in early autumn
weather—hills draped in purple and loud with bees—
burns softly trickling after summer drought—the
first tinge of brown on the older brackens, and hoar-
frost white on their shaded leaves—a serenity as of
fulfilment over all things living.

Duncan tramped the long length of the dusty
road. He slunk past the Macintyres', afraid of being
seen, hearing the barking of dogs before the
rambling whitewashed house.

He was round the corner now, and a sob of joy-
fulness choked his throat. *There* lay Glendarroch
cottage—four-square and white, smoke drifting
lazily from its chimney—a place of security always,
a shelter after storm. *There* was the short green

grass before the buchts, and a white ribbon of a path running steeply up the brae. *There* was the washing, motionless on the sagging line, and the figure of his mother pausing before the cottage door. Far away in the distance on the crest of the hills the bridle-track glinted on its way to the sea. The ewes, bleating and new-weaned, raised their black faces and inquiring eyes—the quiet friendly eyes, the old familiar faces.

Duncan strode on to the brae-foot. There he paused, wondering whether his welcome would be cold. Might they not be angry and send him back to grey imprisonment in unfriendly towns ? Would they insist on his leaving sheep and hills a second time, to relive his suffering in that Auldtown house ? Would his mother show her sorrow and his father disappointment ? Would wee Johnnie's eyes be filled with scorn ?

Then a familiar face peered over the bucht's high wall—Johnnie Gillies, with bonnet cocked at a gay angle, his mouth twisted as though to hide the laughter in his soul. ' Aye, Duncan boy, you're back ! ' he cried, and there was something of the tumultuous joy of spring in the way he said it.

' Aye, father, I'm back.'

' We had a wire about you, Duncan boy. We were thinking you'd be on your way. Ye've been a long time on the road, boy.'

' Aye, father, I missed the boat.'

' Well, away into the house, boy, an' get your breakfast. You'll no' need to be too long over it, Duncan, for we've a long day's work ahead of us, an' I'm needin' your help.'

Duncan walked slowly up the brae. He was smil-

ing to himself because he had found no anger here—
just friendliness and a man's work to do.

Wee Johnnie ran out to meet him, excitement
dancing in his gipsy eyes, jam at the corners of his
laughing mouth. 'You're back, Duncan?' he
whispered. 'My, boy, you were hardy to run off.'

Duncan smiled again. They were all glad to see
him.

He delighted in the smell of wood-smoke, the
sound of his boots ringing on the lobby's stone
floor, the cackling of hens from the sunlit yard. He
entered the kitchen. His mother was at work before
the shining range, a squat and shapeless figure in her
blue print dress. She shifted her weight first to one
foot, then to the other, as though she were already
tired. She did not seem to hear his coming.

'I'm back, mother,' he said.

She did not turn round. 'Aye, Duncan,' she
answered. 'I saw you coming up the road. Sit
down to your porridge, boy; it's poured.'

Duncan sat quietly down, as though he had never
been away.

Mary moved the singing kettle on to the red heart
of the fire. She was sorry, in a way, that Jack's boy
was not to be a gentleman after all. But for herself
she was glad, glad that the long misery of his
absence was done. The glen had come to life again
now that Duncan was home.

Yet it would not do to let the boy know that;
it would be unfair to wee Johnnie, to Jean and to
Hugh. She would not let Duncan see her face
while it showed so much. For in her eyes were
tears of gladness, and her lips moved silently in
thankfulness to God.